fml

Also by Shaun David Hutchinson

The Deathday Letter

Shaun David Hutchinson

Simon Pulse
New York | London | Toronto | Sydney | New Delhi

This book is a work of fiction. Any references to historical events, real people,
or real places are used fictitiously. Other names, characters, places, and incidents are the
product of the author's imagination, and any resemblance to actual events or places
or persons, living or dead, is entirely coincidental.

SIMON PULSE
An imprint of Simon & Schuster Children's Publishing Division
1230 Avenue of the Americas, New York, NY 10020
First Simon Pulse paperback edition June 2013
Copyright © 2013 by Shaun David Hutchinson
For information about special discounts for bulk purchases, please contact Simon &
Schuster Special Sales at 1-866-506-1949 or business@simonandschuster.com.
The Simon & Schuster Speakers Bureau can bring authors to your live event.
For more information or to book an event contact the Simon & Schuster Speakers Bureau
at 1-866-248-3049 or visit our website at www.simonspeakers.com.
Designed by Mike Rosamilia
The text of this book was set in Tyfa ITC.
Manufactured in the United States of America
2 4 6 8 10 9 7 5 3 1
Library of Congress Control Number 2012016007
ISBN 978-1-4424-3287-1 (pbk)
ISBN 978-1-4424-8318-7 (hc)
ISBN 978-1-4424-3288-8 (eBook)

For my brother Ryan,

who always makes sure I take the right path.
Even when it's the wrong one.

Pre-game

I decided for about the hundredth time tonight that I'm not going to Cassandra Castillo's spring break barter party.

Then I changed my mind, because, fuck it: I'm seventeen, lonely, and horny. If I bailed on the party, not only would Coop and Ben never forgive me, but I'd have nothing else to do tonight that didn't involve a bottle of hand lotion and a crusty sock of Catholic shame.

Friday night. I was sitting in a booth at a greasy dive with my best friends, Coop and Ben, praying for the finger of God to wipe us and the whole stupid town of Rendview off the map so that I wouldn't have to make a decision about Cassie's party. The problem wasn't the party. It was the hostess of the party and the fact that, for the first time since freshman year, she was single. And not just single. Newly single. In fact, she had barely been free of the shackles of monogamy for an entire week.

But if I was going to make my move, I couldn't afford to waste time.

Coop interrupted my Cassie-filled daydreams by asking me and Ben a totally irrelevant question. "Who'd play you in a movie about your life?" Coop flashed a grin, unleashing the dimples from which no teenage girl is immune. Which sucks for them because he's totally into dudes. One dude in particular.

Ben snatched a fry off my plate and shoved it into his mouth without so much as a please or thank you. Which is how Ben is. Love him or loathe him, you don't get between him and a french fry. Not if you value your fingers. "Definitely Jake Gyllenhaal," Ben said.

"Just because he plays you," Coop said, "doesn't mean you get to bang him."

"Unless he's a method actor."

"You are pretty good at fucking yourself," I said, and pulled my plate of limp fries out of his reach.

Ben kissed Coop on the cheek and said to me, "You'd be played by a Muppet. And the movie would be called: *Simon Cross and the Blue Balls of Destiny*." Ben cracked up at his own joke and slid out of the booth to go talk to friends at another table.

Coop, Ben, and I had been best friends since grade school, when we all got stuck at the same lunch table with Phil Bluth. Banding together was the only way to protect our precious pudding cups from Phil's grabby hands. We were the Three Musketeers. The Three Amigos. Peter, Ray, and Egon. Until junior year of high school, when Ben and Coop coupled up. I thought it was great that they had fallen in lust and all that sappy bullshit, but I often felt like the third wheel of a trike that longed to be a big, bad, two-wheeled bicycle, riding off into the sunset, leaving me to pedal solo on the lonely road to Loserville. Population: me.

"Earth to Simon." Coop snapped his fingers in front of my eyes and brought me back to our sticky booth in the middle of Gobbler's, which is famous for being one of the few places in town that won't immediately call the cops on kids for hanging out, and not at all famous for their lousy burgers. Rendview is a sleepy beach town on the east coast of Florida, and there isn't much to do except eat, sleep, surf, and get drunk. That last item was on everyone's agenda for the evening. Gobbler's was wall-to-wall with my classmates. It was the last Friday of spring break and we were all getting ready to migrate to Cassie's house for a night of balls-to-the-wall teenage rebellion.

Despite the fact that I couldn't wait to graduate from the soul-rotting drudgery of high school, I felt a bond with some of these guys, forged from our years of shared suffering. Suffering that would come to an end at our imminent graduation.

"Ben's only messing with you," Coop said.

"I'm a loser," I said. "A seventeen-year-old virgin. I'm going to graduate in a couple of months, go to community college, and end up sleeping with someone like Mrs. Elroy because I repulse girls my own age with my wit and charm and concave chest."

"Don't sell yourself short," Coop said. "Mrs. Elroy was hot back in the nineteen twenties."

"Lucky me." I picked at one of my fries but tossed it down without eating it. "Even if I did manage to bag her, she'd end up showing me the door before I've had a chance to say, 'I swear it doesn't usually happen that fast'—though who am I kidding, it always happens that fast—because her husband will be home any moment and, oh wait, I think that's him now. Better jump out the window. Naked. Yeah, good times."

Coop laughed into his napkin, and I thought for a minute that he was going to choke, which would have served him right. But the bastard had the nerve to cough and catch his breath again. "It's not that dire. There are plenty of girls that'll do you."

"If you say Aja Bourne, I'm going to punch your face off."

"No," Coop said. "We'll find you a nearsighted girl who likes to binge drink."

"I'd prefer something less date-rapey."

"Who's date-raping whom?" Ben asked as he slid back into the booth, throwing his ropey arm around Coop's shoulders. Ben is always in motion, even when he's sitting still. It's like his molecules can't stop bouncing around. Our school had suggested he go on ADHD meds back in eighth grade, but Ben's mom had told them where they could stick their pills. Four years later, Ben is about to graduate with a free ride to MIT. Guess he showed them.

"I'm not date-raping anyone," I said, loudly enough that a couple of kids at the closest tables turned to gawk.

Ben was eyeballing my fries, so I pushed the soggy leftovers across the table. "Maybe more girls would be into you if you weren't so obvious about your Cassie fetish," he said

"Ixnay on the Assie-cay," Coop said. I hate how he and Ben treat me like a feral monkey who's going to fling his shit at them every time they mention Cassie's name. Sure, I'm totally into the girl, but I'm not obsessed.

"The party is at Cassie's house," I said. "She was going to come up eventually." I did my best to keep my voice even and calm. I'd had plenty of practice.

Here's the lowdown on the Cassie situation: I love her. The feeling isn't, technically, mutual. Maybe, possibly, somewhere deep, deep down where even she doesn't know they exist, Cassie might have some sweaty feelings for me, but it's highly unlikely. Girls like Cassie don't go for skinny geeks like me, in spite of my awesome hair.

And that should have been the end of it, except that freshman year, I'd done the unthinkable. I'd asked her out. And she'd said yes. We'd gone on one date and I'd nearly kissed her but—

"Are you thinking about mini-golf again?" Ben asked. Without waiting for an answer, he slapped me across the face so hard that spit flew out of my mouth and hit the wall. Someone whispered, "Cat fight," from a nearby table, and hissed.

Coop and I gaped at Ben. "Negative reinforcement," Ben said. "Every time he thinks about, talks about, or looks at Cassie, I'll slap him."

I put my hand to my cheek and wiggled my jaw. "You, sir, are a douchenozzle."

"I could punch you in the balls instead." Ben made a fist and leaned forward.

Coop held Ben back. "Can we save the ball punching for later?"

"Or never," I said.

"But Ben has a point," Coop said. "Just yesterday you were going on and on about how the party is the perfect chance for you to tell Cassie you love her and to finally kiss her, finishing what you started at Pirate Chang's."

Ben gulped some of my soda. "That was years ago, buddy. Time to move on. Your crush, while adorable, is starting to curdle. Pretty soon you're going to be that creepy guy who lives in his parents' basement, wallpapering his bedroom with old pictures of the girl he can't get over."

My friends had a point, but that didn't stop my brain from churning out scenario after scenario—imagined histories of what my life might have been like if I'd kissed Cassie that night instead of letting her get away. I feel about Cassie the way Coop feels about Ben. And even though I know that Cassie doesn't feel the same way about me, I've hoped. For years, every time she talked to me, every time she smiled in my direction, I hoped.

"Let's say you do make a play for Cassie tonight," Coop said. "And, for the record, I'm not saying I think it's a good idea. What about Eli?"

"Don't egg him on," Ben said. "Simon's got as much chance of scoring with Cassie as he has of scoring with me."

"Wow," I said. "Thanks for the support."

"I'm not trying to be a dick—"

"It comes more naturally to some," I said.

"Simon, listen. Cassie is pretty. She's popular. She's smart as shit. She dates guys like Eli Horowitz. Eli Fucking Horowitz, man."

"She dumped him."

Ben chuckled. "Do you honestly believe that means he won't break you into tiny pieces and then break those pieces into even smaller pieces? Look at him."

We all turned to the far corner where Eli sat alone. He looked like reheated dog shit. Like he hadn't shaved since school let out for spring break. Like he hadn't showered or even bothered to put on clean clothes. I was willing to bet the cost of my meal that Eli stank like the insides of my gym shorts. And yet, despite looking like a New York City hobo, he was still built like someone who could and would tear me from crotch to crown. His arms were the size of my thighs and his thighs were the size of my torso. His dusky skin hoarded shadows, making him appear even more dangerous. Which he was. Eli was a wrestling god at Rendview. And an honor student, and homecoming king, and staring at us.

"I could take him," I said, trying to look like I wasn't looking. "Anyway, he's mourning Cassie, not trying to get back with her."

Ben patted my hand. "Simon, I would love nothing more than to see you and Cassie sneak off to a quiet bedroom to ful- fill your porniest fantasies so that you can finally move on with your life, but it's never going to happen. Ever. Not in your life- time or mine. Not in a parallel universe where you and Cassie are the last human specimens on a planet ruled by poodles."

I leaned back in the booth and crossed my arms over my chest. "Your confidence in me is inspiring. No, really, I may weep. Here come the tears."

"Just keeping it real."

"Don't be mean," Coop said.

"Sorry," Ben said, but not to me. He and Coop got those silly looks on their faces that meant they were dangerously close to engaging in some full-frontal smoochery.

Thankfully, a tall girl with long blond hair strolled over to our booth and saved me from that ungodly display. We waited for her to say something, but she stood there awkwardly for a long moment.

"Did you forget your lines?" Ben asked.

The girl shook her head. I noticed a long scar that ran along the bottom of her chin. "Ketchup," she said.

"It's not a vegetable, kids."

I kicked Ben under the table. "Don't mind Ben," I said. "He thinks he's funny when he's mostly just an ass." I grabbed the ketchup from the end of the table and passed it to her.

"You're Simon, right?" the girl asked. I nodded. "I'm Natalie Grayson." She smiled brazenly.

Something about that smile reminded me of— "Wait. We had sophomore geometry together, didn't we?"

"Yeah." Natalie's face lit up.

"What did the guy say when he got back from vacation and found his parrot's cage empty?"

"Polly gone," she said, and we both laughed.

Ben groaned and muttered something under his breath that sounded like "geeks," but I ignored him.

"Are you going to Cassie's party?" Natalie asked.

"Totally."

"What's the deal with the bartering thing?"

I'd already made Coop explain it to me a thousand times. I mean, I got the concept but didn't see the point. "You bring stuff to the party," I said. "And you trade it for other stuff."

"Like what?" Natalie stood holding that ketchup bottle with both hands. I was afraid she was going to squeeze a tomato geyser into the air.

Ben reached into his pocket and pulled out a little plastic bag with a dozen white pills in it. "Once people get shit-faced, I'm going to make a mint with these. People will trade me anything for them."

"Drugs? Really?" Natalie did not sound impressed.

"They're baby aspirin." Ben put his finger to his lips and gave the girl one of his patented winks.

"I still don't get why," I said.

"For fun, dumbass. What'd you bring?" Coop asked Natalie.

She looked over at her table, which was packed with girls I knew by sight but not by name. They were the minor-league hitters. Not A- or B-list girls, but not part of the moo crew either. "I stole some tiny liquor bottles from my dad, and I have a guitar pick signed by Damian Crowley of Noodle Revolution."

Ben faked puking into my empty basket of fries. He hates NR. Hates. So much that he started an anti-fan club.

"You can totally trade up with that," Coop said, ignoring Ben's continued mock vomiting. "It's like that Canadian guy who started with a red paper clip and bartered his way up to a house. You could trade your guitar pick for a hot prom date if you played it right."

"Fat chance," Ben muttered, but we all ignored him.

Coop was giving me a look, this mental nudge that he seemed to think I understood. For the record, I did not. But, apparently, I wasn't the only person at the table who didn't get Coop, because Natalie was looking at him like he'd been speaking Parseltongue.

"Maybe I'll see you at the party, Simon," Natalie said, stuttering her way through the sentence, her earlier store of bravery seemingly all used up. "Thanks for the ketchup."

"Anytime," I said. "You need ketchup, I'm your man. Call me Mr. Ketchup. Or, you know, not."

I watched Natalie walk back to her table, where she said something to her friends that made them giggle and squeal.

An idea struck me. "Coop, you're a genius."

"Tell me more," Coop said.

"That thing you said about bartering a paper clip for a house. Was that true?"

"Indeed." Coop grinned at me, and then at Natalie. "You can do anything you want tonight, Simon."

"Then I'm going to barter for a kiss from Cassie. I'm going to tell her that I love her."

Coop smacked his head on the table. Over and over. Ben finally had to put his palm between Coop's forehead and the wood veneer. "It's okay, baby," Ben said. "Simon's a little slow."

"What?" I asked. "It's a great idea. I'll barter for a kiss, and then, when she's had a taste of Simon Cross, I'll tell her I love her. She'll be mine."

"You don't have anything she wants," Ben said. "She's used to eating prime rib. You're beef jerky. You're not even beef jerky. You're that off-brand meat chew that you get at gas stations."

I was feeling abused and didn't try to hide it. "You don't have to be an asshole about it."

"There are other girls," Coop said. He was looking exasperated, not that I blamed him. When it comes to Cassie, I'm a bit OCD.

"Like who?" I asked.

Ben pointed at Natalie. "Her," he said. "She was practically jerking you off under the table, dude. How are you so stupid?"

"She needed ketchup," I said.

Coop and Ben started talking over each other, and I tuned them out. Had I really become so blind that I'd missed Natalie flirting with me? She'd been cute and nervous, sure, but she hadn't been flirting with me, right?

Whatever. I couldn't think about flirting with someone else. I'm not making excuses for my behavior, but if you've never been in love with the most beautiful girl in the world, then you don't know. It's like, for one second of her attention, you'd cut off your fingers, you'd hold your breath until you turned blue and passed out, you'd run to the ends of the fucking Earth and bring her back anything she asked for. Girls like Cassie aren't just one in a million. They're once in a lifetime.

But I'd had my chance. Had it and blown it.

Ben and Coop expected me to move on from that, but being near Cassandra Castillo was like living. Everything else was death.

"All I'm asking is that you try to go out with other girls," Coop said. "You don't have to fall in love, but maybe you'll see that Cassie isn't as perfect as you think."

Ben rested his arm along the top of the booth, absently rubbing the back of Coop's neck. "She's not all that great," Ben said. "The girl has got issues. I could tell you stories—"

"Don't," I said. Ben has a casual relationship with the truth when it comes to stories. It's not that he lies per se, but he doesn't see the problem with embellishing details or leaving them out altogether if it suits the tale he's telling.

Ben is a master storyteller, but if I want the truth, I go to anyone else.

"I just want what you guys have," I mumbled.

Coop looked at me with shelter dog eyes. The last thing I wanted was his pity.

"Simon, I'm never going to be more honest with you than I am right now." Coop sat up straight and folded his hands on the table the same way my mom had when she'd tried to tell me where babies come from. For two years after that I'd believed I would impregnate every girl I smiled at. It had made first and second grades terrifying. "If you want to go to this party tonight and try to barter your way to a kiss with Cassie, I'll help you."

"Whoa," Ben said. "We have our own plans tonight. *You know.*"

"We'll have time for both."

"I think I'm going to hurl," I said, frantically trying not to imagine what Ben and Coop were going to be doing in a dark room at the party.

"As I was saying," Coop said. "If you want to make some final play for Cassie, then I'm Team Simon." Coop paused and took a deep, meaningful breath. "But there's a girl over there who might actually like you." Coop nodded in Natalie's direction. She and her friends were still giggling. When I glanced at her this time, she waved before looking away. I waved back. "A girl who might like you for who you are. A girl who might even be willing to kiss you, though the thought makes me want to regurgitate my veggie burger."

Ben was nodding along with everything Coop said. "And ketchup girl's got small hands, so that's a bonus."

"How exactly?"

"They'll make even your teeny weenie look like a foot-long."

Coop punched Ben's arm. "I'm trying to be serious."

"So am I. Did you see those tiny little baby hands?" The boys started bickering, and I zoned out again.

It wasn't like the thought of kissing other girls had never occurred to me. I'd gone out on some dates but they'd all been catastrophes. There was the Aja Bourne incident of which we never, ever spoke. Then there was Naomi Cutter, a ballet dancer who was great except for the fact that she'd refused to let me eat in front of her. We dated for three weeks and I lost eight pounds. Before that was Kirsten Gallows, who turned out to be as obsessed with Cassie as I was. There were other girls, but it always came back to Cassie.

Look what she'd done to Eli Fucking Horowitz. The guy had everything. He had more play in his pinkie than I had in my entire body. It would take fifty of me to equal one of him. Yet there he was. Broken. Defeated. A gutted man sitting alone, probably trying to decide whether or not he could stomach going to the party.

If I did manage to find something Cassie wanted, barter for it, kiss Cassie, and finally tell her that I loved her, I'd probably end up like that one day. Like Eli.

"If it makes you feel better," Ben said. "Cassie's got a raging case of herpes."

"You totally just made that up," I said. "And how would that possibly make me feel better?"

Coop checked the time on his phone. He was probably getting antsy to leave. He likes to get to parties early so he can score a good parking spot.

"You've got to make a choice," Coop said.

I looked at Natalie. She was pretty and sincere. She had a killer smile, and she really did seem to like me, lame jokes and all. When she leaned forward, I could see the line of her panties sticking out of her jean shorts, and her slender shoulders outlined under her floral cami. I didn't know much about her except that she was terrible at geometry. And I suppose that was the exciting part. I didn't know anything about her and she didn't know anything about me. We were enigmas to each other. She could turn out to be everything I wanted her to be.

Only she'd never be Cassie.

Then again, Cassie might never be Cassie. I might have spent years in love with an illusion.

I didn't know. I didn't know anything except that I had two choices. I could go to the party with Coop and Ben and try to barter a kiss from Cassie. I could try to make my dreams come true. Or I could embrace reality and move on with my life.

Cassie isn't the only girl on planet Earth. Right?

Ben patted my cheek. It still smarted from where he'd slapped me earlier. "What's it going to be, dude? You going to keep pining for Princess Cassie, or are you going to talk to the perfectly nice, heterosexual girl who might not laugh at you if she saw you naked with the lights on?"

I looked over at Natalie. I looked at Eli. I looked at my two possible futures. "Fuck it. I think . . ."

The Party

Living the Dream

". . . We should go to the party."

Coop and Ben were disappointed. It was written all over their faces. Especially Coop's. But he didn't get it. Natalie's laugh would never be Cassie's laugh. Her smile, her mouth, her eyes, and pale long legs. The sum of those parts would never equal Cassie. And while part of me wanted to forget about Cassandra Castillo and move on with my life, the other part of me knew that, until I told Cassie how I felt, until I tried to barter for one goddamn kiss, I'd never be able to let her go.

As we funneled out of Gobbler's with some of the other kids who'd decided to take off, Natalie waved at me.

I didn't wave back.

Coop pulled his mom's Kia up to Cassie's house at 9 p.m. on the nose. We didn't talk the whole drive. I could tell by the way he was fidgeting that Coop was composing a speech in his head, working up the nerve to say something to me that he thought I wouldn't want to hear.

"Whatever you're going to preach at me," I said as Coop put

the car in park, "I've probably already said it to myself a thousand times. I'm not good enough, Cassie's too pretty, I've got a better chance of sprouting an extra pair of arms than I do of getting her to kiss me. Trust me. If you've thought it, so have I."

And I had. I'd thought it all. I knew all the variables and still didn't care. There was something different about tonight. Something in the air that made me feel like anything was possible.

I was going to turn a paper clip into a kiss, and no one, not even Fate, was going to stop me.

"You're still determined to do this?" Coop asked. "Because I'm sure Natalie will be here soon and . . ." Coop leaned over the back of his seat, wrapping his arms around the headrest.

I nodded. "It's all ending, guys. High school, I mean. Only prom's left, then graduation. You guys are gonna take off to Boston, while I'll be stuck at the world's lamest community college. I'm not sure where's Cassie's going, but I'm sure it's somewhere far."

"Yale," Ben said. "With Eli."

"Well, that'll be awkward," I said. "Anyway, my point is that regrets are built out of the shit we don't do. And if I don't do this now, I'll regret it for the rest of my pathetic life." I grabbed the backpack that held all the things I'd brought to barter and headed up the lawn toward Cassie's front door.

Other kids were beginning to show up, attracted like flies to the intoxicating lure of a parentless house. Music rocked the walls, and I knew without needing to see it that Leo Cartenzo had already set up his turntables in a dark corner and was playing the sound track to our lives. There was a cluster of girls by the garage, performing last-minute makeup checks.

"Wait up," Ben said. He and Coop caught up to me by the front door. The flowerpots, which had been filled with a crayon box's worth of color the only other time I'd been here, were conspicuously absent. That night, Cassie had gone on and on about how much her mother loved flowers. I swept the memory into a dark corner. Tonight I was going to make new memories.

"I'm doing this," I said.

Ben said, "Yeah, whatever. I just wanted to warn you that Cassie's been acting a little off lately."

Coop elbowed Ben in the ribs. "Tell him."

"I was about to," Ben said, his voice layered with irritation. I knew Ben. He wasn't irritated with Coop but with me. Ben wasn't the type to interfere in other people's drama. He liked the rumor mill, true, but he would have happily let me run off and make an ass of myself, and his sum total involvement would have been recording my spectacular failure and posting it to Facebook before the end of the party. That he was trying to warn me off was owed solely to Coop's influence.

"Something's up with Cass." Ben paused. Whether it was for dramatic effect or what, I wasn't biting, so he went on. "This whole idea to break up with Eli and throw a party, it came out of nowhere. It's like she went to sleep as Cassie and woke up as a totally different girl."

"I get it," I said. "Cassie's changed, you and Coop have changed. We've all changed. It's called growing up." I heard the muffled sound of Cassie's voice from somewhere inside. "Listen, if Cassie hates her life, if she's bored and looking for a change, then I might just be the change she's looking for."

Coop put his hand on my shoulder. "Good luck, Simon." It was all he said. But I heard the words he didn't say. I heard him wish me luck because I was going to need it. I was going to need more than luck. I was going to need every ounce of karma that I'd managed to earn over the course of my life; I was going to need the sympathy of saints, some divine miracle.

Turning water into wine was a pathetic parlor trick compared to what I was going to attempt.

But Cassie had liked me once. Liked me enough to go on a date with me. Now I only had to convince her that I was worthy of so much more.

After I found a way to convince myself.

Ben banged on the door, and Cassie opened it right away like she'd been waiting for us, watching for us through the peephole. "Ben!" she squealed, and threw her arms around his neck. I was so close to them both that I could smell her mango shampoo and the bright scent of limes that clung to her skin. She wore a thigh-length black dress that exposed a dangerous amount of her frontal assets and moved at the bottom like she carried her own breeze wherever she went.

Cassie wasn't a ten. They hadn't invented a scale that could rate how beautiful she was. She was an eclipse, the dark shadow of the moon blotting out the sun, and I couldn't stop staring at her, even it if meant burning out my retinas.

"Have you started drinking already, Sy?" Cassie asked, using my nickname. Her voice made me melt. Every time.

"What? Yeah." Then I shook my head. "I mean, no. What's up? Awesome party." I heard the words coming out of my mouth and begged my brain to stop them. Stupid tongue and its infernal word diarrhea.

Cassie laughed. She has this monster laugh that surprises me every time I hear it. You'd look at Cassie and expect a china doll giggle, but she inherited her rowdy laugh from her father. He's Cuban and her mother is black. Cassie calls herself Cubrican. I call her perfect.

"You're such a goof, Sy."

Ben rolled his eyes. "You gonna let us in or what, Castillo?"

Cassie crossed her arms over her chest and jutted her hip out to the left, blocking the doorway with her body. There were some other guys starting to crowd behind us, but I didn't give a shit about them. They could wait. "It's a barter party, boys. Nothing's free tonight."

Coop dug into his pocket and pulled out a ratty sheet of paper. "I have the answers to Keating's killer chemistry final." He dangled the paper in Cassie's face.

"Tempting, Super Cooper, but I'm exempt from the final due to my utterly perfect attendance." Cassie smiled. "But hold on to that, because I'm pretty certain you could trade the underwear off half the soccer team for it."

Ben snatched the cheat sheet out of Coop's hand. "I'll take that."

I started rummaging around in my backpack, but before I could find anything that I thought Cassie would want, she said, "I'll let you in if you do shots with me." Without waiting for us to accept her offer, Cassie took off down the hallway toward the back of the house.

Cassie's parents had done some redecorating since the last time I'd been there. The house was bare, stripped down. I hadn't been given the grand tour the night I'd picked Cassie up for our date, but I remember that the hallway was lined with pictures and paintings and these African masks that Cassie's mother loved nearly as much as her flowers. Cassie had probably taken them all down and stashed them to keep them from being broken, but it made the house feel empty.

The party was in its infancy, but DJ Leo was already in the groove, punishing our ears with remixes of songs I hadn't liked in their original incarnations.

Coop and Ben and I chased Cassie down the hall, past a spiral staircase in the foyer that led upstairs, something to the left that might have been a library, and a room to the right that looked like the kind of fancy sitting room that no one actually sits in. Cassie was already in the kitchen when we got there, lining up four shot glasses into which she sloshed a generous amount of clear, thick tequila. She was chattering about who she thought was going to show, and how Sia Marcus, queen bee of the drama club, was hanging out around the pool doing something dodgy, and how she'd put her mom's favorite couch out on the patio so that people could use the living room for beer pong.

"I'm not really a tequila man," I said when Cassie stopped talking long enough for someone to wedge a word in.

"Then you're not really a man," Cassie said.

Coop said, "Ouch," while Ben cracked up so hard that I thought he was going to suffocate. I could only hope.

There was nothing I could say. No witty comeback that would suffice. Without waiting for my supposed best friends or the girl I was insanely infatuated with, I slugged back that shot, slammed the glass down, and said, "My man parts and I agree: That tastes like ass."

I fully expected Ben to fire off a smartass comment that would make me want to clobber him. Instead he and Cassie drained their shots.

Coop held out his hands. "I'm the DD. No liquor shall pass these lips tonight."

Cassie shrugged and gulped his shot too.

"Isn't it customary for the hostess to at least maintain the illusion of sobriety?" Ben asked. He was trying to make it sound like a joke, but I heard the concern.

"Isn't it customary for guests to keep their opinions to themselves?" Cassie said. I thought we were going to spend the rest of the night suspended in that awkward moment, but Cassie clapped her hands and said, "I love this song! Let's dance!" Ben shot me an "I told you she was nuts" look that I ignored.

I assumed that Cassie's dance invitation was directed at Coop or Ben. On the rare occasions in the past that she'd uncoupled from Eli long enough to dance, it had always been with one of her gays. But neither Coop nor Ben made a move to join Cassie, and I realized that they were both staring at me.

Duh.

This was the ideal opportunity. I was so perfectly conditioned to expect that Cassie didn't want anything to do with me that when she flat out invited me to dance, it hadn't registered.

"If I dance with you," I said, "what're you going to trade me?" I tried to keep my voice loose and easy. It was more difficult than the time I'd tried to eat an entire box of jelly-filled doughnuts in one sitting.

"Trade you?" Cassie asked.

"It is a barter party, Cass. Nothing's free tonight."

Cassie rolled her eyes when I used her own words against her. Her every gesture was overly dramatic and I couldn't decide whether she was playing or intoxicated. The shot of tequila I'd taken was warm pancake syrup, coating my insides and making me feel good. In fact, I was certain that I owed my burst of confidence to Jose Cuervo. If I got out of this party alive, I made a mental note to send the company a nice thank-you letter. But it certainly wasn't enough to make me drunk.

"You should be giving *me* something, mister," Cassie said. She absently put her tongue behind the gap between her teeth, toying with the space, making me lose all sense of time or place.

"You're right," I said, still trying to play it cool. I glanced at Coop for help, but he was watching me with a bemused expression that would have fit Ben's face better. I dug around in my backpack, looking for something I could trade Cassie for two sweaty minutes in her presence, but I didn't have anything wor-thy. I panicked. If I didn't have anything worth trading for a dance, what the hell was I going to give her for a kiss?

I pulled a small velvet sack out of my bag. "I have these dice my mom brought me from Vegas." When Cassie didn't look impressed, I said, "No, huh?" and dropped the dice into my back-pack. "What do you want, then?"

Cassie tapped her chin with the tip of her finger. "Find me a pair of Muet Chaüssures, size eight, and I'll do more than dance." She punctuated the end of that sentence with the most indecent wink I'd ever seen outside of a porno, obliterating the last vestiges of control I'd managed to maintain over my spastic hormones.

"Let's dance," Coop said, clearly disgusted. Not that I cared. I was floating on air. I was a delicate butterfly flapping my wings on winds made of Cassie's sweet breath. Briefly, I worried that the Cassie who had just brazenly and openly flirted with me was some imposter, an alien wearing Cassie's perfect skin, but I let those fears go, because I was on fire. I was in the zone. The Cassie zone. And not even Coop could bring me down.

Ben elbowed Coop in the side. "We have other plans," he said as tactfully as Ben was able.

"Gross!" Cassie said. Then she grabbed my sweaty hand and Ben's hand and pulled us into the family room, a large, friendly space that looked out onto the patio. All the furniture had been pushed against the walls, creating an open area where people who had shown up even earlier than us were already dancing. There weren't many people yet, but the house was filling rapidly, and I knew it was only a matter of time before I wouldn't be able to move without disturbing someone else's air. But it could have been wall-to-wall and I wouldn't have cared. Hanging with my best buds, dancing with Cassie—I was right where I wanted to be.

Normally, I'm not a dancing fool. My mom had forced me to take ballroom dancing lessons when I was in the eighth grade. I'd stepped on Margie Bondar's foot so hard that I broke three of her toes, and our instructor—a British eccentric who twirled around and rambled on like he was the product of an unholy union between Nathan Lane and Robin Williams—branded me unteachable and refunded my fee.

Except, with Cassie and my friends, I danced. Expelling all the fear and anxiety that had lain dusty in my lungs for so long that it felt like the first time I'd been able to breathe in years. Cassie smiled at me and laughed at nothing in particular, and I laughed back. Coop and Ben had their arms around each other, and soon we were all sweaty, lost in the music, all but Coop fueled by the tequila that had been our price of admission. We were all blissfully tangled up in this perfect moment.

Others crowded into the house, glomming on to us like we were the coolest cats in the entire universe, despite my dancing. DJ Leo was smooth, moving from one song to another in a continuous flow that was carrying all the Rendview students along with it. Making us the same. Making us equal.

In that moment, I didn't know how I'd ever gotten it into my head that Cassie was out of my reach. I couldn't fathom how I'd botched my opportunity to kiss her. Maybe it was because back then I'd been little more than a boy. I'd needed time to mature. To become a man. Fully grown and in control of my destiny.

And right now, my destiny was shaking her awesome booty like it was the last night on planet Earth.

When I couldn't dance anymore, I moved to the fringes of the floor. There were more people crammed into Cassie's house than I could count. Popular kids and dorks and in-betweeners, all mingling together, homogenized by the booze and bass and freedom of the night.

But I saw only Cassie. She was the only person for me.

While I watched Cassie dance, my mind wandered back to the day I'd asked her out. I'd been an infant among giants. Even Coop and Ben had seemed so much bigger back then. We'd graduated eighth grade together, but when we hit the halls of Rendview High, they grew up and left me behind. They'd fit in in ways I never would, never could. Until I met Cassie.

We sat next to each other in anatomy. It was the one and only time that alphabetical seating had worked in my favor.

The first time I saw her, the first time that I walked into Mrs. Grimauld's classroom and laid my lucky eyes on Cassie, I knew she was the one. In those days, she'd had short hair that clung to her round cheeks, framing her smooth skin. When I'd realized I was going to have to sit next to her for the entire year, I panicked. There was no way I was going make it through the entire hour, let alone two semesters, without a permaboner.

Yet somehow I survived. Freshman year was the year I developed a sudden and intense aversion to tucking in my shirts.

The thing about Cassie was that she was funny and smart and never talked down to me. The other girls treated me like I was their little brother. Or, worse, like I didn't exist at all. But Cassie talked to me. She saw me for what I could be, not what I was.

I'm not sure what possessed me the day I grabbed destiny by the cojones. While we were dissecting our worm—a long sucker Cassie had named Wormy Worthington the Third—I asked Cassie to go out with me. The words were all smooshed together like the letters had linked arms and formed a long chain. I didn't know where the question had come from. It had bubbled up out of me spontaneously. Sure, I'd fantasized about asking Cassie out, but never seriously. I was a nobody. It was absurd to think that Cassie would go out with me.

I waited for the blowback. The laugh. The sympathetic smile. The words that would banish me irrevocably to that frigid nightmare world whispered of among guys with the deepest shades of dread: the Friend Zone.

But Cassie had said yes. She'd smiled warmly at me and changed my life. "Sy, you're so adorable. Of course I'll go out with you."

Those words were seared onto my brain. When I died, they'd be etched on my grave marker. I think everyone has a couple of moments that truly change their life. Those words changed mine.

Cassie still smiled at me like that. She saw me standing on the edge of the dance floor and waved me over. The shot of tequila that had been in my system was soaked into my shirt now. I saw everything with perfect clarity. Past, present, future. All mine. All open.

I moved my lazy feet and pushed through the thick outer layer of sweaty dancers to get to Cassie. The knot of bodies was tighter than it had been just twenty minutes earlier, but with a burst of strength, I cut a path straight to Cassie. Hands groped me and the smell of body odor and dozens of different perfumes and colognes mixed together assaulted my nose, making my eyes water.

When I got to Cassie, I stood in the middle of the dance floor, waiting for her to notice me again. I was always waiting for her to notice me.

"Cassie!" I called. I was done waiting.

Cassie opened her eyes. Her lashes cut long shadows on her face. "Simon!" She held out her hands to me, and I took them. Spots danced across my vision.

The music was heroin. The receptors in my brain fired volleys of chemicals, making me love every single person in the room. Making me love Cassie more—something I'd thought impossible.

The distance between us closed with each beat. Our breaths were counterpoints to the music. Our hearts keeping time. Our eyes locked on only each other. All the shit that had happened between the moment on Pirate Chang's killer eighteenth hole and this second was nothing. Erased. I had bridged those other million agonizing seconds like they had never happened.

Holding Cassie's hand, dancing. Staring into her eyes, not blinking. My heart beating so fucking hard that I wondered if it were possible for it to explode.

I thought back to Gobbler's. To Coop and Ben—who had

conveniently disappeared—telling me that I was doomed to failure. To Natalie Grayson, who was dancing over by the French doors, pretending like she wasn't watching me. To that moment I'd almost decided to get up and go to Natalie's table, because I was sure that Cassie was out of my reach.

I thought about how I'd almost fucked this up. Dancing with Cassie and being near her, being so close to her that I could kiss her right now. We'd been closer only one time. Tonight would change that.

Because Cassie was looking into my eyes. She was putting one arm around my neck, the other against my chest. She was doing that thing with her tongue behind her teeth again. She was practically begging me to kiss her.

And then she was yelling at me.

"Ow! Fuck, Simon!" Cassie shoved me away; I fell into Kate Jordan, who cursed at me. I didn't give a shit about Kate. Cassie was standing awkwardly, favoring her left foot.

"Damn, Cassie, I'm so sorry. I have stupid feet. Dumb, clumsy feet. I'd cut them off if I could."

Cassie rolled her eyes and grabbed my arm, taking a tentative step. "I thought Ben was the drama queen," she said. "I'll be fine. Help me get some ice."

I bent down so that Cassie could put her arm around my shoulders, and we limped into the kitchen, which was packed with people trading for drinks, talking, and grazing from artsy ceramic bowls filled with assorted tasty snacks.

"I'm so sorry," I said again.

Cassie kicked off her shoe and wiggled her toes. "Nothing broken." But I could see her skin turning red and was willing to bet it would bruise.

I found a dish towel and wrapped it around some ice cubes. Cassie held it to the top of her foot, clearly not caring that she looked silly. She was the hostess and could do anything she wanted.

We stood in the kitchen while the party happened around us. I was terrified that I'd blown my chance with Cassie but still riding the high of dancing with her. My choices were to retreat or press on, and retreating was simply not an option.

"Told you I was a sucky dancer," I said.

Cassie chuckled, which alleviated some of my guilt. "Maybe you better make one of those Muet Chaüssures a size nine. I think my foot's going to swell like a bitch." She tried to slip the injured foot back into her heel, but winced and gave up for the time being.

This moment wasn't as perfect as on the dance floor, but Cassie was still smiling. She was still looking at me like I was more than Simon Cross.

"Cassie? I have something to ask you." I wasn't that bumbling freshman anymore. I had years of experience with rejection now. But the words still stuck to the roof of my mouth. I still trembled like a boy.

"Anything," Cassie said. She was looking over my shoulder, though. Something had caught her eye, but I had already pro-grammed my course and I couldn't abort now.

"I want to barter for a kiss. From you." Saying it took all the air in my lungs. I suffocated waiting for her answer.

Cassie was still looking past me. Her smile had disappeared; her face had hardened. "What?" she asked. The word slashed across my cheek like the end of a whip.

"A kiss," I said, my confidence flagging. "What can I barter?" I turned to see what had stolen Cassie's attention, but deep down I already suspected the answer.

Eli Fucking Horowitz. He was the dark cloud over my picnic, the razor blade in my apple, the piss in my cornflakes.

He was the one thing I couldn't compete with. I'd already lost Cassie to him once.

"Sorry," Cassie said. "I have to go."

I tried to think of something to say to keep her from leaving, but Cassie was already gone, swept up in the current of bodies rushing from one part of the party to another.

"How about a paper clip?" I said to no one in particular, and watched Cassie disappear, along with my chances of kissing her.

Reality Bites

"... I'm gonna go talk to the ketchup girl."

Ben and Coop looked like they were going to crap their pants when I got up from our booth and marched over to Natalie's table. Natalie's friends fled like I was covered with massive, oozing pustules. But I didn't care because I felt powerful. I wasn't Simon Cross. I was SIMON CROSS! I didn't need Cassie. Holding out for Cassie was like waiting to win the lottery: The odds were not in my favor, and I could waste decades trying, only to end up a bitter, lonely man with nothing to show for his life.

I sort of thought I deserved more than that.

Maybe I was deluding myself. The thought crossed my mind. Asking Natalie Grayson to accompany me to the party wasn't going to expunge Cassie from the dark, dank recesses of my brain. I still loved Cassie, and not even ten Natalies could change that. But asking out a girl not named Cassandra Castillo, well, it was definitely a step in the right direction.

Things happened quickly after I managed to open my mouth and say words. I'd hitched a ride to Gobbler's with Coop, but he was antsy to take off. Natalie told me that I could ride with her. Everyone was starting to head out to Cassie's party anyway, so I accepted the offer. We chatted in fits and starts on the short drive toward Cassie's neighborhood, then Natalie suggested we park on the beach road for a few minutes so that we could get to know each other better. It seemed like a brilliant idea. Girl plus car plus a nearly full moon over the beach. What could go wrong with that?

"So then River was like, 'You should totally go over and ask him to come to the party,' and I was like, 'He's probably going with his friends,' and I'm so glad I asked you for the ketchup even though I hate ketchup—hate it—because otherwise I just know that I would have ended up dancing with Ed Swinder. He always tries to touch my boobs and blame it on someone pushing him into me—like I don't know."

I sat in Natalie's truck, on the side of the road, watching the waves pull away from the shore while my date babbled. She talked about her friends and what kind of music they'd listened to while they got ready for Cassie's party, which led her on a thrilling tangent about how she'd come to be wearing those little jean shorts rather than the festive skirt she'd been planning to wear all week long. I wanted to puncture my eardrums with a chopstick.

"Maybe we should get going," I said.

Natalie glanced at the clock on the radio. "It's like nine,

Simon. The party won't get good for a while. Besides, we're having fun, right? Now, what was I talking about?"

"I honestly don't know."

"What?"

"Skinny jeans," I said, defeated. It might not have been so bad if there had been some interesting music playing or if I could have read the encyclopedia. But I was stuck listening to Natalie go on and on and on about clothes while I focused on her lips and wondered why people don't build emergency ejection seats into cars for moments like this.

"Right," Natalie said. "So then I got the fours and they were too small and I was like, 'Hello, these can't be fours because I'm a four and they don't fit.' And that stupid biznatch had the nerve to suggest that I needed a bigger size. Can you believe that?"

"Please kill me." I hadn't meant to say it out loud.

"Exactly," Natalie said. She eyed me. "You like music?"

"Coop's the music geek."

"What about TV? I love reality shows."

"Have you ever noticed that people on TV never actually watch TV?" I waited for Natalie to say something or nod her head or spontaneously vomit baby ducks onto the gray cloth armrest, but she only stared blankly at me with her sort-of-blue eyes. "I have a theory," I said, "that the reason people on TV are so productive is because they never watch TV."

Natalie's waning smile began to dip into a frown. "So, no favorite shows, then?"

I shook my head.

Things got quiet. In spite of the awkwardness, I was relieved. I didn't regret that I'd gone over to talk to her, but I was ready to admit that it might not have been on my top-ten list of best decisions. Still, I wondered if she might let me kiss her. I wasn't particularly interested in the words that passed through her lips, but the lips themselves were pretty hot.

"I'm really glad I asked for the ketchup," Natalie said. She wore her puppy-eyed optimism openly. It was simultaneously sexy and annoying.

"Me too," I said, and I was surprised to find that it wasn't a lie. I wanted to give Natalie the benefit of the doubt. Her verbal spew could have been the result of nerves, which was something I could understand.

Natalie smiled. She had a great smile. Like she'd been saving it up over a hundred rainy days for this moment. For me. "My friend Keisha told me that you were all hung up on Cassie and that you'd be up her ass now that she's single."

"Yeah," I mumbled. The funny thing was that, until Natalie brought her up, our conversation in the truck was the longest I'd gone without thinking about Cassie in a while.

"I don't get what guys see in her," Natalie said. "She's kind of a biznatch, if you know what I mean. Strutting around Rendview like she owns it, because she's popular and her parents are loaded and she's queen of the universe. She's not even that pretty."

"She's prettier than you," I said.

Shit.

What I'd meant to say was that people often misconstrue Cassie's confidence for bitchiness, and that she's pretty in an unconventional way. That Cassie is a complicated girl people have to get to know to really get to know, you know?

Clearly, those were not the words that raced to the tip of my tongue and plummeted out of my mouth. I'd said that other thing. The bad thing.

"What?" Natalie said. All joy and optimism gone. Vanished. Like my chances of scoring more than a swift punch to the crotch.

"That didn't come out right," I said. There was no doubt in my mind that I had the power to put the night back on course by telling Natalie that I'd gotten tongue-tied, that I'd meant to say that she, of course, was prettier than Cassie. That, compared to Natalie, Cassandra Castillo was a pockmarked hag who cooked fat German children and ate them for her supper. But years of being in love with Cassie had wrecked my ability to act properly around other girls.

In other words, I choked.

The awkward second turned into an uncomfortable moment, which quickly became an unbearable minute in which my social blunder morphed from comical misstep into a catastrophic thermonuclear explosion, obliterating any chance I may or may not have had to salvage the situation.

Natalie huffed and turned the key. Her truck roared to

life, the growl of the engine an expression of the anger bloom-
ing inside of its owner. "My friends were right."

"Probably," I said, honestly. Sadly. Her friends shouldn't
have been right. I should have been capable of going out
with a perfectly pretty, perfectly nice girl like Natalie without
Cassie getting between us. But I wasn't, and it made me want
to bash my head against the pavement to save myself from a
future where all I did was fuck things up. Maybe, probably,
Natalie Grayson and I wouldn't have had a long-term future,
but we could have had one fun night together.

Sometimes I hated being me.

"Get out."

"What?"

Natalie unlocked the doors with a click. "Get. Out." She
looked straight ahead, her hands firmly at ten and two.

I pushed the door open but stayed in my seat. Natalie
couldn't be serious about kicking me out of the car. Certainly,
I'd said some dick things, but I wasn't really a dick. She
wouldn't strand me in the middle of nowhere. Would she?

"I'm sorry," I said. I meant it.

Natalie sighed, and I felt hopeful. I even reached for the
handle to shut the door. "You've got your phone, right?" she
asked.

"Yeah."

"Then call someone who gives a fuck." Natalie revved the
engine and clutched the gearshift, putting the transmission
into drive. I grabbed my backpack and leaped out of the cab

into the road, not even looking to see if I was jumping into the path of an oncoming car. Truthfully, death by Cadillac wasn't the worst thing that could have happened to me right at that moment.

Without a second's hesitation, Natalie pulled a U-turn and floored it. I didn't think she was coming back.

Whining about my predicament would have been counterproductive to getting to the party, so I opted not to indulge. Plus, I knew I'd deserved to be kicked to the curb.

I rang up Ben and Coop first, but neither answered their phones, which meant either the party was kicking ass and was too loud for them to hear anything, or they were in a dark room groping each other so hard they'd gone temporarily deaf.

The rest of my phone list was sad and short. Friends I rarely talked to and girls I'd sort of dated.

My finger hovered over Aja Bourne's name, but I was not yet that desperate, and I shoved my phone back into my pocket.

I was also not yet desperate enough to call my parents. I knew they were sitting at home watching reruns of bad sitcoms and eating unbuttered, unsalted popcorn, and would have gladly picked me up and taken me to the party. But the only thing more degrading than being chucked into the road by Natalie would have been showing up at Cassie's party in the mom-mobile.

The option wasn't off the table, but I'd probably crawl ten

miles with two broken legs and a stomach covered in road rash before I'd give it serious consideration.

I started walking north toward Cassie's house. It was only a few miles, and I figured that if I didn't stop for any mope breaks, I could make it before the party ended. I envisioned arriving at Cassie's door, finding Ben and Coop partied out and wondering where I'd gotten to. They'd be racked with guilt, apologetic that they'd convinced me to talk to another girl. Cassie would be waiting on a chaise lounge, exhausted from fending off other boys all night. I'd attach myself to her lips like one of Ripley's aliens and never, ever let go.

Or, you know, I'd show up and the keg would be dry, and I'd spend the remainder of my night listening to everyone tell me how great the party *was* because my best friends were too busy to pick up their goddamn phones.

I checked again to see if Coop had called back, but he hadn't. It felt like I'd been walking for hours, but it hadn't even been fifteen minutes. I kept hoping Natalie would realize that I wasn't a complete dick and that leaving me on the side of the road had been a terrible mistake. But I knew that would never happen. I was about to give up and call my dad when a white car with a rusted hood and one dead headlight skidded to a stop, nearly mowing me down.

The driver's-side door opened. "Falcor, wait!" A whitish dog the size of a football darted out and ran straight into the base of a palm tree. The dog stood, stunned for a second, and then lifted his leg and peed on it.

"Show that tree who's boss," I mumbled.

"Can you grab him?" a voice called from inside the car. I couldn't see a face because of the cyclopean headlight that was trained on me like a laser.

"Sure," I said. "I hope he's got all his shots."

"I hope you've got all yours," said the voice, which sounded distinctly feminine.

I approached the dog slowly. "Nice doggie." If the dog noticed me, he gave zero indication. After finishing his pee, he began running in tight circles, barking with wild abandon. I picked him up and he seemed startled. He gave a little growl and licked my hand.

Falcor was maybe the ugliest dog I'd ever seen. His freakish underbite and smooshed nose made me think he definitely had some shih tzu in him, but he was misshapen, like someone had put him together wrong. And his eyes were all pupil, black. Creepy.

"Here," I said, walking up to the open car door.

"I seem to be having a seat belt malfunction." The girl inside the car was struggling with the locking mechanism, pulling it and beating at it with a pair of shiny handcuffs that I thought better of asking about.

I crouched down so that I was eye level with her. Falcor wiggle-wormed in my arms, but I held him tightly. "Want some help?"

The girl looked at me. Her eyes were big and brown and I don't think I saw her blink once. There was something about her. Like the dog, she seemed off, the way a movie and the sound are sometimes slightly out of sync.

"I can get it," the girl said. "Are you a rapist?"

"What?"

"A sexual predator. You're not going to kidnap me and take me to an abandoned house and have your fiendish way with me, are you?"

"Jesus Christ! Of course not!"

"Oh." The girl eyed me up and down like maybe she wasn't sure she believed me. "I guess you're okay, then."

I shoved the dog at her and said, "Here's your dog." Then I stood up to leave, hiking my backpack up on my shoulder.

"Hold your horses, bucko." The girl gave the seat belt a series of taps, and it released her. "I'm Stella." She climbed out of the car, her movements oddly insectlike, and when she stood up straight she was so short that I could have rested my chin on the top of her head.

I briefly entertained the idea of giving Stella a fake name in case she turned out to be an escapee from an asylum for the criminally insane or something, but I couldn't choose between Alejandro Von Tittlesworth or Roger, so I told her the name I'd been saddled with at birth.

Stella cocked her head to the side. "You look familiar. Are you an actor?"

"No," I said, unsure what to say next. Stella was equal parts confusing and exciting.

"Hm. You look like that guy in the gonorrhea PSAs." Stella

lowered her voice and put on a grim expression. "I may look like a nice guy, but I've been in more dark holes than a professional spelunker. And that was just last week!"

"Gonorrhea free," I said. "In fact, the closest I've ever come to catching an STD was the time I accidentally used the same spoon as Foster Jefferies at lunch. He has chronic cold sores."

"So, if you're not out here collecting sexually transmitted diseases, what are you doing?" Stella kicked at the sidewalk with the toe of her lime-green sneaker. She was a kaleidoscope of colors, from her red hair to her yellow tank to her limey shoes. It looked like she'd been dressed by a color-blind kindergartner.

The thought of concocting a lie occurred to me. It more than occurred. I thought lying might offer me the only opportunity to escape with my dignity more or less intact. But in the end I told Stella what had actually happened. There was some kind of gravity in her smile, in her eyes, that sucked the whole stupid truth, in all its excruciating glory, right out of me.

"You're a dick," Stella said when I'd finished.

"I just have dick tendencies," I said. "I'm actually pretty nice."

Stella seemed to consider this. "You did save my dog from that vicious tree."

"What's wrong with him?"

"Blind," she said. "He was born that way."

"He's fugly."

"You're not so great yourself." Her smile revealed her lie, and I couldn't help but grin back.

"I should get going," Stella said.

"Yeah, okay. I should call the Taxi de la Parents, anyway. Get them to come pick me up."

Stella leaned against her car and pursed her lips at me. They were nice lips, not too thin, but not overly full, either. Stella was different. Not Cassie, for sure, but not like any other girl I knew either. Other girls worked tirelessly to keep up with every ridiculous fad so that they could cling to popularity. But Stella wasn't trying to be anyone other than herself. And that gave me a boner.

"You're not so bad for a dick," she said. "Wanna ride?"

"Dick tendencies," I corrected. "To the party?"

"It's on my way?"

"Really?"

Stella shook her head. "Not really, but I was about to spend my entire night listening to ABBA and putting makeup on dead people."

"Ew," I said reflexively.

"I know. My mom's a funeral director, and she always ropes me into helping her with the bodies. She claims I have a natural talent for making the best of a dead situation, but I think she's just too cheap to hire an assistant."

"I was talking about ABBA," I said. "But the corpses are freaky too."

Stella slapped me on the arm. It stung, but I refused to flinch. "ABBA is only the best pop band of the last fifty *forever*."

"You have a sickness," I said. "My dad listens to them nonstop during tax season. He works out of the house, and for three agonizing months we all become dancing queens. It's a serious disease."

"I think I love your dad." Stella pulled her keys from her jeans pocket and jingled them. "You want a ride or not?"

I accepted without hesitation.

The Castillo house is a startling departure from the norm in the garden of McMansions that line Windsong Lane. Mr. Castillo had not been content to build a house that looked like everyone else's. The Castillo house stands out with its clay roof tiles and bright Spanish flair.

The front lawn, which had been meticulously manicured the last time I'd been there, was scarred by tire tracks and littered with cars of every make and model.

Stella pulled to a stop in front of Cassie's house. Falcor was sitting quietly in her lap, resting his head on the e-break.

I toyed with the zipper on my backpack, opening it and closing it. I knew this was the part where I was supposed to get out and go into the party. But I didn't want to. I wanted Stella to put her foot on the gas and take us anywhere else. Some of that was because I was having fun talking with her, but most of it was because I knew that if I went into that party, I'd see Cassie, and I'd want Cassie, and I'd spend the entire night mired in the soupy pit of despair. Which was exactly what I'd been trying to avoid when I'd nutted up at Gobbler's and talked to Natalie.

"Come to the party with me," I blurted. And even though I

knew I'd said it, I wasn't sure that I'd meant to. I was glad that I had, though, if that makes sense on any planet other than the one I inhabit.

"I have Falcor," Stella said. Falcor's ears perked up at his name.

"There are bound to be crazier things inside than a blind dog. It's a barter party."

Stella rolled her eyes. "I'm not dressed to party. I don't even have my saddle."

"You look fine."

"You sure know how to make a girl feel special."

"I only meant—"

"No, Simon, stick to your guns. I look *fine*." Stella dragged out that last word and then licked her pale peach lips in a mockery of sexy that drew reluctant laughter out of me.

"There'll be booze and dancing and bartering," I said, managing to make what Cassie had declared would be the greatest party of our high school lives sound überlame.

I unzipped my backpack and dug around until I found the small velvet bag I'd been looking for. I pulled open the drawstrings and emptied a pair of dice into my palm. "My mom got me these from Vegas. They were used at a real craps table. Mom said she saw someone win ten grand with these babies." I held the dice closer to her face, trying to make them seem as enticing as possible. "For the superlow price of spending one hour at this party with moi, these dice can be all yours."

Stella frowned at the dice and then took them from me.

She shook them in her closed fist, listening to the sharp clack they made. "I'll stay twenty minutes," she said. "And no dancing."

"Deal."

Stella pocketed the dice and looked for a place to park.

We found a spot on the side of the road and walked up the driveway. Music pounded at the windows and the doors and even the roof, straining the joints and leaking out of every crack it could find. It was the kind of music Coop abhors, the kind that thumps out of control, with lyrics that dig into your ears and squat there for days.

"Did she hire a DJ?" Stella asked.

"That's DJ Leo," I said. "He wants to be the next Daft Punk or something. No one really invites him, he just shows up."

Stella turned her ear to the house. "He's brilliant."

I took Stella's free hand and led her to the doorstep. As I reached for the doorknob, I was momentarily stunned by the memories of the last time I'd stood in that same spot. I half expected Mr. Castillo to be waiting behind the door, holding a Louisville Slugger in one hand and a fat cigar in the other.

But he wasn't. When I opened the door, the party rushed out like the leading edge of a tsunami. The sounds and smells and music and laughter carried on a wave of entropy that would eventually dissolve into utter chaos.

And then there was Cassie.

She stood in the space between the door and the jamb, leaning with one arm up and one arm hidden behind her back. She was wearing a black dress that hugged her curves and left very little to my overheated imagination. She smiled at first with her honey-colored eyes, and then with her lips, revealing that little gap that I'd been in love with for years. Even Cassie's imperfections were perfect.

"Simon! And other girl!"

The smell of tequila wafted from Cassie like a heavy fog, and I wondered how much she'd had to drink. It was barely ten.

"Heya, Cass." I coughed and said it again, unsure of my voice.

"Welcome to my barter party," Cassie said.

"Thanks," I said.

Stella whistled a tune, and I admit that I'd momentarily forgotten about her.

I was about to introduce Stella when Cassie said, "There's a price for admission." She had a devious look in her eyes. "And I think I'll take a kiss." I forgot about Stella all over again.

Everything was moving so quickly, and I couldn't get a grip. I hadn't even gotten through the front door and Cassie wanted me to kiss her? My lips and her lips. I'd resigned myself to forgetting about Cassie, and now she was inviting me to kiss her. It was maddening and terrifying and other words that I was sure I'd missed on my SATs.

"Really?" I asked.

"Nothing in life is free, Simon Cross," Cassie said. "Pay up, unless you want to spend your night on the front lawn."

Ben and Coop had been so wrong. They'd said it was

impossible. They'd said it was never going to happen. But here I was, about to make my dreams come true.

Except Stella, with her stupid dog, pushed past me, stood on her tiptoes, and kissed Cassie right on the mouth. Cassie didn't even seem surprised. The girl I'd brought to the party was making out with the girl I loved. There was full tongue involvement. Okay, maybe there wasn't, but in the days that followed, when I remembered it, there would be.

People on both sides of the door catcalled and whistled. And I could only stand there and watch, embarrassed to the tips of my toes. Not only had I failed to kiss Cassie—again—but someone else had done it in my place.

What. The. Fuck.

Stella winked when she was done. "I'm Stella Nash," she said to Cassie. "Nice to meet you." Then she wiped her lips with the back of her hand, pushed her way into the bowels of the party, and disappeared, taking with her any chance I'd had of kissing Cassie.

Living the Dream

Cassie had chucked Eli Horowitz like an ugly sweater, and the douche was still managing to cock block me. He hadn't needed to say a word; he'd simply walked into the party and stood there being all Horowitzy while I asked Cassie the price for a kiss. And it wasn't like she'd said no to the kiss. That, I could have handled. I could have scooped the battered remains of my ego off the kitchen floor and retreated to a dark corner, maybe chatted up Natalie or resorted to making out with Aja Bourne. But Cassie hadn't even heard me. She'd blown me off without taking one serious second to consider my proposal. Like I meant nothing to her. Less than nothing. I might as well have been DJ Leo, except he, at least, had some skills, whereas I had dice.

I stood in the kitchen, replaying the way Cassie had looked when she'd seen Eli standing by the French doors in the family room. Eli Fucking Horowitz. Seriously, if I had a time machine, I wouldn't waste my effort righting the wrongs of the world's ridiculous history, I'd travel back and wipe out Eli. I'd punch through the time-space continuum and take a chainsaw to the whole Horowitz family tree.

I might have wasted my entire night coming up with progressively more violent ways to delete Eli from my life if a girl in a bikini, chasing a guy wearing nothing but a towel, hadn't run through the kitchen and bumped into me, spilling something red and sticky onto my jeans.

"Thanks," I called after them, as if they could actually hear me. I groaned and snatched a napkin from the counter to dab at the slowly spreading stain, but the napkin was useless. As useless as I felt.

It was all too much. Cassie and Eli and the party and the people and the music pounding at my ears. I needed a break before I broke someone's jaw. Before I had the kind of meltdown that would cost my parents a fortune in therapy bills and antidepressants.

God, I was being so melodramatic. And I melodramatically stormed through the family room and opened the first door I found. Which happened to be Mr. and Mrs. Castillo's bedroom. I turned to leave—aware that Mr. Castillo would likely flay me alive if he found out I'd been in his bedroom—when I caught sight of Eli again. He was standing against the far wall with his arms crossed over his ridiculous chest. I followed his gaze to where Cassie had stopped to have an animated conversation with some girl I didn't really know. The fact that Eli was watching her pissed me off. There were only two logical reasons that explained why he'd decided to show up. He was either trying to make Cassie jealous or trying to get her back.

If he'd been trying to make her jealous, he would have shown up with another girl on his arm. Someone like Lacy McDougal, a.k.a. Cassiebot 2000. Which would have made Cassie go ballistic.

That meant that Eli was definitely trying to get back together with Cassie.

I watched Eli watching Cassie for another minute before ducking into the bedroom—Mr. Castillo be damned. I needed a moment to calm down, clear my head, and clean the stain off my jeans, and this was the perfect place to do it.

The room was bigger than my living room, dining room, and kitchen combined, and that wasn't counting their bathroom, which was divided by a luxurious, sloping tub. A king-size bed dominated the room, and it looked so soft that all I could think about doing was jumping on it. Seriously, it called out to me. Begged me to hop up and defy some gravity. The lure was so great that I momentarily forgot how angry I was at Eli and his stupid, cock-blocking ways.

"What are you doing in here?" Cassie walked up behind me. She didn't look angry, but it was clear that she didn't approve of my choice of hiding spots.

I tried to tell her that I'd come to clean my stained jeans, but I sputtered and stalled. I was too overwhelmed by my feelings for Cassie. It was all I could do not to admit right then and there that I'd been in love with her since the very first moment I'd seen her. I wanted Cassie to feel the same way about me that I felt about her. I wanted her to know. But how could I tell her that when I couldn't even tell her about the stupid stain?

"I was contemplating taking a jump on your parents' bed." Fortune favors the bold. Plus, I couldn't think of anything better.

Cassie made a pinched face. "What?"

I pointed at the bed. "Jump. The bed's begging us to jump on it. Come on." I held my hand out to Cassie and prayed for her to take it. I didn't expect her to. The idea was dumb, idiotic, but a voice in my head told me that at this second, this moment, Cassie didn't need me to kiss her, she didn't need my romantic declarations of Shakespearean love, she didn't need me to eliminate Eli from the infinite arrow of time. All she needed was to jump.

Cassie glanced at the bed and shook her head. "This is stupid, Simon."

"Stupid awesome."

This was not a Cassie thing to do. She protested school budget cuts of the arts programs, she rallied for organic cafeteria food, she studied hard and got good grades, she was proper and cool and classy. She always did the right thing. I knew she had a rebellious streak and I knew she'd been drinking, but I didn't know if that would allow her to jump on her parents' bed with a loser like me.

"No," Cassie said. "No." I felt her slipping away, retreating back into the party, where she was safe, where I might not be able to reach her again. I knew I was being a flaming imbecile, but for the second time in less than an hour, Fate had thrown Cassie and me together. Had given me the rare opportunity to show her that she was oxygen and I was hydrogen and that we belonged together. Molecularly.

I might not get another chance.

"Yes," I said, holding my hand out to her again. "One jump. If you hate it, we'll stop."

"Simon—"

"A trade, then," I said. "Jump on the bed with me and I'll go vegan for a month."

Cassie paused. "You? Vegan?"

I nodded. "One jump," I said. "And I'll eat nothing with a face for a whole month."

"Two months," Cassie said. "And if you welsh, I'll tell everyone in school that you wear silky pink panties."

"That's not true!"

Cassie shrugged. "Dear, sweet Simon. It doesn't need to be true for people to buy it." Her smile was so genuine that it was nearly impossible to believe she was so deliciously devious.

"Deal," I said. "Two months for one jump. Unless you like it, in which case, I'll be more than happy to provide subsequent jumps at a greatly reduced rate."

Cassie arched her sculpted eyebrow at me, looking rather like a Bond villain about to spill her evil plan for world domination. "I didn't realize this was a pay-per-jump establishment."

"We can discuss alternate payment plans later."

"My mom's head will explode."

"I'll never tell," I said. I drew an X over my heart. "You have my word. The only way your parents will ever find out that we jumped on their bed is if they have a camera in here somewhere." I looked around conspiratorially.

Cassie feigned shock. "Why would my parents have a camera in their bedroom?"

"Duh," I said. "For when they put on their after-hours sock puppet shows. They're all the rage on YouTube. The Castillo Tube Sock Variety Pack. Over a hundred thousand hits and counting."

"Now you're just being silly," Cassie said, but she was smiling. For that, I'd be as silly as I needed to be.

"Stop stalling. You owe me a jump." I kicked my shoes off before climbing up on the bed. Cassie bent down to take off her heels, wincing as she pulled the shoe off her injured foot. It didn't look as bad as before, but I could see that it hurt.

"Sorry. Again."

Cassie didn't say anything as she used the headboard to haul herself up.

The ceiling in the Castillo bedroom was vaulted, and there was a skylight over the bed that let in all the stars. They seemed so bright and I wondered if any of this was real. This whole thing felt more like my dreams than reality. The lights were brighter, the lines sharper, the sounds clearer, and Cassie actually wanted to spend time with me. But dream or not, I didn't care.

My socked feet sank into the thick comforter and I took an experimental hop. The bed was springier than I could have hoped for, and a smile took root on my face and grew.

"I haven't jumped on a bed in forever," I said.

Cassie got her balance, but held on to the headboard for support. "I've never jumped on a bed."

"Never?"

"Nope."

"I'm shocked," I said. "Speechless."

"Not so speechless," Cassie said.

"You know what I mean." I ran my hands through my hair and tucked it behind my ears. "I find it impossible to believe that you've never jumped on a bed before. That's, like, child abuse. Your parents are totally going on my naughty list. What kid hasn't jumped on a bed?"

"There are a lot of things I never got to do," Cassie said. "Maybe this was a bad idea."

"Oh, hell no," I said, and took her arm, guiding her to the center of the bed. "We had a deal, and if you back out now, I'm stealing a car, driving back to Gobbler's, and ordering a Big Bacon Belly Exploder, with extra bacon. Anyway, you know you wanna try this."

"Ugh. You're like a bad drug dealer."

"Careful, Cass. One jump and you'll be hooked. Next time I see you, you'll be breaking into furniture stores, stealing jumps off the discount mattresses."

"Or turning tricks for jumps on strangers' beds."

"Yikes," I said. "This is gonna be fun, but I'm not sure it's worth turning tricks for." I cocked my head to the side and broke out my special occasion smile. "Who am I kidding? I'd trade hand jobs at truck stops for jumps. I'm Simon Cross, and I'm a jumpaholic."

Cassie laughed, which made me smile even bigger. So big, my cheeks hurt. "Are you going to tease me all night or are we going to jump?"

"You can't just jump into this sort of thing," I said.

"You can't jump into jumping?"

"It's an art; it must be respected." I held out my hands and Cassie took them. "Okay, so here's what we're going to do. When I count to three, you're going to jump as high as you can. Got that? On three."

Cassie rolled her eyes dramatically. "I think I can handle it."

"Okay." I tightened my grip on Cassie's hands, but not too hard. They were soft and so small. My own fingers fit around Cassie's like a perfectly tied knot. "One," I said slowly, drawing it out theatrically. "Two." I grinned at Cassie, memorizing her face. "Three!"

I jumped and Cassie jumped. We jumped. The two of us, connected by hands and happiness and our declarative FUCK YOU! to gravity. Our smiles and laughter filling the void between our bodies, joining us, entangling us. One and the same.

And then my feet hit the bed and I bent my knees and jumped again. Again. Again.

Again.

With Cassie.

Because she couldn't resist jumping with me. She couldn't fight the pull of fate, the density of her soul locked in battle with her insatiable desire to leave this earth behind. Even if only for a moment.

At least that's what I thought I saw in her eyes as we hovered in the air for those brief moments. Maybe it wasn't real.

But maybe it was.

"Oh. My. God!" Cassie yelled as we hopped like demented

bunnies. The bed groaned and creaked, and I laughed, and Cassie squealed with delight.

When we were in the air, everything disappeared. History, our history, vanished. The hours, days, and years that had existed between the time I'd turned chickenshit at Pirate Chang's and this moment right now were nothing. We'd bridged the two points in time and space and come together. Here. In the air.

I wondered if Eli was standing outside the door, listening to the sounds of us jumping, which to anyone else might have sounded like we were doing something less vertical. I hoped that he was standing there, right outside of the Castillos' bedroom, imagining all the things I might be doing to Cassie and that she might be doing to me. The same way that I'd been forced for three long years to endure watching Eli touch Cassie's neck in a way that made the tips of her ears turn pink. Watching him say something that made her laugh. Something that only the two of them understood.

But Eli had had his chance. This was my time to soar.

"I can't believe I've never done this," Cassie said. Stray bits of hair stuck to her slightly damp forehead.

"Awesome, right?"

"Higher," she said as an answer, and I squeezed her hand and pulled her higher into the night sky, ignoring the ceiling and the limitations of mass and molecules and that buzzkill Newton. Leaving the house and the party and the whole damn world behind.

Because Cassie was the girl for me. The girl for forever.

So I kissed her.

Or I tried.

What really happened was that we were jumping on the bed, had been jumping on the bed for a full minute. And I was looking at her and thinking about her, and this little voice in my head, a voice that I should have known better than to heed, told me to go for it. And I listened. Midjump, I craned my neck for the kiss, sure that Cassie would kiss me back and we'd spend the rest of the night in the fluffy comforter, rolled up like sushi.

"What are you doing?" Cassie dodged my lips and shoved me into the headboard. "What the fuck do you think you're doing?" She was Shiva, the angry god, and she was going to tear my arms from my scrawny frame and choke me with my own hands.

"I love you, Cassie," I said. Because trying to kiss her hadn't been bad enough. There had been a moment, a second, where I might have been able to pretend that I hadn't meant to try to kiss her, that it was all some monumental misunderstanding. Or I could have blamed it on that shot of tequila or the music or the stars or anything. But I didn't. No. Because I was a moron. Certified. When I died, scientists were going to cut open my skull and scoop out my brain, pickle it, and study it as a prime example of the long-term effect of love on the brain of a moron. Because surely, I was the biggest moron who had ever been in love with a girl.

Cassie stopped jumping. She was tethered to the earth now, a prisoner of gravity once again. "I know, Simon. You wear your feelings for me like a neon sign over your heart. What do you want me to do about it?"

The words were deadly shards of glass. They sliced my skin,

and I watched as my blood fountained from a million tiny wounds, spreading over the bed like a new duvet.

"I thought—"

"You thought that since I dumped Eli, you'd lure me into my parents' bedroom and make everything in my life all better because we jumped on a fucking bed? And then what? We'd ride the mattress into the sunset? You're like everyone else. No, you're worse because you're so naive."

I grew smaller. I grew small. Insignificant. A worm not worthy of even her pity.

"I only wanted to make you smile," I said. And I meant it. "I wanted to make you happy."

Cassie laughed. It was dark and devoid of joy. "I don't need you, Simon Cross. I'm capable of taking care of myself." Cassie sat down and slid off the bed, slipping her feet back into her shoes, ignoring any pain from her injured foot. "You don't love me. You love some girl you invented in your stupid pea brain. But I'm not that girl. She doesn't exist."

When I said, "I do love you, Cassie," my voice was as small as I was. It barely registered above the bass line of DJ Leo's latest song. I wished that guy had a mute button. "If you'll just let me show you."

Cassie crossed her arms over her chest. "How about a barter, Simon?" Her voice kept cutting me.

"Anything."

The anger Cassie had loosed was fading, wrestled back into Pandora's box along with that tiny flame of hope upon which my future happiness now rested. "Prove that you love me, Simon. Prove irrefutably that you love me, the real me, not just some idea of me, and I'll give you anything you want."

And then she left.

I was still standing on the bed, watching the space where Cassie had been, when Coop and Ben walked through the door hand in hand. Coop frowned at me while Ben just chuckled.

Ben dropped Coop's hand and leaped onto the bed. He hooted and jumped as I stood there bouncing in his wake, still stunned. He didn't jump with the same kind of innocent joy Cassie had. Ben was a madman.

I pushed Ben aside and got down off the bed.

Coop grabbed my sleeve. "Simon, what's up? You okay?"

Explaining what had happened wasn't at the top of my list of superfun things to do, so I stormed into the adjoining bathroom to get away from the boys. I shut myself in and sat on the floor.

Hardly a moment had passed before Coop slid open the door and poked his head in. "Hey."

"What if I'd been pooping?"

Coop plopped down cross-legged on the immaculate white tile. "Remember the eighth-grade DC trip?" I nodded. "Remember the free oysters in the hotel?"

I chuckled. "We ate like a pound of those suckers. Stupid food poisoning."

"Right," Coop said. "I've seen things coming out of both your ends that would make a garbageman bleach his eyes out."

"Point taken."

Silence.

"Cassie hates me." I told Coop everything. More than he probably wanted to know. When I was done, he patted my arm.

"You're an idiot."

"Don't I know it," I said.

"But you're my best friend," Coop said. "And Cassie doesn't deserve you."

I rolled my eyes. "You're supposed to say shit like that."

"Yeah," Coop said. "But this time, I also happen to mean it." He was quiet again. "What are you going to do?"

I shrugged. "Kidnap Cassie and put her in your trunk? I'll keep her in a deep pit in my backyard. Nothing says 'I love the real you' like kidnapping."

"This is Florida," Coop said. "You can't dig a pit in your backyard."

"I don't know," I said. "This was supposed to be different."

Coop nodded. He knew what I'd expected. He'd probably also known I'd been delusional. "Quick question: You got a condom?"

Oddly, it was a relief to talk about something other than my monumental failure in the Cassie department. "No. My mom found the one I kept in my wallet and chucked it. Apparently, I'm too young to be having sex. She informed me that if she found out I was doing it with anyone, she'd neuter me."

"Ouch. Someone should tell your mom that not having a condom won't keep you from having sex."

"Luckily for her, social awkwardness is one hundred percent effective."

Coop stood up and helped me to my feet. He put his arm around my shoulders and said, "Don't waste the whole night, Simon. If you love Cassie, prove it. If not, then have some fun. But you're only seventeen once. And for a dick, you're a pretty awesome guy."

Only, I didn't feel pretty awesome. I felt like an ass. But Coop was right. It was time to crap or get off the pot. Cassie had issued me a challenge. And even though I was sure she figured I'd never be able to do it, I was going to prove to Cassie that I really loved her.

I was going to earn my kiss or die trying.

Reality Bites

"Did that just happen?" Cassie asked as she stood in the doorway, staring at me, absently touching her lips with the tips of her fingers.

"No," I said. "That was a figment of your imagination. Here comes your real kiss."

For a moment, I thought that was going to work, but then Cassie smacked my shoulder and giggled. I didn't know what else to say. I was struck mute by the fact that Stella had managed to accomplish in ten seconds what I'd failed to do in three long, lonely years. I played the ridiculous scene over and over in my head: Cassie, standing by the doorway, smelling of tequila, looking beautiful—more beautiful than I'd ever seen her—telling me that I had to kiss her to get into the party. And then Stella, a girl I'd only just met, wedging herself between us and stealing that kiss like it was nothing.

"Sy?" Cassie pulled me aside as a group of girls I half recognized pushed their way into the house and were absorbed into the party.

I pinched my arm hard, which made Cassie giggle again. "I don't even know that girl," I said. "I mean, I know her. I didn't pick her up on the side of the road. Actually, she picked me up off the side of the road. But there's a perfectly good explanation for that. Stop me from babbling any time."

Cassie rolled her eyes and pulled me into the house by my sleeve. "Same old Simon." Her smile was a shooting star— brilliant and gone before I could capture it. Cassie was beautiful without thought, without effort. And I was in her thrall.

As Cassie closed the door behind us, I stood in the foyer and looked around. The last time I'd been to the Castillo house, I'd barely made it past the unwelcome mat. Mr. Castillo had answered the door sporting a surly face, glaring down at me like I was wearing a T-shirt emblazoned with the words: "Future Baby Daddy." Cassie had been beautiful that night too. But that was years past and this was now.

And in the now, the house was a wall-to-wall collection of people I barely knew in varying states of drunkenness and undress. The party was in overdrive. It usually took a couple of hours for people to start losing articles of clothing, but one girl was already down to her bikini top. I wondered what she'd bartered in exchange for her shirt. I was about to ask Cassie when I was interrupted by a crash from the room to my left.

"Contact Scrabble," Cassie explained, as if that was somehow supposed to make sense. "The debate team started a Scrabble game in the library, but Jody got the lacrosse guys involved and, well . . . Contact Scrabble."

"Should I break it up?" I asked, as if there was any way that I could do such a thing. Jody Johnson was a beast of a guy who spoke exclusively in grunts and wedgies.

Cassie shrugged. "Why bother?" She moved as if we were touring the Louvre rather than an illicit, underage party. "Over there is the beer pong table," she said, pointing to the room across from the library. I took a peek. All the furniture had been pushed up against the walls and a green Ping-Pong table sat in the center of the room, under a crystal chandelier that was begging for some drunk dick to swing from it. Dean Kowalcyk and his harem of girls were the sole occupants of the room, which was fine by me. Dean and I had briefly been mortal enemies in seventh grade, and I'd avoided him religiously since.

"You invited Dean?"

"He invited himself," Cassie said. She stood in the foyer and looked down the hall toward what appeared to be the kitchen. "They all did. I don't know half of these people." For a second, I thought Cassie was going to lose it. Maybe I was being melodramatic—it had sort of been that kind of night for me—but I felt like I could see her standing on the precipice of some kind of emotional breakdown. She stood at the edge, looking over, thinking about jumping, and then used her own smile to tether herself to the now.

I wasn't just imagining it—there was something wrong with Cassie. It was so obvious that even blind Falcor could have seen it. And a better man would have put aside his own selfish desires and tried to help Cassie. But I was not a better man. Not at that moment. I was still wearing blinders forged from the feelings of the more-than-a-crush I'd been harboring for Cassie since the first time I saw her. And I couldn't help but hope that whatever was going on with Cassie might make her willing to kiss me. I'm not making excuses, but sometimes guys don't always think with the brain that they ought to.

"Whatever," Cassie said. "It's a party. Drink?"

Without waiting for my answer, she took off down the hallway toward the kitchen, seemingly unconcerned with whether or not I followed. I tried to trail her wake, but where she had sliced like a knife through the hordes mingling in the narrow hall, I felt like a salmon struggling upstream, petrified that even if I made it to my destination, a motherfucking bear was going to rip me out of the water and eat my head off.

Ben Kwon isn't a bear, but when he grabbed me by the collar and pulled me into the dining room, I jumped.

"Simon!" Ben said. He was slick with sweat and his eyes were bloodshot. "Got a condom? Tell me you have one in your wallet for that just-in-case that never comes. Unless you've managed to dip your fries in ketchup girl? Did you? Do you? Don't toy with me, Simon."

I ducked out of Ben's grasp and clapped my hand over his mouth. I needed to get my bearings. I wanted out of this room; I wanted to get to Cassie before the party swallowed her up.

But Ben was staring at me like we were trapped on the moon and I have the only oxygen on the whole bloody rock.

"Why do you need a condom?" I asked, regretting my question immediately.

Ben tossed his arm around my shoulder and tried to wrap me up in a sloppy hug. I could smell the same tequila on him that I'd smelled on Cassie. "Simon, buddy, bro. Got a condom or not?"

"No."

"Useless," Ben said, and he let me go.

I tried to leave, but Ben yanked me back. I fell into him and he stumbled into the table, knocking a can of soda onto the floor. "Are you drunk?" I asked, righting myself and putting some necessary distance between us.

Ben stood up and brushed imaginary lint off his shirt. "I'm only a little tipsy. Cassie made me take tequila shots when I got here." Ben tapped his chin thoughtfully. "I don't know what's up with party girl, but I'm digging it."

"Cassie's acting odd," I said. "Very un-Cassie-like."

"Let me tell you something about women."

"Because you're the expert."

"In this room," Ben said, "I'm the expert." He grabbed a warm Sprite out of an open box and chugged half, following that with an impressive belch. "It's senior year, Simon. Cassie dumped Eli. She's finally realized that this is supposed to be the best year of our lives. A little late if you ask me, but better late than sober."

I frowned. "I don't know."

Ben put the soda on the table and sat in one of the high-backed chairs. "Maybe this is the real Cassie, and that other uptight girl was just an ugly outfit she was wearing to impress people."

"You're pretty much talking out of your ass."

"It is my best feature." Ben leaped at me and tried to wrestle his way into my back pocket. "You sure you don't have a condom back there?" Ben was stronger than me, but I was wiry and fast, and I ducked out of his grasp. "Don't hold out on me," he said.

"I don't have a condom!" I skirted the wall, trying to keep some distance between us. "And for the record, it's gross of you to ask me to help you and Coop get busy. You're practically my brothers. You should be ashamed."

"I have no shame." Ben broke out in a toothy grin and said, "Let's go find my boyfriend."

We dove back into the party, letting the crowd and the rhythmic beat of the music carry us down the hall and to the kitchen—the usual hub of a party. People were dancing in the family room, playing beer pong in the living room, and brawling over the use of proper nouns in the library, but the kitchen was where everything else was happening. In the breakfast nook, some football jocks were sitting at a circular table, playing Bullshit for shots. It was pretty much a foregone conclusion that they were going to be comatose before midnight.

I kept an eye out for Cassie but I'd lost track of her. It was her house, so she had to be somewhere, but she definitely wasn't in the kitchen.

A girl that I'd had health with in tenth grade was hanging around the keg with a bunch of other in-betweeners—kids who weren't exactly popular but weren't all that unpopular, either. They were the kind of kids who no one would remember when we left high school. I'd have been one of them if it hadn't been for Ben and Coop. Those boys were one of the reasons I hadn't taken the long slide into high school obscurity.

"There's my Coopy Bear," Ben said. He pulled me with him to the other side of the kitchen, where Coop was talking to—shit. Shit, fuck, damn. Coop was chatting up Stella. She was cradling her stupid blind dog in her arms, laughing at something Coop had said.

It was fight-or-flight time, and my lizard brain wanted to run, to get as far from that girl as my feet could carry me.

But that was stupid. Idiotic. Stella was just a girl. A cool girl. She couldn't have known that I'd wanted to kiss Cassie for the better part of my high school career.

I took a steadying breath and tried to smile, even though I knew that I likely looked like I was trying to hold back poo.

Ben rushed Coop and kissed him so hard that both boys fell into the stove—which thankfully was off. It was obscene and a little uncomfortable. I wondered if they realized that the rest of us were still here. On the plus side, Ben and Coop playing tonsil hockey was the perfect antiboner.

I turned away. Stella couldn't seem to stop gawking.

"Get a room!" shouted one of the jocks.

Coop managed to disentangle himself from Ben's arms. "Simon! You made it. Stella's been telling me you nearly didn't."

"Yeah," I said.

Coop frowned at me. As our DD, I knew he hadn't been drinking, and I was thankful for that. I needed one of my friends to be sober. "What I can't figure out," Coop said, "is what you could have said to make Natalie dump you on the side of A1A."

It was bad enough that everyone knew I'd blown it. Indulging Coop's desire for the gory details was something I had zero intention of doing. Instead I grabbed a warmish beer from a passing junior and chugged it. "Ben, isn't this that song you like? The one with the words?"

Ben's ears perked up like Falcor's, and he zeroed in on the dance floor like he had GPS. DJ Leo was just a nerdy, short kid with glasses who always had headphones in his ears and slept through his classes. But for tonight, he was a minor-league legend.

"I love this song!" Ben grabbed Coop's hand and dragged him away. Coop shot me an evil glare that said, "You've won this round, but I will find out the truth." And I knew that Coop eventually would. Just not right this second.

The moment they were gone, disappeared into the dancing shadows, I turned to Stella and lost the ability to say things. When I looked at Stella, I saw only Stella kissing Cassie. Cassie kissing her back. It was like watching the worst best movie ever.

"Cool party," Stella said. "Does your friend Cassie always kiss strange girls?"

"You kissed her."

"I'm pretty sure she asked for it."

"She was asking me."

"She didn't ask you by name—oh." Stella's shoulders drooped and she bit the corner of her lip. "You wanted to kiss her, didn't you?"

The question was rhetorical. Of course I'd wanted to kiss her. There wasn't a guy at the party not named Ben or Coop who wouldn't have climbed over a pit of bloodthirsty unicorns to get that kiss. "No," I said. "It's no big deal."

Stella looked at me like she was seeing right through my words to the truth of everything about me. It was unsettling and annoying and I wished that I'd called my parents when I'd had the chance. "You like her."

I could have lied. I should have lied. I'd met Stella only an hour earlier and for all I knew she could have been some kind of crazy stalker chick who had formed an unhealthy emotional attachment to me and would spend the rest of the night hunting Cassie so that she could kill her and wear her skin like a prom dress. Or not.

"Kind of." Which was an understatement. "We went out in ninth grade and I almost kissed her and I thought that if I had another chance—especially since she just broke up with her boyfriend—that . . . you know."

"And I took that chance," Stella said. "Hear that, Falcor? I'm so dumb."

"You're not dumb."

"I'm pretty dumb."

I caught Stella's eyes. They had these dark swirls like the planet Jupiter. And even though she was the one who'd ruined my perfect chance with Cassie, I was the one who felt like an asshole. "You're not dumb. For all I know, you wanted to kiss her as badly as I did."

Stella made this face that was equal parts "meh" and "maybe." Then she said, "I prefer girls with more facial hair. And by girls I mean boys. And by facial hair, I mean money. Would it help if I told you that Cassie was a terrible kisser?"

"Maybe a little."

Stella wiped her mouth with the back of her hand. "Yuck! It was like kissing a dead cat. Gross. So bad that I may never kiss another living human being again."

"I suppose it's a good thing you work with dead human beings."

"In the morgue, 'no' always means 'yes.'" Stella was smiling again and I had to forgive her. There was no way to stay mad at this girl. Not even for stealing what may have been my last, best chance to kiss Cassie.

"You can tell me the truth. It was good, right?"

"I don't really have a frame of reference," she said.

"Never kissed a girl before?"

"Never kissed anyone."

I rolled my eyes and chuckled. "Funny."

Stella stared at me like she had the first time we'd met. Unblinking. And I knew that she'd been telling the truth as sure as if she'd beamed her entire kissless history into my brain via psychic laser.

"For really real? No one?" I didn't mean to sound so judgmental, but even I had kissed other people. Other girls. And maybe even Coop once on a dare.

"No one. Not even Falcor, and I've tried enticing him with peanut butter."

It simply didn't compute that Stella had never kissed a guy. "Are you one of those abstinence groupies? Like no sex till marriage?"

Stella sighed. "I go to an all-girls school. And I'm not a lesbian. My kissing opportunities are limited to dead guys or the occasional Jehovah's Witnesses who wake me up at seven on a Saturday morning. I love those guys."

"Aren't we a pair?" I said, trying to defuse the awkwardness that had sprouted between us. I leaned against the counter and folded my arms over my chest, watching the party move and groove around us like a living thing rising toward its inevitable climax. The half bottle of beer I'd chugged was tearing through my veins, making me feel dangerous. Reminding me that I am SIMON CROSS. I'd talked to Natalie Grayson. I'd hitched a ride with this strange girl and traded my Vegas dice to get her to accompany me to the party. I felt like I was finally taking control of my life rather than just letting it steamroller over me. I'd been pining for Cassie for all of high school. Pining but not acting. Tonight, however, that was going to change.

"I propose another trade," I said.

Stella looked up at me. "Go on."

"I'll find you a guy to kiss if you help me kiss Cassie." It was a bold proposition. It could backfire horribly. It could turn into a disaster of epic proportions. It could ruin my entire high school life, leaving me a broken shell of a man with nothing left to live for but Butterfinger bites and *Firefly* reruns.

Or it might just be crazy enough to work.

Stella might just be crazy enough to make it work.

"What do you think?" I asked.

Stella was watching me through narrowed eyes. The girl was impossible to read. But I knew she'd say yes, because Fate was cheering for Team Simon. I had the ball, all I had to do was shoot and not fuck it up again.

A small smile crept up the corners of Stella's mouth. It spread across her face like sunrise. I briefly wondered if there existed any guy at the party who was even remotely worthy of planting a kiss on that mouth.

"Can I take that as a yes?" I asked.

Stella didn't need to answer, it was in her eyes. But she said it anyway, and it changed my life.

Living the Dream

There was a yawning gulf between knowing that I needed to do something to prove myself to Cassie and actually getting off my ass and doing it. The girl I adored believed I didn't know her, that I wasn't in love with her. But she'd given me an opportunity. The opportunity to earn my kiss. All I had to do was show her that I wasn't another jerk who had crawled out of the shadows to have a go at her because she was finally single.

But I had no idea how to begin to do that.

Coop and Ben had abandoned me, and a few feet from where I stood, Natalie laughed at something another guy said. I felt a twinge of regret. No, not regret. Curiosity. I couldn't help wondering what my night might have been like if I'd followed Coop's advice and talked to her at the diner. Would we have spent the entire night chatting and laughing and sucking face? Or would it have been an unmitigated disaster? There was no way to know. And none of that would matter if I managed to prove to Cassie that I really did love her. All I could do was keep moving forward and hope for the best.

"Can I score a little of your beer?" someone asked. I looked down at this short, skinny kid who spoke with a slight lisp. He was standing in front of me, holding out a red cup that was filled nearly halfway with something brown and unappealing.

"Come again?" I asked. I'd never seen the kid before, but he glanced around nervously, like he was afraid that I'd stomp him if he made direct eye contact. He looked like a freshman, which was odd because underclassmen weren't usually invited to senior parties or any party outside of a Chuck E. Cheese's.

The kid pointed at my cup. "Can you give me a splash of your beer?"

"Why?" I asked.

"Forget it," he said, agitated. I was clearly no longer worthy of his fear.

"Sing the song, Urinal Cake!" Blaise Lewis shouted from his spot at the breakfast nook. He was sitting with his jock buddies, holding court.

"That's the worst nickname ever," I said to the kid. He was staring at his feet, looking more irritated than embarrassed.

I should have done what the kid had asked and poured some of my beer into his cup, but I didn't, so I suppose it was my fault that he had to sing. Urinal Cake had a surprisingly clear tenor.

"Blaise is a god, Blaise is my master, he's a champ with the girls, no one does it faster. On the field, and with the ladies. Even with the grannies, who are sometimes in their eighties. As his slave, from you I beg, a pour from your drink, or a squirt from the keg." As if that rhyming monstrosity wasn't bad enough, Urinal

Cake then knelt in front of me and held his cup in the air. Blaise and his asshole friends were cracking up so hard that I could only hope they choked on their own tongues.

"Whatever," I said, and poured some of my beer into the kid's cup. I had a feeling it would be worse for him if I didn't.

Urinal Cake stood up and tossed me an insincere thanks before moving along to someone else.

It would have been funny if I hadn't felt so bad for him. One of the things that had saved me from being known as Simon Hymen throughout my high school career was Cassie. Going on just one date with that girl had pulled me out of the social gutter. Having Coop and Ben as friends had helped too, but without Cassie, I might have ended up like Urinal Cake. In him, I saw the path my life nearly took, and it made me shudder.

I wandered over to Blaise's table. "Are you seriously going to make him drink that whole cup?" I said it casually, trying to keep my disgust on a short leash.

Blaise nodded with his huge, toothy grin. He had the emotional depth of a tapeworm. "That's Urinal Cake."

"I'll bite. Why do you call him Urinal Cake?"

It was like Blaise had been dying for someone to ask that question all night. He rubbed his hands together and took an anticipatory breath as he prepared to tell me the origin story of Urinal Cake. But then Derrick Fuller blurted out, "Because we made him eat one," and stole Blaise's thunder.

"Dick!" Blaise punched Derrick in the neck. It was a sloppy swing that barely clipped him, but Derrick pushed the table forward and stormed out of the kitchen. "Little bitch," Blaise said as Derrick left. And as soon as it was over, Blaise's smile returned.

I honestly wished I hadn't asked, but now I had to know the rest. "Why again?"

"Why not?" Blaise said, as if that explained everything. For the record, it did not. "He was a champ, too. The kid puked only once. We didn't make him eat that."

"You're a saint," I said, but my sarcasm was wasted on these guys. "What does he get out of this?"

Blaise shrugged and looked at his remaining friends. None of them had any answers either. In fact, I was certain that one of them was sleeping with his eyes open. "He gets to hang out with us, I guess."

"Lucky kid."

It was probably the end of our conversation anyway, but Blaise caught sight of Urinal Cake talking to a cute junior girl and called for another verse. It started with "My tongue is blue and my face got zits. Now do me a favor and—" I left without waiting to hear the rest.

It was hard to move through the house. There were people lining every wall, dancing in every room, mingling in tight, oblivious groups. Thinking about how many people were in Cassie's house made my chest tighten. Made it difficult to breath. So I kept moving because it was the only thing to do.

I still hadn't figured out how I was going to show Cassie that I really loved her, that I loved the real her. Truthfully, I was beginning to believe that maybe Cassie was right and I didn't know her at all. Before the party I'd have said that Cassie was a funny, sweet, sincere girl who played by the rules but occasionally toed the line. I'd have said that she had a soft spot for losers, a heart-on for Eli, and a sense of self that was unassailable. I'd have told you that I knew who Cassie was because Cassie knew who Cassie was.

That was before the party. Doing things like throwing a barter party in her parents' absence and dumping Eli and making me take shots to enter the house. Those were not typical Cassie moves. Hell, even that dress she was wearing was very un-Cassie-like. It was almost like she was searching for something. If I knew what it was, I could help her, but I was clueless.

My doubt didn't deter me, though. In fact, it only strengthened my resolve. I wanted to prove that I loved her no matter who she was.

First, I had to find her again. I ducked into the library, by the front door, which turned out to be a mistake. A handful of Scrabble tiles flew over my head, barely missing me, and hit the opposite wall with a clack.

"Blingy is *not* a real word!"

"Your mom's not a real word!"

I scrambled out of the way as one Scrabble player launched himself over the table and tackled another. Chairs tumbled and drinks spilled onto the expensive Oriental rug, and a chant of "Fight, fight, fight!" broke out. It reminded me of watching my grandparents play bridge.

Either way, Cassie wasn't there, so I retreated across the hall into the living room. It was an intimidating chandeliered room that I'd have been scared to sit in even if my junior high nemesis and his girlfriends weren't lounging on every available surface, watching a fierce beer pong battle unfold.

Dean nodded at me when I caught his eye. He held out a tightly rolled joint, but I shook my head. "Makes me paranoid," I said.

Dean took the hit for himself and whispered something to a girl I didn't know. "Where's your boyfriend?" he said to me.

"I'm not gay," I said through clenched teeth. Dean isn't particularly big or strong, but it's common knowledge that he's practically a sociopath. Even Blaise avoided tangling with him. Rumor had it Dean had been expelled from his elementary school in Miami for pulling a knife on the lunch lady over burned turkey casserole.

Dean feigned surprise. "Right. I always get you and those other homos confused." The big-haired girl on his lap giggled. "You sure some of that queer hasn't rubbed off on you, Cross? There's no shame if you like polishing knobs. The world's all about tolerance and shit now, right, Crystal?"

The girl on his lap mimed a vulgar visual aid.

"Classy," I said. "You kiss your uncle with that mouth?" I might have been afraid of Dean, but I wasn't going to take crap from Crystal.

"No," Crystal said. "I kiss your uncle, and he loves it."

I did my best to look shocked. Big eyes, jaw drop. The works. "That's quite a talent since my uncle died when I was two. But hey, necrophilia. I'm betting that'll look totally bitchin' on your beauty school application."

Dean laughed so hard that his face turned three shades of red before Crystal smacked him in the ear. He pushed her out of his lap and gave her a menacing frown. I almost felt bad for the girl.

"You don't know me," Crystal said with so much sincerity that I thought for a moment I'd misjudged her. She looked up at me through her lashes and ran out of the room.

Dean punched his right fist into his left hand. "I kinda liked that one. Now we're gonna have to have a lesson in chivalry and stuff."

"Leave him alone, Dean," said a voice from the corner. A familiar voice. A voice that made me cringe.

"Shut up, Aja," Dean said. He looked as annoyed as I felt, but he relaxed somewhat. "This ain't your thing."

Aja rose from the shadows where two friends had been standing in front of her, blocking her from my view. She was rocking these skinny, low-cut jeans and a loose-fitting tee that showed an indecent amount of skin.

"Don't fuck with me, Kowalcyk." Aja flicked her words like daggers. "I know your dysfunctional little secret." She held up her pinkie finger and frowned in a way that only Aja could. The girl didn't know the meaning of scared.

Dean didn't flinch. He didn't even blink. "My secret wasn't that little when I was—"

"And I'm out," I said, turning to leave. I made it as far as the stairs before Aja caught up to me. She pinned me to the banister and snaked her arms around my waist.

"Going so soon, Smoochie?" Aja's breath was hot on my neck and I did my best to conjure thoughts of that one time I walked in on my Grandma Mary coming out of the shower—all the vaguely recognizable parts sagging in ways that would haunt me for decades. "I've been looking for you all night."

Aja smelled like beer and the perfume I'd given her last Christmas. "Found me," I said, my voice breaking. "Yay."

"Don't act like you're not happy to see me."

"Don't flatter yourself," I said. But Aja always flattered herself. If Crystal Whatsername had a self-esteem deficit, Aja had a surplus. And her surplus was pressed up against my ribs.

I took Aja by the arm and led her outside where the air was cooler and I felt like I could breath.

"What the hell are you doing?" I asked.

Aja smirked. "I'm messing with you, Simon. Obviously, your sense of humor is still as underdeveloped as your—"

"I'm leaving." I went for the door, but Aja grabbed my wrist and jerked me back to her, latching onto my face with her lips. She had hooks for hands and it took me a couple of seconds to push her away.

"Damn!" I said when I'd regained possession of my tongue. "I'm not into you, Aja. We're through."

Aja crossed her arms over her chest, baring her teeth at me. There were only a few people outside, mostly just a group of smokers huddled together by the garage. "It's Cassie, isn't it?"

"Aja—"

"It's always fucking Cassie with you." Aja's nostrils flared, and I knew where this was heading. We'd had this fight before. More than once. "That girl isn't worth the effort you've put into chasing after her. We could've had something great, Simon."

I shook my head and tried to reach out to her, but Aja pulled away. "I don't like you like that," I said, feeling like a jerk. "Even if Cassie wasn't in the picture, we wouldn't have worked out. You know that."

"For your information, I'm not into you anymore either." But I could hear the hurt, the hurt I'd caused, and I sort of hated myself for it.

Aja and I had the kind of past I wanted desperately to forget, but that didn't mean I could leave her here feeling like shit. So I walked up behind her and put my arms around her. "It was never about you," I said. I wrapped my arms tighter and let her lean her head against my chest. "You're a cool girl when you're taking your meds."

Aja chuckled. "Dick."

"So I've been told."

We stood like that until a cough from behind us shattered the moment. Aja let go of my arms and I let go of Aja. Coop stood in the doorway wearing quite the surprised expression.

"Coopster," Aja said.

"Aja," he said flatly. He gave me a look that let me know I owed him an explanation later.

"We were only talking," I said, cramming my words into one breath.

Coop nodded. "Sure." He stood there like he'd forgotten whatever it was he'd been doing before he saw me with my arms wrapped around Aja like a bow.

"Is everything okay?" I asked.

Aja watched us with a bemused expression. She'd never liked Coop, and the feeling had been mutual. She'd gotten along with Ben well enough, but there were few people who couldn't get along with Ben.

"Right," Coop said. "You have to come with me. Now." He narrowed his eyes and motioned toward the back of the house with his head. Whatever was going on clearly didn't involve my ex-whatever.

"Go," Aja said. "Before Coop messes his panties."

"Nice to see you, too, Queen of the Damned," Coop said. "Come on, Sy."

As I turned to leave, Aja said, "I hope she breaks your heart."

Coop practically ran through the house, leading me to the family room, where half the freaking party had gathered around Cassie and Urinal Cake and Blaise. There was no way this was good.

"So you'll make a freshman drink this crap, but you won't drink it yourself?" Cassie stood like a superhero, hands on her waist, chest puffed, and the steely glint of justice burning in her eyes. Ben was her trusty sidekick.

The freshman in question looked über-uncomfortable. His devotion to Blaise and his crew was clashing with how badly he didn't want to drink what was in the cup he was holding.

"It's just a little fun," Blaise said. His eyes kept darting to the red cup in poor Urinal Cake's hand. It was filled to the brim and had unrecognizable chunks bobbing at the top. It nauseated me to look at it and I couldn't imagine drinking it. Not even for Cassie. "I don't know why you're getting all worked up."

Blaise couldn't have chosen a worse thing to say to Cassie. The self-righteous ember in her eyes flared. She took the cup from Urinal Cake and held it out to Blaise. "Drink it."

"No." The confrontation was spiraling madly out of control. Blaise's pride wouldn't allow him to back down, and he wasn't bright enough to think his way out of the combustible situation. But Cassie should have known better. She had always been the kind of girl who stood up for lost causes, but she wasn't reckless. She had always known where to draw the line before, but from what I could see, the line was way in the rearview.

Cassie held the cup right up to his face, sloshing some down the front of his white dress shirt. "Drink it, bitch."

Ben tossed Coop a look that even I could read. He'd sensed the inevitable train wreck we were all in the path of, but was unable to stop it. The other kids hanging around were laughing at Blaise, egging Cassie on, unaware of the potential apocalypse about to be unleashed. Urinal Cake just stood there, staring at Cassie with naked adoration. Coop shrugged helplessly; there was nothing any of us could do.

"What did the blind, deaf kid with no legs get for Christmas?" Ben shouted. He was grasping at straws, but no one was listening.

Blaise turned to his friends, maybe for help, maybe to gauge just how badly they'd torment him on Monday if he walked away. But walking away was never an option. Blaise took the cup from Cassie and held it in the air for everyone to see. More of the rancid brew sloshed over the side, dripping onto his shoes.

"You want me to drink this?" Blaise asked.

Cassie smiled. It was nothing like the smile I'd fallen in love with in freshman anatomy. It was wicked and cruel. The hair on the back of my neck stood up. "You're going to drink every drop out of that cup, Blaise. And then you're going to lick the bits stuck to the sides. And maybe that will teach you to pick on people your own size."

"Cassie, this might not—" Ben started, but Cassie redirected her angry glare onto him for barely a second, and the words turned to dust in his mouth.

Instead of shaming Blaise, all Cassie had done was make him angrier. I wasn't sure who I felt sorrier for. Urinal Cake was saved for now, but Cassie couldn't protect him forever.

"You think you're some kind of badass, Castillo?" Blaise asked. He held the cup at Cassie's eye level and slowly turned it on its side, letting the foul mixture spill onto the carpet, creating an expanding stain that would surely never come clean. "You're nothing without Eli. Nobody. On Monday, no one is going to remember that you even exist, you stuck-up bitch." Blaise poured the last of the drink onto the carpet, tapping the plastic bottom to get out every last drop.

The party went quiet. No music, no talking. I was pretty sure that no one was even breathing for that impossible moment. All eyes were on Cassie, waiting for her reaction. The kids on the patio and the in-betweeners in the kitchen held still. Even the Scrabble guys had paused their game to come bear witness. Ben inched back, out of the line of fire.

I'd like to claim that I rushed to Cassie's aid. I'm not sure what would have happened if I had. She might have been grateful or she might have seen it as an attempt to undermine her. Only, rescuing Cassie never crossed my mind. Cassie was the hero, not the princess in the tower. It was one of the reasons I loved her so damned much.

But I was still shocked as hell when she clocked Blaise in the nose. Her tiny fist came out of nowhere. There was no warning. Nothing. Just silence and then a single fist of fury.

Blaise clutched his nose, too stunned to fight back.

"Yeah, that's right!" Cassie shouted. "Who's the bitch now?"

The moment Blaise's shock passed, he lunged at Cassie. His buddies were on him before he was able to lay a finger on her. The spell of silence was broken, and the party erupted into motion. Blaise's friends dragged him out to the patio, Coop and Ben rushed to Cassie and tried to get her under control even as she continued taunting Blaise, and DJ Leo kicked the music back on.

I spotted Eli standing against a far wall, watching. His face showed no emotion. He could have stopped the whole thing. Blaise wouldn't have challenged Eli.

"A little help here, Simon," Coop said, and I turned back to where Cassie was trying to convince Coop and Ben that she was calm and didn't need them to hold her arms. Her eyes told a different story, as they were locked on the French doors Blaise had fled through.

With nothing left to see, the crowd dispersed, lured back to the dance floor.

"Calm the fuck down, bruiser," Ben said.

"Fine," Cassie said. "I'm fine. Leave me alone."

Ben let Cassie go and stepped off. He held up his hands to protect his face and I'm pretty sure he was only half pretending to be afraid she was going to deck him too.

"You okay?" Cassie asked Urinal Cake. He nodded. "What's your name?"

"Freddy," he said. "Freddy Standish."

Cassie smiled at Freddy. "Don't let assholes like that push you around. Not ever."

Freddy beamed. I knew exactly what he was feeling. I knew every emotion that was welling in his young heart. And I was jealous. I admit it. I was jealous of that scrawny, skinny kid that Cassie had rescued from humiliation. But it wasn't as if Cassie actually liked Freddy. She'd helped him out of pity.

Coop lifted Cassie's fist, which was still tightly balled up, and said, "Let's get some ice on this." He led Cassie into the kitchen with Ben in tow. Freddy and I watched the boys nurse Cassie's bruised knuckles. Coop had gone into full-on mother hen mode, and Ben was already reimagining the story. By the end of the night he'd probably be telling people how Cassie had beaten the shit out of the entire Rendview Warriors football team with one fist behind her back.

"She's amazing," Freddy said.

I patted him on the back. "You have no idea." But I did. Too bad I still wasn't any closer to proving it.

Reality Bites

Stella and I stood in the middle of the kitchen, watching the party happen around us. Blaise and his friends—whom I mentally organized in decreasing order by IQ—had moved on from their exhilarating game of Bullshit and were now abusing a pathetic freshman they called Urinal Cake for some reason that was blessedly unclear. Their specific method of torture involved making the kid run around and collect drips and drabs from the cups of everyone at the party, which Blaise had declared he was then going to make Urinal Cake drink. As if that wasn't enough, Blaise and his crew forced him to perform a ridiculous song and dance routine.

I felt bad for poor Urinal Cake. But not bad enough to do anything about it. I had my own problems.

Falcor was pretty much the belle of the ball. Hardly anyone could pass by us without stopping to pet him or coo at him or try to sneak him beer, which Stella discouraged by mentioning that Falcor had a severe gluten allergy and that feeding him anything with wheat would result in massive quantities of toxic diarrhea spewing from his tiny butt in a matter of minutes. It worked like a charm.

Stella and I made small talk, but I think we were both killing time, stalling, trying to figure out how to fulfill our respective ends of the bargain. The barter had seemed like a great deal at the time—I'd find a guy for Stella to share her first real kiss with and she'd help me with Cassie—but in practice, it turned out to be far more difficult.

Part of the problem was that Stella didn't know anyone at the party. She didn't go to Rendview and it turned out she'd lived in town for only a couple of years. So she had an excuse, whereas I should have been able to find her a guy in the time it took for Urinal Cake to sing his little song. Stella was a cute, funny girl with red hair and a blind dog. Who wouldn't want to get with her? The trouble was that while I knew a lot of guys at Rendview, I didn't actually have a lot of friends outside of Ben and Coop. And neither of them was Stella's type.

"What about him?" I asked, pointing at a lanky dude I'd had European history with sophomore year. All I remembered about him was that he could recite every detail of every NASA mission. Ever.

Stella shook her head. "Too tall. Also, too much fuzzy lip hair."

"I don't think that's hair," I said.

"Reason number three, then." Stella tapped her teeth with the end of her fingernail. "Can you sing?"

"Have you ever heard the sound a cat makes when it's in heat?"

"Unfortunately."

"That's how I sound when I sing."

"Oh," Stella said. I was frightened by the fact that Stella's only idea so far seemed to involve me singing. Anything that involved me singing or dancing or performing magic tricks or wrestling polar bears was probably a bad idea.

I clutched a mostly full cup of weak beer that I'd been nursing for the last thirty minutes. Getting some liquor in me probably would have helped to boost my confidence, but I decided that I was going to need a clear head if I ever got my chance to tell Cassie I loved her.

"What about that guy?" I asked, pointing out Rory Johnson.

Stella seemed to consider him. I'd sat at a lunch table with Rory in eleventh grade, when, due to a tragic scheduling error, I'd been put in a different lunch than Ben and Coop. He chewed with his mouth open and spit when he talked, but he drew the most demented underground comic books. Plus, I knew for a fact that he had three dogs. So there was that.

"I'm pretty sure he wouldn't be interested," Stella said. I was about to ask why when I realized that he was staring at Nic Fulson. Specifically Nic Fulson's ass.

"Ten-four," I said. "God, this is tough."

"Tell me about it," Stella said. "Can you write poetry?"

I grimaced. "I'm not much of a poet. In fact, poets everywhere would shower you with gifts if you made certain I never, ever attempted to write in any form of rhyming couplet." Stella sighed, dejected. I scanned the family room for Ben or Coop—they were more suited to this type of job—but neither was dancing. I finally spied Ben out in the courtyard talking to a couple of girls, looking frustrated. Probably still trying to get that condom. Coop was by the front door hamming it up with Cassie.

"In fact," I said, "the less you make this like a bad teen movie, the better."

Stella flashed me a wry smile. "Does that make you Molly Ringwald or me?"

I chugged the rest of my beer, unsure how to answer. "How about my old lab partner Ewan McCoy? He's funny and cute, if you like that sort of thing. Ben's mentioned multiple times that he'd do Ewan."

"He's got potential," Stella said. "Tell me more." So I told her about the time he'd refused to speak in anything but Mandarin for an entire week. And about the time he'd snuck into the chem lab and turned all the furniture upside down.

"I'd date him," I said. "I mean, I wouldn't. I mean, you know what I mean."

Stella and I covertly followed Ewan into the living room to watch some beer pong. We hung back by the wall, on the opposite side from Dean Kowalcyk and his girl of the week.

I could practically see Stella working out a pro/con list in her head as she looked at Ewan. For her sake, as well as mine, I hoped that she went for him. The longer it took me to find her a guy to kiss, the longer it was going to take for her to keep up her end of the deal.

I glanced down at my watch. It was nearly eleven. The party was beginning to hit its stride. People were drunk, but not too drunk. The music was perfect and every song seemed so danceable that even people like me who hate dancing couldn't resist moving to the beat a little. Cassie's party hadn't peaked yet but it was definitely reaching for the crescendo. Everywhere I looked were happy faces, people making out and drinking and smoking pot in dark corners. The party spilled to the outside, to the night, and it was like Cassie's house was too small to contain all the concentrated awesome. Everyone was beautiful, everyone was amazing. We were all gods: immortal, perfect, and so fucking alive.

"Come on," I said. "I'm going to introduce you to him." Before Stella could say no, I dragged her to the corner where Ewan was chilling with some of his friends. He bumped my fist. "Ewan, this is Stella and her blind dog, Falcor."

Ewan nodded casually. "You the hottie who made out with Cassandra?" His words were sharp and not slurred at all, which meant he was probably just holding that can of beer for show.

Stella jutted her hip out in a totally cute way. "Made out? No. Gifted her with the best kiss of her life? Absolutely."

The guys with Ewan chanted "Stella! Stella! Stella!" while Ewan's grin covered him from top to toe.

"Cool pup," Ewan said.

"The coolest. We do yoga together. Warrior pose is his favorite."

Ewan frowned. "Not downward dog?"

"Too obvious."

Stella and Ewan were getting on like I didn't exist. Ewan even turned his back to his friends to give Stella his undivided attention. "I have any classes with you?"

"I go to Saint Anne's," Stella said. "Nothing but bitchy rich girls all day."

"Sounds like my sisters, minus the rich part. Got eight of 'em."

"Your parents ever hear of birth control?"

Ewan shrugged. "Seems like every time my pop winks at my mom, he knocks her up."

"Sounds like the worst superpower ever," Stella said. Ewan laughed and asked her about her favorite band, at which point I realized I was no longer part of the conversation.

Clearly, Stella didn't need me anymore, so I slipped away to look for Coop. I found him by the front door, sitting on the spiral staircase, nursing a Red Bull. His shirt clung to his chest and arms. Sometimes I forgot how ripped the guy was, and it made me regret not learning to play the guitar. Maybe if I'd taken lessons with Coop I'd have had arms like his rather than arms like bar stool legs.

I plopped down next to Coop and stole a sip of his energy drink. I admired his dedication to being our sober driver, especially when everyone around us was drinking their body weight in beer, running around like they were partying down to the end of the freaking world. I should have been blowing up the dance floor or chatting up the girl of my dreams, but instead I was sitting on the edge of the chaos with my best friend.

"Where's Stella?" Coop asked. Despite asking the question, he looked almost too preoccupied to hear my answer.

I glanced through the spaces between the banisters to see if I could steal a glimpse of Stella and Ewan, but they'd moved into a blind spot, and all I could see was the beer pong table, some of the kitchen, and the glass doors leading to the courtyard.

"She's hanging out with Ewan McCoy."

Coop let a halfhearted chuckle slip out. "What'd you do to piss her off?"

"Nothing," I said, trying not to be offended by Coop's assumption. "I introduced them."

"Oh," Coop said. "Why, exactly?" Coop leaned back against the steps and rested on his elbows so that he could better shine the spotlight of his curiosity on me.

"We had a deal," I said. "She's never kissed a guy before, so I promised to find her one. And in return, she agreed to help me with Cassie. Though, in retrospect, I should have gotten her to help me before introducing her to Ewan." Not that I believed Stella was really up to the challenge anyway. Her ideas had all been less than inspiring, and to win Cassie's heart I needed something brilliant. A foolproof plan for a fool.

When I looked up, Coop was watching me with the most disappointed expression I'd seen on his face since the time I hooked up with Aja Bourne at Maria Hernandez's *quinceañera*.

"Don't start," I said.

"Simon—"

"I love her."

"I thought you quit this shit when you talked to ketchup girl."

I buried my face in my hands and then looked at the ceiling, anywhere but at Coop. His judgy eyes were too much. Partly because I hated disappointing the kid, but mostly because he was right. He knew it, I knew it, even Falcor knew it. But the heart wants what it wants, and my heart beat for only Cassandra Castillo.

"I tried, Coop," I said. "I wanted to let go of Cass, but I can't. Things didn't work out with Natalie, she wasn't my type, and—"

Coop held up his hand. "Shut up."

"Coop—"

"Shut. Up." Coop took a deep breath, the way he does onstage before he begins to sing. He told me once that when he did that, he imagined he was breathing in all the hopes and dreams of the people in the audience and breathing out all his fear. I wondered what he was breathing in from me. "Fuck it, dude. You're hopeless."

Not much I could say to that. Coop's disappointment in

me was bottomless, but I had no shame. "If you were me, and Cassie was Ben, you'd be sitting right where I am and I'd be where you are. Only I wouldn't be looking at you like you were the biggest piece of shit on the planet."

A couple tried to climb the steps but they were so busy groping each other that they didn't see me or Coop, and we had to scoot all the way to the side to keep from being stepped on.

"You're still a moron," Coop said.

"True," I said, nodding. "Where's Ben?"

Coop shrugged. "Somewhere. Bartering. Trying to figure out how to get some pictures from Jordan that he took of Camille when they were together. Jordan wants tickets to the Mustache Pirates' show in Orlando next month, but the tickets sold out in under five minutes—even I couldn't get them, and now they're like five hundred bucks on eBay. But according to Lee, Katia's got tickets because her brother is a roadie for Captain Fingerbang, who's opening for the Mustache Pirates for the Southern part of the tour. The real problem is that Katia wants this purse that's sold only in Europe and costs more than my first semester at BU. Maya Faustino has the purse in question because her dad's an editor at large for a fashion magazine, and Ben thinks he can convince her to part with it, though I think she'd rather give up one of her feet than that ridiculous leather bag."

Trying to follow that convoluted spew was exhausting, and I was a little more than impressed that Coop was actually able to keep track of it all. "So I'm guessing that Camille has the condom Ben assaulted me for earlier?" Coop frowned at me but nodded. "You're sober," I said. "And you have a car. Just drive to the store and get some."

"That's no fun," Coop said. "It's a barter party. Buying them defeats the purpose."

I screwed my face up into my best "What the hell are you smoking?" expression. "I thought the purpose was to have sex. Lots and lots of Coop-on-Ben action in a dark room. Get your priorities straight, dude."

"Yeah," Coop said. "You're right." Except Coop didn't sound convinced, and he was avoiding looking at me. One of the best parts of having a best friend who knows you inside and out is that he can always tell when you're full of shit. And Coop was so full of shit that it practically fell out of his mouth every time he peeped.

"You do want to sleep with Ben, right? You haven't changed your mind, have you?"

Coop and I didn't spend a lot of time talking about his relationship with Ben. Partly because I knew less about relationships than . . . well . . . anyone, but also because Ben was my friend too, and that made it awkward. But we had talked about losing our virginity. Ben had been rooting for sexy times since he and Coop first kissed, whereas Coop was something of a traditionalist—or prude, depending on who you asked. Coop wanted to be in love, to know he was in love, and to know it was going to be forever. Last time I'd checked, he had all those feelings for the incomparable Benjamin Kwon.

"I don't know," Coop said. "I love Ben. God, I love him. But it's like . . . where's this going?"

I was floored. It wasn't even my relationship and I still felt like Coop had sucker punched me. "Where are you and Ben going? Is that what you're asking?"

"Yeah." Coop hung his head and I gave him some room to breathe. "Graduation's not far off. We're growing up, Simon. How many high school relationships do you know that work after high school?"

"Whoa, Cooper. Just slow down here." I was shocked that I was about to be the voice of reason, but it did happen occasionally. "You're not getting married. It's just sex. You love Ben and Ben loves you and I can't imagine two people who deserve to get biblical more."

Coop chuckled. "I'm pretty sure the Bible has rules against what Ben and I are planning to do."

"Yes, well, two-thousand-year-old rules are meant to be broken."

"True," Coop said. He relaxed a little and took another of his deep breaths, letting all his tension go. "When did you become an expert on this shit?"

I shrugged. "What's that supposed to mean?"

Coop rolled his eyes like I should have known exactly what he meant, but since I didn't, he said it out loud. "You've had two opportunities to get with girls that actually liked you, but instead, you're going to spend your whole night on a fruitless quest to win the heart of a girl who will probably never feel the same way about you that you feel about her."

"Two? Natalie and who else?"

"The girl you showed up with?" Coop smacked his head. "You're a moron."

"Stella's cool and all, but she and I would never—"

"Bullshit," Coop said. "She's perfect. Weird, hot, and totally into you."

"No way," I said, slightly uncomfortable with the way Coop had turned the focus of the conversation to me. "She's hanging out with Ewan."

Coop's groan was drowned out by a rambunctious collection of howls from the living room and we both turned in time to see Trey Howser drink the last cup on the table and then fall to the floor.

"You really are going to die a sad, lonely virgin," Coop said. I turned back around. And I didn't argue. I couldn't. Not with Coop, anyway. Over the years, we'd dissected every moment of my one date with Cassie and every interaction I'd had with her since. If she smiled at me in the hall or when we were hanging out at Ben's, I picked it apart until Coop threatened to garrote me with a guitar string.

After a minute, Coop said, "So, just out of morbid curiosity, what was Stella's plan for helping you score the girl of your dreams? I mean, a girl who brings a blind dog to a party has got to have something slick up her sleeve." There was a note of sarcasm in his voice that I chose to ignore.

"Her best idea involved singing—"

"Don't."

"Obviously."

I was saved from further interrogation by Ben running down the hall from wherever he'd been, yelling, "Someone give me the password to AJ Tucker's Facebook account! It's a matter of life or death!" He skidded to a stop, nearly slamming into the front door. When he saw us, he bounded up the steps to slap a quick kiss on Coop's lips and whisper something in his ear. Then he jumped down the steps and ran back the way he'd come, shouting, "The purse is mine!" and laughing manically.

Coop chuckled. "And that's my boyfriend."

"How could you not want to have sex with him?" I asked. I was being sarcastic but Coop answered soberly.

"It makes it real."

"You've been together for three years," I said. "*That* makes it real."

Sitting on the steps felt lame now. There was a party going on, and Coop and I were sitting around talking about our feelings. Not even talking. We'd spent most of our time dancing around the things neither of us wanted to talk about. "I need a drink after all this whining," I said. "Unless you want me to go buy you some condoms. Do they make micro-size?"

"You should talk. I've seen you naked."

I stood up in mock outrage. "You said you didn't look! Anyway, that lake was freezing. There was definite shrinkage."

"Calm down, Tiny Tim, I'm only messing around." Coop used the railing to haul himself to his feet. "I should find Ben before he sells my mom's car for the condom."

"That car's not worth a condom," I said. "It's not worth a used condom."

Coop grimaced. "Gross."

I jumped down the last couple of steps and came to a stop by the front door. It was cracked open and smoke from the nicotine junkies was seeping inside. Cassie hated smokers, so I kicked the door all the way closed.

When I turned around, Coop was standing uncomfortably close. "Can I give you some advice without you getting all pissy?"

"Always."

"Forget Cassie." Coop had more to say, so I kept my mouth shut. "I know I said I'd back you if you decided to go for it, and I still will, but you should forget her. Put her out of your mind. You'll be better off."

"What if I can't?"

Coop sighed. "Then you need to forget about grand gestures or your deal with Stella. No plans, no singing. Just walk up to her and tell her how you feel."

"Just like that?" I asked.

"Just like that." Coop patted me on the arm and headed toward the back of the house, trading fist bumps and smiles with most of the people he passed.

And then I was alone. It was a huge party with more

people than I could count, but I was alone. Stella, who didn't know anyone at this party an hour ago, was having more fun than I was. Which made Coop's advice that much sweeter. If Stella could walk right up to Ewan and strike up a conversation, I could tell Cassie—the girl I'd known for years—that I loved her.

With that in mind, I marched through the house on a mission to find Cassandra Castillo and make her mine. I dropped by the kitchen for a shot of vodka that burned like a jalapeño on the way down but then spread through my limbs, carrying courage to every cell in my body. Cassie wasn't in the kitchen, but Ben and Coop were, and I passed Coop a knowing smile. He mouthed "good luck" before returning to Ben, who was yelling at Maya that she owed it to his penis to give him her purse.

Stella and Ewan had disappeared from the living room, and I didn't see them dancing, either. I maybe felt a slight pang of jealousy as I imagined where they might be and what they might be doing. But it passed and I genuinely hoped that if Ewan turned out to be Stella's first kiss with a guy, that he made it a damn good one.

As I searched the first floor of the Castillo house room by room, my courage began to flag. Cassie was nowhere. Not by the pool or in her parents' room, which was occupied by a group of kids who looked kind of shady, like the types who rummage through other people's medicine cabinets for pills to steal. But they weren't my problem. Finding Cassie before my spine turned to jam was my one and only goal.

My focus was so myopic that I nearly walked right by Cassie on my way upstairs. She was sitting in the courtyard, this little space in the middle of the house that's open to the outside. An oasis, Ben had called it. Tonight it was decorated with Japanese paper lanterns that cast long shadows on the walls and across Cassie's face. She was sitting on a bench almost facing me. It was like she was looking just past me. Her dress had slid up her leg to reveal a smooth, touchable thigh. But I wasn't thinking about that. Not at all. I was thinking about what I was going to say. So far, I hadn't come up with much.

My breaths came quickly and I wished I'd taken another shot for luck. I didn't know why I was so scared, though. Nothing I had to say should come as a shock to Cassie. She couldn't have been blind to the fact that I'd loved her since day one. Cassie probably knew how I felt better than I did.

I guess that I wasn't scared of telling her; I was scared of what she'd say after. I was scared she'd laugh. Or tell me to go to hell. Or kiss me and tell me she loved me back. In some ways, that last one was scariest of all. No matter what, it was a gamble I'd been scared to take for far too long.

With clammy hands, I turned the handle and pushed the glass doors open. The words were in my mouth before I even looked around. Cassie glanced up, but she wasn't exactly happy to see me.

"Cassie, I—"

"Sy, you know Eli, right?" Cassie looked past me again, and

this time I looked with her. Eli. He was sitting across from her, staring at me with naked annoyance.

"Yo, Simon." He gave me a chin nod and said, "We're having a private conversation, dude. You mind?" His tone wasn't mean, it wasn't rude, but there was no room for argument. I was being dismissed, and if I didn't turn around and leave immediately, Eli would likely stuff me headfirst into one of the potted birds-of-paradise decorating the courtyard.

"Sorry," I said. My declaration of love turned tail and ran, just like I did, making sure to shut the doors behind me.

Living the Dream

Ben and I stayed out of the way, watching Coop treat Cassie's knuckles with ice and quietly lecture her about fighting. It was admirable that Cassie had stopped Blaise and his idiot friends from forcing Freddy to chug the cup filled with tiny pours from dozens of different drinks, an act that would have surely sentenced the kid to a night dancing the porcelain ballet, but Blaise was a dick and he could have seriously hurt her.

Which was probably what Coop was telling her in the corner by the sink. The last thing I wanted to do was get between Coop and one of his little lectures. While it was true that Coop would always be there to help pick up the pieces in the aftermath of whatever crazy scheme his friends got tangled up in, the price of that help was a long-winded treatise on everything we'd done wrong in the history of ever. And right now, Cassie was getting an earful.

"Think we should rescue her?" I asked Ben.

"What?" Ben looked at me like he was seeing me for the first time that night. He'd been somewhere else and I didn't know where.

"Cassie?" I said, pointing.

Ben shrugged. "I'm not getting in the middle of that. Besides, Bruiser's proven she can take care of herself."

I wished that I shared Ben's confidence. If anything, Cassie's uncharacteristic outburst proved how unstable she was, how much she needed help. Maybe Coop's help, maybe mine.

"Wipe the drool, Simon," Ben said. I brought the world back into focus and found that Cassie was staring at me staring at her. She rolled her eyes and I caught a flicker of a smile before she turned back to Coop, nodding in agreement—which was pretty much the only way to shut Coop up once he got rolling. "I asked if you knew Chuck Bell," Ben said.

"Not really. Why?" Chuck wasn't the kind of guy Ben associated with. He wore his oddness like a Boy Scout merit badge, proud to be different, happy to be a one-man freak show. I respected Chuck but I'd never hang out with him.

"I'm betting he has a condom," Ben said.

"Go offer him something for it."

"It's not that easy," Ben said. He was getting his evil-genius look. The pinched-faced, distant expression he wore when he was calculating odds, mapping trajectories, and usually figuring out a way to drag Coop and me into a shitstorm of trouble. "If I flat out ask him for it, he'll know that I want it and jack up the price." Ben patted down his pockets. "Which would be trouble since I'm pretty much cleaned out. Ain't got nothing left to barter with but my sweet, sweet ass."

"And we all know that's not worth a charcoal briquette in hell."

"Ha, ha." Ben punched me lightly in the arm, his heart not really in it.

I'd been holding up the wall for the last five minutes and I stood up straight. For a second, I felt untethered and light, like gravity had relinquished control of my body. I chalked it up to the liquor I'd drunk earlier, but even I knew that most of that had run its course. "I'll go ask him," I said.

Ben grabbed a handful of my shirt and yanked me back. I shoved him off and smoothed down my tee, making sure Ben hadn't stretched the collar.

"Do you want it or not?"

"Don't worry about it," Ben said.

"Don't you want to get your freak on?"

Ben snorted. "No one gets their freak on anymore, Simon. It's no wonder you've never been able to hook up with Cass."

"Oh, burn," I said. "But you have a life partner and you're still a virgin." I made an L with my right hand and held it to my forehead. "You must be so frustrated. All those nights, making smoochies, unable to seal the deal. If Coop was my boyfriend, we would have done it ages ago."

"Simon," Ben said slowly. "That's about the gayest thing you've ever said. And you've said some ridiculously gay things before. Sometimes, I think you're actually gayer than Coop and me combined. Maybe it's our fault. We've kept you from mingling with your own kind and warped your poor heterosexual brain." He patted me on the cheek and headed over to the keg.

While Ben flirted shamelessly with the girl who was manning

the keg, I risked a glance back in Cassie's direction and tried to read Coop's lips. Cassie was smiling now, laughing a little, and I had a moment of panic imagining Coop telling Cassie all my deep, dark secrets, like the time I farted in his car and accidentally crapped my pants. It was only a tiny bit of poo, but the way Coop told it you'd think I had the Old Faithful of shit exploding from my shorts. But the fear passed when Ben returned and handed me a red plastic cup of beer.

"I was serious earlier," I said. "I'll go talk to Chuck for you."

"No." If he hadn't said it quite so forcefully, I probably wouldn't have thought anything of it.

"Why?" I asked, suddenly more interested in why Ben didn't want me to help him get the condom than in the topic of Coop and Cassie's conversation. "Ben? Are you scared?"

"Of what?"

"Sex. Are you afraid to sleep with Coop?" But Ben didn't need to answer because the answer was in his darting eyes, his flushed cheeks, his fidgety free hand. It was written all over Ben's body. He wasn't simply scared, he was terrified. I pulled Ben into the family room, where we could talk without being overheard. "But you're always pressuring Coop to do it."

The fear that had been so plain a moment ago was replaced by a devious smile as Ben pushed me against the wall, invading my personal bubble. "It's you, Simon," he said throatily. "It's always been you."

I struggled to shove Ben aside, but he had muscles that I didn't even know existed. He licked his lips, which were so close that I could smell the beer on his breath.

"So, this is weird," I said.

"Don't tell me you haven't felt it." Even though I knew deep down that Ben was messing with me so that he wouldn't have to talk about what was actually on his mind, there was a fraction of a second when I thought he was going to kiss me. And it's not like it would have even been the first time, but that had been a case of mistaken identity because he'd been drunk and I'd been wearing one of Coop's hoodies. Then that moment passed, because it was Ben for Christ's sake, and I knew better.

"Get off me or I'll tell everyone about your secret stash of *My Little Pony* DVDs."

Ben busted up laughing, but it was forced. Everything about Ben tonight was too much. His smile too big, his voice too loud, his movements too wide. "I had you going for a minute," he said.

I gulped my beer. It was barely cold but it felt amazing going down. "If you don't want to talk about why you're afraid to sleep with Coop, just say so."

"I love him." Ben's whole carefully crafted facade crumbled with the words and I saw the real Benjamin Kwon. Not the guy who hid behind jokes and pranks, the guy who ate up compliments, always craving more. Just Ben, my friend. Stripped down, acoustic.

And then he was gone again. But the words, they were out there. The words I'd never heard him say before.

"Shit," Ben said. "You weren't supposed to hear that."

I put my hand on his arm but he pulled away. "It's cool," I said. "They were meant for Coop."

"They're words," I told him. "You can say them again. It's not like you've wasted them."

Ben rolled his eyes. "I'm not a moron. It's just—I've been saving those words for Coop. Saying them over and over in my head, waiting for the perfect moment to unleash them. I thought tonight was going to be it. We'd find a condom and a quiet room. Cassie told me about the spare room off the garage that no one uses. I bartered everything I brought for candles and flowers and shit, and I even paid a kid to set it all up for me. I was going to tell Coop—you know—and then we'd fuck like bunnies."

I held up my hand. "Thanks for the unnecessary yet horrific visuals." I peeked around the corner to make sure Coop and Cassie were still occupied. The lecture portion of the night appeared to have passed, and Cassie was wearing her bruised knuckles like a prom queen crown. I wanted to ditch Ben and join them so badly my teeth hurt. But it was rare that Ben needed me. "What's stopping you?"

"You were right," he said. "I'm scared. Terrified." He paused and scrubbed his face with his hand. "I applied to MIT without a safety school, Simon. I jumped out of an airplane. But sex with Cooper Yates is the scariest thing I can imagine doing."

"I get it," I said.

"You don't get shit," Ben said. "You think you know things, you think you love Cassie, and you think everything in your life is going to turn out like a movie. You know fuck all about love, Simon. Less than."

I'd rather Ben have slapped me in the face. His words hurt ten times worse. But I came back swinging. "I'm not stupid," I said.

"You're worse because you don't even know how dumb you actually are."

"Drop it," I said. Anger was bubbling up and the last thing I wanted to do was get into a fight with Ben.

Dropping things was not Ben's strong suit. "You don't know what love is. You're hanging on to the memory of a night you almost kissed her. That was over three years ago. Do you think Cassie remembers? Do you think she even cares?"

"Fuck you, Ben." My voice became ice, I became stone. But I couldn't deny the truth of what he'd said. Cassie probably didn't care. She most likely didn't remember that night despite the fact that I remembered every second of it in such painful detail that I could describe each individual dimple on the blue golf ball I used to win our bet at the eighteenth hole. I sat on the floor and hugged my knees to my chest.

"Cassie's my friend," Ben said. His voice had softened but it still had an edge. "And so are you. It might be kind of cool if you two hooked up." Ben sat on the floor beside me. "But you have to stop living in the past. You have to figure out who Cassie is and stop worshipping who she was. And if you still love her after that, then good for you."

It was a lot to take in, more to think about than I had the brainpower to compute. I finished off my beer instead. "Coop loves you back," I said. "He says it all the time."

"Yeah," Ben said. "That's what freaks me out the most. The moment I say it back, it becomes bigger than him, bigger than me."

"It already is," I said. I checked to make sure Ben was paying attention. "There aren't many constants in this world, dude, but you and Coop are one of them. Say it, don't say it. Have sex or don't. But Cooper Yates is always going to be sickeningly, maddeningly in love with Benjamin Kwon."

There was an awkward moment after I'd finished talking where I didn't know whether Ben was going to cry or try to hug me, but he shattered it by putting me in a headlock and raping my ear with a wet willy. His finger made a squicky sound as he dug it around my ear canal. It was the grossest thing to happen to me all night. Then Ben let me go and said, "Thanks."

I cleaned Ben's spit out of my ear with the corner of my shirt. "Now get out there and find a way to get your freak on with my best friend."

Ben didn't waste another second with me. He ran into the kitchen, pushing past anyone in his way. He swept Coop up and kissed him in front of everyone. A couple of guys catcalled and some of the girls whistled, but two guys kissing wasn't the most interesting thing going on at the party. When the boys separated, Ben took Coop's hand and led him from the kitchen. I hoped they found their condom.

I waited a full minute before I got up and made my way to

Cassie as she moved in the direction of the dance floor. The rage that had possessed her earlier seemed to have subsided. She actually looked a little ashamed when she saw me.

"Nice right hook, Rocky." Without asking, I took her hand and looked at her knuckles. They were swollen and purple and looked pretty painful. Worse, even, than the foot I'd stepped on earlier. "They hurt?"

"They'll heal," she said. "Unlike Blaise's face."

I laughed. "I think it's his ego that really took a beating. Punched by a girl. He's never living that down."

Cassie wavered between pride and embarrassment. "I'm no girl," she said. "I'm a warrior woman. An Amazon. If Coop and Ben hadn't stopped me, my parents would be picking pieces of Blaise off the ceiling fan."

"Cassandra Castillo, champion of freshmen."

"Seriously, that song was the worst."

"The song?" I said. "I thought you were pissed about Blaise making the kid drink that cup of swill."

Cassie nodded. "Sure, but that song was driving me insane."

I chuckled. "You surprise me daily."

Then she surprised me again. "Want to dance?" I didn't know whether she'd forgotten what had happened in her parents' room or if she'd forgiven me or maybe even just written it off as something regretful that had happened in the heat of the moment. Not that I regretted it, actually. But either way, I was willing to take what I could get. And maybe Ben had been right. Maybe I needed to forget the girl in anatomy, the girl at the mini-golf course, the girl Cassie had been. I wasn't the same boy I had been, was I? I needed to get to know this Cassie, the one asking me to dance.

I glanced at her injured toes. "Remember? Simon dance bad."

Cassie looked down. "My feet are evil and must be punished."

"Then I'm definitely your man." I took Cassie's good hand and led her to the dance floor.

For the first time that night, I could see DJ Leo. He was standing in the corner, dripping sweat. Except for the fight, the music hadn't taken a break all night, and I guessed that neither had he. DJ Leo was the reason Cassie was smiling right now, the reason she had her arms around my neck.

I didn't know the song, but I jumped along anyway, allowing the rhythm and the sound to move my bones, shedding my insecurity, forgetting the past, letting the Cassie I'd built up in my mind fade away, to be replaced with the one breathing my air.

We danced for what felt like hours, though it might have been only a couple of songs. The seamless way one became the next befuddled my sense of time, my ability to judge where I was or what I was doing. There was nothing but Cassie.

I could have danced all night, but Cassie motioned that she needed a drink, so we floated off the dance floor. Instead of going for another shot, she grabbed a bottle of water from the fridge and chugged it. The plastic made crinkling noises as she sucked it dry.

"About before," Cassie said when she was done. "What I said—"

"Forget it. I was stupid."

Cassie touched my hand. "No, you weren't. You were only being honest."

With Cassie touching me, it became difficult to keep my thoughts straight, but I struggled not to stutter or make an ass of myself again. "Yeah, but you were still right. I don't know you." I quickly added, "I want to, though."

It was a bold move. I hadn't forgotten her other challenge, but I couldn't prove to Cassie that I really loved her until I could get to know the real her. I expected Cassie to move on, to leave me like she'd left me twice that night already. But she started doing that thing with her tongue and her teeth again.

"What do you propose?" she asked. It was such an innocuous question that it caught me off guard.

I hadn't thought about the how. I had no plan. Nothing. I swept the room with my eyes, hoping something would leap out at me, that I'd have a sudden moment of inspiration. DJ Leo was still spinning; people were still dancing, drinking. And then I saw Eli Fucking Horowitz in the courtyard, watching us. If I didn't come up with something quickly, it would only be a matter of time before he swooped in and did what I was unable to.

"Beer pong," I said.

"Beer pong?" Cassie looked confused. "Are you trying to get me drunker?"

"That's just the added bonus. We'll play for answers. Sort of like truth or dare without the dares. Plus, there's beer. And Ping-Pong." I gave Cassie a chance to absorb my proposal and then said, "Unless you're chicken."

Cassie grinned with the same manic energy she'd greeted me at the door with. "I hope you don't play beer pong like you play mini-golf." Before it registered that she'd accepted my challenge, she was off.

"I do," I said, and ran to catch up.

Reality Bites

Of course Eli and Cassie were back together. I should have known that he was going to show up and sweep Cassie off her feet and that I didn't have a chance in hell. I never had a chance, not really. Especially with Eli in the picture. I was a wholly straight guy, 100 percent attracted to girls with their perfect, God-given girl parts, but if Eli had shown up at the party and asked *me* to take him back, I'd probably have said yes. He was that good-looking. And that smart. And that nice.

And I was just Simon Cross. A delusional dweeb who didn't deserve a girl like Cassie.

When I realized that I'd been spying on Cassie and Eli for long enough that any rational person would consider it creepy, I trudged back to the kitchen and grabbed the first drink I found, not caring who it belonged to or what it was. I tipped back the bottle; empty. All Cassie and Eli were doing was talking, but I knew what came after that. He'd apologize for whatever he'd done, she'd make him beg, he'd beg, she'd take him back, and before the stroke of midnight they'd be up in her room—the rest of the thought was simply too much for me to bear. I could not, would not, think about what came next. I wanted to drink, to be drunk. I wanted to wake up in a puddle of my own puke, the entire night nothing more than a bad, blurry memory.

"Trade you a beer for a smile," Aja Bourne said, sliding into view, holding out a full red cup. Aja's smile I got for free. Her teeth gleamed against the backdrop of her lush lips and black hair. She was the last person I wanted to see, and yet I was glad she was there.

"Aja." I reached out to take the beer but she pulled it back. "Smile first."

"I'm not in the mood for games," I said. "Give me the beer or leave me the fuck alone." Most girls would have told me off for speaking to them like that, but Aja had grown up with four brothers and was more man than Ben, Coop, and me combined.

Aja seemed to consider it and then handed me the cup. "Who pissed in your cornflakes, Smoochie?"

I took a cautious first sip—a little because it was warm and a little because I didn't trust Aja not to roofie me—but then gulped the rest. At that point in the night, even roofies would have been an improvement. "Don't call me Smoochie."

"Princess Teeny Bladder?"

"Thanks for the beer." I turned to leave but Aja sighed through her nose, a thoroughly irritating sound that made me hate having ears.

"Simon, wait."

"Don't waste your breath, Aja. I'm not drunk or desperate enough to hook up with you right now." I forced a wry smile and held up my empty cup. "Try me again after a couple more of these."

Aja was not amused. I'd spent enough time with her to be able to interpret the subtle gestures that indicated her mercurial moods, but even if I hadn't, I'd have been able to comprehend the meaning of the one-finger salute she shoved in my face. "For your information, I'm here with someone."

If she was trying to make me jealous, it had worked. Not that I was jealous in the sense that I wanted to be with Aja. Listen, somewhere out there was someone who was absolutely perfect for Aja Bourne. I wasn't him. She knew it, I knew it, everyone knew it. But the idea that Aja could find someone and I couldn't was too much for my pickled brain to absorb.

"Good for you," I said. "I hope he isn't charging you by the hour."

Aja laughed mockingly. "*She* isn't a prostitute. Not all of us have to resort to paying a girl to get her to take off her clothes."

"Am I supposed to be shocked?" I asked. For the record, I wasn't. Intrigued, maybe. Curious if the girl was someone I knew. But definitely not shocked.

"Not everything is about you," Aja said. The lines around her mouth deepened, and her eyes got paradoxically narrower and wider. But then her anger faded, replaced by a softness that I could only describe as pity. It wasn't a natural expression for her. "You may be the hero in the story of your life, Simon Cross, but in everyone else's you're just a pathetic secondary character who never achieves enough depth for the reader to care about."

I stood momentarily stunned into silence. Getting another beer forgotten, the party forgotten, Eli and Cassie forgotten. Partly because Aja's astute observation had cut me to the bone, and partly because it had come from Aja, a girl I'd never describe as having an abundance of insight. Aja was a lot of things—tough, brave, sarcastic, a great kisser—but this was a side of her I'd never seen. Maybe if I had, things would have been different.

"Who are you and what have you done with Aja Bourne?"

I was serious but it made Aja laugh. She had a laugh similar to a pig squeal, and it thawed the deep freeze that had formed between us. I even managed to squeeze out a genuine smile of my own.

"So, who's the girl?" I asked. I was still jealous of the fact that both Stella and Aja had managed to find someone while my night was little more than a collection of disasters strung together by a weak thread of hope that Cassie could actually have feelings for me. But everyone deserved happiness, even the girl who had called my house after I'd broken up with her and told my parents that I'd given her crabs, which wasn't true by the way.

Aja craned her neck to look over the crowd. She pointed

across the family room to the patio, where I'd seen some kids from the drama club earlier. "Sia Marcus."

"Sia? The type A with the diva complex who believes that the entire world is a cast of extras in an epic play starring her?"

Aja nodded sheepishly. "I know, I know."

"Wow. And how is that working out for you?"

She shrugged. "We've only hung out a couple of times. We're not actually dating or anything. I don't know. But she's not as uptight as people think." A genuine note crept into her voice as she talked about Sia. The hard edges were blunted.

"You really dig her," I said. It wasn't a question. It wasn't a guess. It was a plain statement of fact that was practically written in the air around her like an aura.

Aja glanced toward the patio again. "Maybe. It's complicated. I've never been with a girl before." She smirked. "But then again, neither have you, so you're my least likely candidate for advice."

I clapped my hand to my chest. "Ouch. You wound me with your sad-but-true words."

"Dork."

Our conversation had reached a crossroads and I wasn't sure which path to take. It was the first time in months that we'd talked for more than ten minutes without ending up fighting or making out. It was refreshing, actually. Also weird.

"So, I heard a rumor you got beat up by Natalie Grayson," Aja said, taking the lead as usual.

"From who?"

"Everyone. I heard that you tried to cop a feel from her at Gobbler's and she clobbered you."

I wasn't surprised. Once a story gets out into the open, it has a way of mutating, taking on a life of its own that can't be stopped. Sort of like a hydra. Cut off the head and it grows three new ones.

"It didn't happen like that," I said. I told Aja the fast version, aware that not even facts could stymie the spread of a juicy rumor.

"That's almost worse," Aja said when I'd finished. "You kind of deserved it."

I nodded. "Yeah."

"But I'm glad you're trying to move on. I figured that with Cassie and Eli on the outs you'd go public with your twisted obsession."

I dropped my chin and looked at the ground. The kitchen was starting to feel claustrophobic. The whole house was. The heat from so many bodies was taxing the AC and turning la casa de Castillo into a sauna.

"You're not moving on, are you?" she said. I shook my head. "Oh, Simon."

"Can we not talk about this?" I asked. Cassie had always been a point of contention between Aja and me, and I wanted to get out of this conversation without it turning into a brawl.

Aja nodded. "I should go. Sia's plotting something on the patio. She won't tell me what it is, but she says it's going to blow our minds."

I pointed down the hall. "I have to pee anyway. They don't call me Princess Teeny Bladder for nothing."

"Later, Simon." Aja moved first, heading in the direction of the patio. She got as far as the family room before pushing her way back to me. Quickly, so quickly that after, I wasn't sure it had actually happened, Aja kissed my cheek and whispered, "You're better than Cassie."

I'd been lying when I told Aja I needed to use the bathroom, but less than a minute after she left, I had to go so badly that only my pride was keeping me from doing the potty dance. There was a bathroom off the hallway, and the line was ten deep. I took my place at the end, behind a couple of girls who looked at me before whispering to each other and laughing, not bothering to hide the fact that I was the butt of their joke. Obviously, that Natalie rumor was spreading like mono. Whatever. It was not the first or worst rumor that had ever made the rounds about yours truly. I got my phone out and was surprised to see I'd missed a text. I didn't recognize the number but it read: "I'd call heaven and tell them they lost an angel, but I'm kind of hoping you're a slut."

I laughed and typed a reply.

ME: STELLA?

STELLA: WHERE ARE YOU?

ME: HOW'D YOU GET MY NUMBER?

STELLA: I STOLE YOUR PHONE IN THE KITCHEN.

ME: WEIRDO. HOW'S EWAN?

STELLA: CHATTY. HOW'S CASSIE?

ME: I'M IN LINE FOR THE BATHROOM.

I avoided her question because if she was having fun with Ewan, I didn't want to be Debbie Downer. But within ten seconds of my last text, Stella was standing beside me, wearing a slick grin.

"Where's Falcor?"

Stella looked around and then motioned toward the front of the house. "I loaned him to one of Ewan's tragically unhip friends to help him pick up girls. He's the worst. That pickup line I texted you? His second best."

"What's his first?"

"Hold on." Stella shook out her limbs and then leaned against the wall doing what I assumed was her best impression of the sleazy guy. "I may not be the hottest guy at this party, but I'm the only one talking to you."

"Wow," I said. "Do you think that ever works?"

"Only on girls of the inflatable variety."

"I need to find me one of those girls." The line was moving slowly and my bladder was on fire. I wasn't sure if I was going to be able to hold it.

Stella rolled her eyes. "I haven't forgotten about our barter."

"It's not a big deal," I said. "Forget it."

"No way," Stella said. "Nashes don't welsh."

"It's not welshing if I release you from the terms of our arrangement." I waved my hands in the air dramatically and said, "You are released." Since I already knew there was no way I was going to get Cassie now that Eli was back in the game, I tried to change the subject by asking about Ewan.

Stella made some faces as she formulated her answer. "He's funny," she said. "But he knows he's funny so he's not actually that funny. Know what I mean?"

I shook my head. "Not really. Did you kiss him?"

"No, but I let him kiss Falcor. Anyone who wants these lips has got to pass the Falcor test first."

The thought of Ewan swapping spit with Stella's dog made me laugh. But I was sobered by the image that followed, the one of Ewan kissing Stella. I felt like some kind of over-protective older brother. Which was stupid since I'd practically forced Stella and Ewan together. I just had to accept the fact that Stella and Ewan were going to get lip-locked while the only tongue action I was likely to be involved in was with a box of Double Stuf Oreos.

"I have an idea about Cassie," Stella said. She was looking impatient with me because I'd zoned out.

"I told you to forget it." But Stella made it clear without saying a single word that she wasn't the kind of girl who forgot things. So I said, "Her ex-boyfriend is here." I pointed to the window overlooking the courtyard. I couldn't see if Eli and Cassie were still there or not, and I didn't care. In my mind, he'd already won.

Stella didn't know Eli, though, so she didn't know enough to let his presence deter her from her goal. "So?"

"So, he's Eli Fucking Horowitz. I haven't got a chance against him."

Stella jumped from the line and peeked out the window. She actually had the nerve to wave at them. I bowed my head in shame while simultaneously wondering what Cassie's reaction had been. When Stella returned, she said, "I see your dilemma. He's hot. I'd kiss him any day."

"I'm out," I said. Not only did I not want to stand in line and listen to Stella wax poetic about Eli's hotness, but I honestly thought I'd piss my pants if I didn't get into the bathroom soon, and there were still six people in front of me. I pushed through the party, ignoring Stella's appeals to come back, making my way out to the patio and around the side of the house where I found a quiet row of bushes in which to relieve myself.

When I'd finished and zipped up, feeling a million times better, I turned around and nearly bowled Stella over.

"Jesus Christ! I'm a little busy here."

"Which is why I didn't disturb you." Stella didn't look the least bit embarrassed, which was fine since I was embarrassed enough for the both of us.

I was angry and annoyed. Not at Stella but at everything that had happened. At myself for not being able to get over one stupid girl.

"Listen, I'm just going to leave."

Stella met my irritation with a bright smile. She was exactly like Falcor; nothing fazed her. "I'll drive you."

"No," I said. "Go hang out with Ewan. He really is a cool guy." I tried to push past her but Stella wouldn't budge. "Move."

"Make me, tough guy." Stella was so tiny that I could have pushed her aside and retreated to my house to spend the rest of the night replaying every mistake I'd made. But she had been nothing but nice to me all night, and she deserved better.

I crossed my arms over my chest. "What?"

Stella stood there for a full beat before she said, "Are we done having our hissy fit now?"

"You don't understand," I said. "I was going to tell her. I was going to walk up to Cassie and tell her that I love her. No games, no gimmicks, definitely no singing. Maybe it would have even worked. But now that Eli's got his hooks in her, I haven't got a chance."

"If you always quit when something gets in your way, it's no wonder you've never kissed her."

If Ben or Coop or even Aja had said something like that to me, I would have flipped out on them. But with Stella, there were no judgments. She was simply stating what she saw. The truth. Which was that I did give up. I always gave up.

"I don't know what to do."

Stella made a square with the pointer and thumbs of both hands, and looked at me through it the same way a photographer looks through the lens of a camera. I didn't know what she saw but she did that for almost a whole minute, which felt like an hour.

"I think I have a plan," she said. "But you have to trust me, and you have to do everything I tell you."

It could have been the night or the beer I'd had. Or maybe

it was the stars weaving fate around me and laying it across my shoulders like a quilt on a cold night. Honestly, though, it was probably Stella. How she was like no girl I'd ever met. How she didn't seem to recognize limitations or acknowledge that hopelessness in the face of overwhelming odds even existed. I did trust her even though I barely knew her. Because sometimes when you meet someone, someone special, you recognize them. Like some part of you knows them from another time or another place.

That's why I agreed to Stella's plan before she'd even laid out a single detail. With Stella at the lead, I would have agreed to anything.

Especially if there was even the smallest chance that her plan might succeed and that I might finally kiss Cassie.

Living the Dream

Challenging Cassie to a game of beer pong was probably the stu-
pidest thing I'd done in a night littered with the corpses of stupid
things I'd done. And not a simple game of beer pong, either—a
beer pong hybrid involving questions and answers. Cassie outlined the rules while some friends of hers got the table ready,
but I wasn't paying attention because I was too busy trying not to
spontaneously combust from fear.

For a brief moment after I'd laid down the challenge, it had, in
fact, seemed like a good idea. Cassie believed I didn't know the
real her. Ben believed the same thing. And despite the fact that
collecting information about Cassie had been my unofficial hobby
through most of high school, I'd also begun to believe that I didn't
actually know the girl I was madly, deeply, dangerously in love
with. The real Cassie. The one who'd chucked Eli out on his ass
and jumped on a bed with me and thrown what might go down
as the best party anyone in our class had ever thrown—though to
be honest, the bar was pretty low.

But reality had set in rather quickly, and I scrambled for a way to take back my challenge without looking like a coward. Maybe I didn't know Cassie, and maybe I had to know the real Cassie before I could prove to her that the love I'd confessed during our perfect antigrav moment in her parents' bedroom was the real deal. But there absolutely had to be a better plan than the one I'd thought up.

The only problem was that even if I thought of one, it was already too late. The living room was stuffed with people dying to witness my inevitable defeat. Blaise and Urinal Cake and Aja and Natalie—clinging to Ewan McCoy's arm—and just about everyone except for Coop and Ben. They were probably the only two people at the party who could have put a stop to the shellacking I was about to take, but they were absent. I hoped that meant they'd finally bartered for a condom and were locked in that quiet room off Cassie's garage.

I couldn't believe this was where I'd ended up. Standing in front of the beer pong table, still holding a stupid red paper clip. Metaphorically speaking, of course. The truth was that I didn't even have a paper clip. I'd lost my backpack somewhere along the way—not that I could have MacGyvered my way out of this mess with any of the useless crap I'd brought anyway.

I'd resigned myself to my drunken fate when salvation appeared in the unlikeliest form: Dean Kowalcyk.

"Ain't nothing free, Castillo," Dean said. "Your rules, not mine." Dean was still sitting in his chair, relaxing like a boss. Crystal hadn't returned, but she'd been replaced by another girl. They were Lego pieces to Dean, interchangeable. The horny part of me that spent more time thinking with his little brain than his big brain admired Dean's game. But the rest of me was disgusted by him and hoped that karma would eventually teach him a much-deserved lesson. However, right then and there, I could only hope that his douchebaggery would provide me with the exit strategy I needed to avoid humiliation.

"It's my party, *cabrón*," Cassie said. "And my table. I'll play if I want." Cassie had the same look in her eyes she'd had when she'd confronted Blaise. The problem was that Dean was not Blaise. Even if Cassie did deck Dean, he wasn't going to turn tail and run. If any of the rumors about Dean were true, then there was no way to know what he'd do if Cassie didn't back down. Punch her back? Kill her? Burn her house to the ground with all of us locked inside? I didn't know, and I didn't want to find out.

"What do you want for the table?" I asked. A moment ago, Dean had been my salvation, now he was my opponent. It was no longer about escaping a beer pong match with my pride intact; it was about escaping with all my teeth.

Dean scanned the room with a calculating stare. If there had been fewer witnesses, Dean might have chosen his price differently, but the crowd gave him an opportunity he was clearly unable to pass up. He turned to Cassie. "I want a kiss."

"Not a chance," I said immediately. I'd hardly had time to process his request before my unequivocal denial burst from my mouth. But there was no way I could stand there and watch him kiss Cassie. The room was quiet—the house was still vibrating with music and laughter and the energy of the night, but the living room, and everyone in it, was completely silent. Until I opened my mouth and kept speaking. Seriously, Coop should have sewn my lips shut. "I'll eat my own underwear before that happens."

When I glanced over at Cassie, she was looking at me with something that resembled respect. Maybe a smidgen of awe. Tonight, I'd seen a side of Cassie that I'd never seen before, and now she was witnessing a hitherto unseen side of Simon Cross.

Dean didn't share Cassie's sense of wonder at my transformation, and Aja wasn't going to be able to save me this time around. When he stood up, Dean towered over me. I wasn't short—in fact, I was taller than both Coop and Ben—but Dean was Iowa-basketball-player tall. His clothes were baggy, but he moved with predatory grace. Images of Dean tearing my Superman underwear right off my body and stuffing them down my throat flashed in front of my eyes, and I knew there was nothing I could do to stop him.

"What'd you say, faggot?"

"Excuse me?"

I knew that in a fight, I didn't stand a chance. While Dean was bench-pressing freshmen for fun, I was eating my bodyweight in Chipotle. I hadn't thrown a single punch in my entire life. But being friends with Coop and Ben—having had to endure the looks and taunts and hateful graffiti scrawled on their lockers in the first few months after they'd come out—had instilled in me a savage hatred of *that* word. So much so that when I heard it, rational thought fled.

The tension in the room became unbearable. People had

come to watch Cassie kick my ass at beer pong and maybe unearth some juicy, long-buried secrets, not to see me have my vital organs rearranged by a sociopath.

Dean got right up in my face, so close that I could have counted every hair on his chin. "I called you a faggot," he said. "You're a faggot, hanging out with your faggot friends, spending all day watching *Ellen* and giving each other blow jobs."

No one laughed. The days of people hating on the boys for being gay were long gone. Coop and Ben were liked. Hell, they were serious contenders for prom king and king. But no one was willing to take on Dean. They were the smart ones.

I'm not sure what would have happened if I hadn't glanced at Cassie. If I hadn't seen the look in her eyes that I'd seen only one time before, standing on the bow of Pirate Chang's freakishly realistic fiberglass pirate ship. Recently, I'd thought a lot about the many turning points in my life. What would have happened if I'd asked Natalie Grayson to the party? What would have happened if I hadn't tried to kiss Cassie on the bed? What would have happened if I had kissed Cassie on the eighteenth hole? But this moment was one that shined like a beacon. What would have happened if I hadn't looked over at Cassie? Truthfully, I just don't know. Because I did look. Only I didn't see her. I saw me as she saw me. I saw the kind of guy who would never back down from a giant dick like Dean Kowalcyk.

I saw Simon Fucking Cross.

"Say it again," I said to Dean, not recognizing my own voice. "I don't think I heard you the first time."

"Faggot." He was grinning, his smile a chaotic line carved from his stubbled, sunken cheeks. "You're a fag. You've probably sucked more dick than this bitch." He hiked his thumb at Cassie and settled back on his bones, like a soldier standing at rest.

Coop had been in a couple of fights in middle school, and he always claimed that he didn't remember anything that happened during them. He could recall the before and the after but never the punches he threw or the kicks he took. His memories, he'd told me, were out of focus.

I'm not sure if Coop was bullshitting me or if I'm some kind of freak, but I remember every second of what happened before, during, and after Dean called Cassie a bitch. Hell, my fist was on the way to Dean's nose before he cleared the "tch."

Dean never saw it coming. He was strong and I was a wuss and he didn't believe that I had the balls to take a swing at him. The cartilage of his nose crunched under my knuckles like rotted rubber. Dean grunted in shock and stumbled backward. My fist exploded in pain but I felt invincible. I'd slain the giant; I slew Goliath. I was a bona fide badass.

Until Dean regained his feet and launched himself at me with preternatural speed, fueled by a potent cocktail of rage and humiliation. I didn't even have time to protect myself before he was on me, his first punch catching me under my ribs, driving my breath from my lungs. Luckily, I was able to hold on to the contents of my stomach, but only because I was preoccupied with protecting my body from the next anticipated blow. But Dean was a pro. He punched me in the jaw and I bit the tip of my tongue so hard that I tasted warm, coppery blood.

The rest of the party faded away as I focused on survival. I tried to throw a second pitiful jab, but Dean shrugged it off and laid into me with a flurry of punches that landed so fast I couldn't register the pain before the next one hit. I collapsed to the carpet, trying to minimize the damage.

What scared me most wasn't that he was a freakishly strong psycho who'd been voted most likely to end up on death row before his twenty-first birthday. It was that he didn't say a single word as he beat the shit out of me. I registered every kick, every punch. I registered Cassie trying to pull Dean off of me. But his silence is what stuck. And the thought that he wasn't going to stop until I was dead.

Except, then it was over. As quickly as it began, the fight was done. I tasted blood, unsure whether it was coming from my nose or my tongue. I risked a quick glance around the room. Dean was standing over me, holding out his hand.

"You're still a faggot," Dean said. "But you got balls." Dean's nose was barely red. My ineffectual punch had done little more than bruise his ego.

I took Dean's hand and let him help me up. The first person I looked for was Cassie. Her face was splotchy and her dress was disheveled. But under her concern she was smiling at me. For me. I'd lost the fight but it had been so worth it.

The room was still silent. I didn't know when DJ Leo had stopped the music, but the quiet that had earlier been contained to the living room had now infected the entire house. I cleared my throat of the mucus and blood that coated it.

"So, the table is ours, right?" I said.

Dean laughed and broke the silence. The music resumed and everyone who had gathered around us let out the collective breath they'd been holding. Dean returned to his chair and motioned at the table with his chin. "All yours," he said. "Try not to embarrass yourself."

"No promises," I said.

Cassie kept trying to dab at my nose with a napkin to stanch the dribbles of blood that were leaking down onto the front of my favorite shirt. I briefly entertained the notion that standing up to Dean to keep her from having to make out with him for possession of the beer pong table was all the proof she needed to know that I really loved her. She disabused me of that notion by slapping my arm and calling me an idiot.

"You're welcome," I said back. There was a gaudy mirror on the wall that I used to survey the damage to my face. It wasn't as bad as it felt. My cheek was developing a colorful bruise, and my nose was a leaky faucet of blood, but I hadn't lost any teeth or broken any bones. A definite win in my opinion. The napkin Cassie had given me had soaked through within seconds so I stripped off my ruined shirt and held it to my face.

"Here," Cassie said. She handed me a bottle of water that I used to clean some of the drying blood from my chin.

I plugged my nose up with another napkin and turned back to the table. "We going to play or what?"

Cassie put her hands on her hips and shook her head. "You're in no shape to do anything except find Coop and have him drive you home."

Though much of the crowd that had gathered had faded back into the party, enough remained to make backing out of our beer pong game impossible if I wanted to hold on to any of the points I'd gained by fighting the scariest guy in school.

"The cups are set up," I said. "Let's play. Unless you've got something to hide."

Taunting Cassie was a bad move, but my whole body hurt and I couldn't think up any other way to keep her around. If I'd been playing the long game, I would have taken the points I'd earned, kept my title of Hero of the Beer Pong Table, and lived to try another day. But I knew—I felt it in my battered bones—that everything, my whole life, my chance to kiss her, was down to this one night. If I gave up now, I might as well give up forever.

Cassie shrugged. She didn't look angry, but the admiration she'd had for me a moment ago was dwindling fast. "Fine," she said. "But you asked for this."

Though it didn't look like that much beer in the cups on the table, I knew it was still enough to do some damage. The pain from my fight further impaired my already questionable beer pong skills. If I had any chance of getting answers from Cassie and not pickling my brain in the process, I was going to need serious luck.

"Here's the deal," Cassie said. "If I put my ball in your cup, I get to ask you a question. You either answer or drink. If you lie, then you drink all the cups and the game is over."

I nodded. "Got it. Let's play." I tried to sound cool but with a bit tongue and one plugged nostril, everything I said came out sounding like the Swedish Chef.

"Flip to see who takes the first shot?"

"Ladies first," I said.

Without hesitation, Cassie picked up the orange Ping-Pong ball and executed the most perfect throw in the history of beer pong. She made it look effortless, even with swollen knuckles. The ball sailed in a tight arc into the center of the plastic cup at the apex of my beeramid.

Shit was about to get real in the living room.

"Your question," I said. "I've got nothing to hide."

Cassie took only a second to come up with her question, and it was immediately evident that she wasn't going to lob me any easy pitches. "Are you still a virgin, Simon?"

There was no way not to answer the question. She knew I was, so I couldn't lie. I couldn't drink, either. If I did, everyone would assume I was a virgin but was too afraid to admit it. There was only one thing to do. I said, "Yes," and owned it.

My answer earned a couple of snickers from people who didn't matter. All that mattered was proving something to Cassie. That I wasn't going to back down, no matter how difficult she made it.

I fished the ball out of my cup and casually tossed it at one of her cups. It hit the rim and bounced onto the floor.

Cassie smirked and said, "Too bad, Sy."

"It's cool," I said. "I'm learning a hell of a lot about you right now, anyway." Which was the truth. Behind Cassie's stony veneer was a girl who was petrified. Of what, I didn't know. I knew I hadn't hallucinated the way she'd looked at me right before Dean beat my ass, the same way I hadn't imagined the way she'd looked at me when I'd sunk the shot on the eighteenth hole at Pirate Chang's. It was like she'd realized in the time between accepting my challenge and actually playing that I might uncover something about her or, worse yet, that she might uncover something about herself.

"Whatever." Cassie picked up the ball again and sank it into the second cup.

"You've obviously missed your true calling as a beer pong pro," I said. "You're some kind of freaky savant."

Cassie sighed and said, "No, you just suck at this." She smiled and asked her next question. "Are you really wearing Superman underwear?"

I silently vowed to torture Ben. I was going to tie him to a chair and force him to watch every Alvin and the Chipmunks movie on repeat until he went mad from the incessant squeaking. But not for telling Cassie about the underwear. I didn't care if the whole world knew that I was sporting my lucky Man of Steel briefs. I was pissed because what I was wearing under my jeans was likely one of many secrets about me that Ben had revealed to Cassie. And if Ben had armed her with an unlimited supply of ammo, I was sunk.

I had only one play to make. I picked up the cup and chugged the beer. When I was done, I set it upside down and said, "Why don't you come over here and find out for yourself?"

My false bravado didn't impress Cassie as much as it did the rest of the onlookers. She rolled her eyes while they hollered and laughed. Even Aja was giving me some respect. Not much, but some.

"Throw already," Cassie said.

Since I lacked Cassie's skill with the Ping-Pong ball, my only shot was to play the odds. I took aim at the middle of Cassie's beeramid. Luck is the only way to describe how my orange ball managed to bounce around and fall into a cup. Not the cup I'd been aiming for, not even close, but I'd take what Lady Luck gave me. All I had to do now was ask my question.

When Cassie had told me that I didn't know her, I knew she wasn't talking about what kind of music she listened to or who her favorite actress was or what she wanted to be when she grew up. I knew those things. The Kooks, Charlize Theron, and a journalist. Those were the sorts of things anyone who was her friend on Facebook knew about her. No, Cassie had been suggesting that I didn't know the answers to the bigger questions—the million little pieces that make up a person.

But of those million little pieces, I wanted to know about only one.

"Why did you dump Eli?"

I'd certainly fantasized that Cassie would break up with her boyfriend for me. That she'd wake up one morning and realize that something in her life had always been missing, and that the only time she'd been truly happy was the one night we spent together playing mini-golf. But I wasn't stupid enough to believe it would ever really happen.

Instead of answering the question, Cassie picked up the cup of beer I'd hit and chugged it. Then she chugged another. And another, until all of her cups were empty. She wasn't smiling, she wasn't frowning. Without needing her to say it, I knew the game was over.

"Fuck you, Simon," she said. "Fuck Eli, fuck Rendview, and fuck everyone at this stupid party." She looked around the room as if realizing for the first time that her house was filled with people. If she hadn't been drunk before, she was going to be soon, and I could see her desire to be anywhere else. But before she left, she said, "You should have kissed me that night at Pirate Chang's."

I didn't get to tell her how many times I wished I had before she fled.

The moment the drama was over, people forgot us. Someone else took possession of the table, and Dean lit up a joint to pass around the room. The crowd began funneling back to the kitchen or the dance floor or the patio or wherever they thought would be more interesting than the room in which I'd been humiliated multiple times.

A symphony of thoughts fought for my attention and I needed quiet to hear them. I ran up the stairs, taking them two at a time, and ducked into the last room down a long hallway, not caring who it belonged to. I slammed the door behind me and leaned against it, sliding slowly to the carpet, trying not to hyperventilate. When I caught my breath, I looked around. The pictures on the mirror over the rosewood dresser announced loud and clear that I'd taken refuge in Cassie's bedroom. I got up to leave immediately, but when I turned the knob, it came off in my hand.

"That happens sometimes," said a deep, familiar voice from behind me. I slowly turned around, horrified to find Eli Horowitz sprawled on the floor between Cassie's bed and the wall.

I tried to push the knob back in but the tiny bits fell to the ground. There was no way out. I was trapped.

"Balls."

Reality Bites

When my mom found out that Ben and Coop were gay, she spent a month hinting to me that it would be okay if I were too. For a while, I had a complex about it, convinced that my mom secretly wanted a gay son because she believed that it would entitle her to an all-access pass into an elite club. She could tell people that her son was a homosexual and bypass the normal line at her hairdresser or get special discounts on shoes. I spent a ridiculous amount of time trying to convince her that I was completely, totally heterosexual, going so far as to purposely leave straight porn lying around where she could find it.

If my mom could see me now, standing in front of Mrs. Castillo's lavish closet, it would have undone all my hard work. Still, though I hated to admit it, I looked fucking hot in a skirt.

The skirt was part of Stella's plan, which she'd yet to fully explain. The first thing we'd done was find Ben and Coop and recruit them to our cause. Ben hadn't taken much convincing;

Coop had. I told him about seeing Eli and Cassie on the patio. Coop maybe didn't totally support my telling Cassie how I felt, but he recognized the devastating implications of Eli being back in the picture. Eli Fucking Horowitz was a stumbling block I couldn't overcome without help.

Ben and Stella had suggested I wear something from Cassie's closet, but I was too tall. Mrs. Castillo's clothes probably weren't much better, but Stella had declared that they'd do. Now she and Ben were arguing over what shade of lipstick I should wear while Coop stood by the door and tried not to laugh.

"I have two questions," I said to Stella when I'd finished admiring my ass in the mirror. Mrs. Castillo probably hadn't worn any of these clothes since college, but they didn't look too bad on me.

"Only two?" Coop asked.

Ben faced me, holding out a tube of lipstick. "Yes, you're pretty. And no, I won't sleep with you."

"Thank you," I said. "And ew."

While he was distracted, Stella snatched the lipstick from Ben and tossed it behind her. He looked appalled and bent to retrieve it. "Do you like having hands?" Stella asked.

"Whatever," Ben said. "If you want him to look like a two-dollar hooker, by all means, go with Passion Pink."

I couldn't tell why Ben and Stella were bickering, but it had been nearly constant since they'd entered the same room. "I prefer the term 'working girl,'" I said, trying to defuse the tension.

Stella ignored everyone and pushed a chair across the room so that she could stand on it and apply the winning lipstick. She smeared it across my lips and it felt like bacon fat. Of course, it wasn't the first time I'd dressed in women's clothing, but that had been Halloween and I hadn't so much dressed up as a girl as dressed up as a zombie Charlie's Angel. It had been Ben's idea, and he, Coop, and I had won first place in the Rendview Junior High costume contest.

"Back to my questions," I said when Stella had finished with the makeup. "Where'd you get the wig, and why do I have to be the one to dress up like a girl? Especially since you already mostly look like a girl."

Instead of answering me, Stella hopped down off the chair to admire her handiwork. When she was satisfied, she slipped the lipstick into her purse and said, "I'll hold on to this."

"The only person this is going to fool is your stupid blind dog," Coop said from his post by the door. His job was to make sure no one came into the bedroom. He didn't have the fashion sense Ben did anyway, and if he'd picked out my clothes I'd have ended up in a burka cut from the Castillos' sheets.

"Falcor isn't stupid," Stella said. "He's very smart, actually."

Ben bit back a laugh. "Then how come I caught him trying to hump the beer keg earlier?"

"It's a party. Half your class is out there humping the keg." Stella disappeared into the closet muttering something about my hairy belly button. The blouse they'd dressed me in didn't quite give me the necessary coverage.

"Remember Stevie Kayne?" Ben asked. I nodded. "I loaned him my Halloween wig when the drama club did *Hairspray*. He brought it to barter."

"So you got it from Stevie?"

Ben shook his head. "He'd traded it to Naomi for a bottle of absinthe that I'm pretty certain is fake. Naomi traded the wig to Jamison Belko for some of those berries that are supposed to change the way everything tastes."

Stella popped her head out of the closet. "Those things make vinegar taste like apple juice."

"Cool," Coop said.

"I hate apple juice," Stella said before retreating into Mrs. Castillo's closet again.

"So you got the wig from Jamison," I said. "Got it."

Ben shook his head. "No. Jamison traded it to—"

"Don't care," I said. "Next question."

Coop whistled—the signal that someone was coming. Ben and I ducked into the closet with Stella while Coop got rid of whoever was out there. Without the slightest bit of hesitation, Ben began rummaging through Mrs. Castillo's personal things. Stella had apparently found nothing to replace my blouse with because she was empty-handed. She didn't seem in any hurry to finish, and if I hadn't known better I'd have thought she was stalling. It was odd since I knew for a fact that Ewan was out there waiting for her to return.

"Why are you doing this for me?" I asked in a whisper.

"You're nice," she said. Stella toyed with one of her dreads. I'd have thought they'd smell bad but they had the faint scent of fresh wood. "Also, we had a deal."

I looked at where we were and what I was wearing. "This definitely goes above and beyond our deal."

"The Nash family motto is: Never give up." Stella frowned. "It's actually: Never give up cake. But that doesn't exactly apply here."

Stella made me smile. I didn't always understand her, but I definitely seemed to smile a lot when I was around her. She was so different from other girls. I didn't feel the need to try around Stella. When I embarrassed myself in front of Cassie, I felt as if the entire world was judging me. But with Stella, I could stand in a closet wearing women's clothing, and it was cool.

Coop whistled twice to let us know the coast was clear. Ben pushed past Stella and me to get out.

"It was Aja," Coop said. "With Sia Marcus." He was making his "I've eaten something bad and I don't know whether to spit it out or swallow it" frown.

"Yeah, they're a thing now," I said. "Maybe." Despite enjoying Ben's clear astonishment that I, for once, was the one with the gossip, I quickly changed the subject. "So I'm dressed like . . . well, like this. Now what?"

We all turned our attention to Stella. She'd kept the plans close to her vest, indicating only that Ben's and Coop's participation was crucial. "Simon's gays, you'll be responsible for separating Eli from Cassie and getting him up to Cassie's bedroom."

Knowing that part of Stella's master plan did little to illuminate how this was going to help me with Cassie. "No can do," Ben said. "Eli's on her like peanut butter on jelly."

"Seriously," Coop said. "How are we even supposed to do that?"

Stella stroked her chin as if she had an evil, pointy beard. "Me thinks you need proper motivation." She reached into her purse and pulled something out, keeping it hidden in her palm, stage magician–style. "Complete your task and this will be yours." She revealed one plastic-wrapped condom. "Ribbed for her pleasure. Or rather, his pleasure."

Ben tried to grab it, but Stella snatched it out of his reach and put it safely back in her purse. "You've had that the whole time?" he asked. Stella nodded. "Why didn't you tell me?"

"You didn't ask." It sounded logical to me, and Ben certainly did look motivated to do whatever it took to pry Eli from Cassie, including set the house on fire if necessary, which I hoped he wouldn't have to resort to.

Coop furrowed his brow and said, "I think I have an idea. Can I borrow Falcor?"

"My stupid dog, you mean?" Falcor was on the bed, sleeping in a nest he'd made out of the comforter. Coop didn't take back his assessment of the dog but did his best to look appropriately chastised. "Sure," Stella said. "Don't lose him."

Ben was jumping up and down like a kid at Christmas. He could hardly contain his excitement as he scooped up a grumpy-looking Falcor in his arms. "Let's go!"

Coop paused. "Let me just get a minute with Simon." He waited for Ben and Stella to leave and then he got all serious on me. "You sure this is worth it?"

"It's worth it," I said without hesitation, sure that it was. In fact, at that moment, I'd have been hard-pressed to dream up anything I wouldn't have done for the chance to tell Cassie I loved her.

"Because, here's the thing . . ." Coop took a deep breath before continuing, steady again. "I promised I'd help you and I will. But after this, I'm done."

"Yeah," I said, patting him on the arm. "I get it."

Coop shook his head and looked me right in the eyes. "No, you don't," he said. "I'm done with us. With you, Simon."

Up to that point, only half of my attention had been on the conversation, but now Coop had it all. "Come again?"

"Listen," he said. "It's just that you shouldn't have to crawl through the mud under barbed wire to get the girl you like to give you the time of day. And if you go through with this, well, I can't hold you together for another three years. It's time to move on."

I was stunned, and pissed, but mostly confused. "You're telling me that if I tell Cassie I love her, you and I won't be friends anymore?"

Coop nodded.

"Then I guess I'll find another ride home." My voice was emotionless. I didn't know what to feel. Mostly, I didn't believe it. Coop and I had been friends for so long that I couldn't imagine life without him. But when it came down to him or Cassie, I chose Cassie.

With a terse nod, Coop took off to fulfill his part of the mission and earn his condom.

"You ready, hot stuff?" Stella asked, popping back into the room.

I was as ready as I was going to get, but I had a fleeting moment of indecision. A second where I considered calling the whole thing off. It's difficult to explain, but I had this thought, this picture of Cassie and me twenty years in the future. We'd gotten together at the party and gotten married and had kids. And I was sitting with them—daughters, of course—telling them the story of the night I told their mother I was in love with her. And when that premonition or whatever you want to call it had passed, I wondered whether this was the story I'd want to tell my children. That I had to dress in drag to get a shot at winning their mother's heart. In that moment, I wondered if Coop was right. But the hesitation passed and I wrote it off as nerves.

Stella patted my ass and I jumped. "Whoa there, little lady. You gotta pony up the dough to touch these goods." I smoothed down my blouse, uncomfortable with how much my own fake breasts were turning me on. A boner in this skirt would ruin everything. "This plan is bound to fail," I said.

"But it'll make a great YouTube video." Stella held up her phone and I couldn't tell if she was actually filming or just screwing with me.

I took a couple of steps in the heels, realizing for the first time that I was actually going to have to walk in these things. Lucky for me, the bed was there, because I face-planted into the warm spot Falcor had been sleeping on.

"Up-skirt shot!" Stella shouted, and her flash lit up the room. I wasn't sure how much she'd seen until she said, "Come on, Man of Steel. Let's do this thing." She was out the door before I could stop her.

"Where are we going?" I yelled even though I knew Stella wouldn't answer me. The only way to know was to follow. Fear of being left behind overrode my fear of breaking my ankle, and I chased Stella into the hall.

I hoped that in the dark, I made a passable woman. In regular light my disguise was hardly a disguise at all. I'd put the fate of my sexual destiny in the hands of a madwoman.

Stella put her finger to her lips. She peeked around the corner and then said, "Come on." She pulled me down the hall and into the garage.

"Where are we going?" I said when the door had closed behind us. The garage smelled like old grass and gasoline. It was dominated by a huge workbench that was neatly organized.

"Maybe you should have shaved your legs," Stella said. She looked me up and down and then shook her head. "Nah. This is good."

If this was good, it was only because it had lapped bad and come back around again. "Where are we going?"

"Cassie's room."

"Isn't that where you told Ben and Coop to send Eli?"

Stella nodded.

"Why?"

"That's the plan."

"*What's* the plan?" My voice went up two octaves and broke. "Are you insane?"

"Clinically, yes." Stella grabbed my hand again and pulled. "Come on!"

I followed Stella out into the night, where I was immediately attacked by hungry mosquitoes. We waited at the edge of the house while Stella made sure it was all clear. Of course, her idea of clear and mine were radically different. There was a small crowd of smokers that we had to pass, but she withheld that information until it was too late for me to turn back. My only saving grace was that Stella was so brightly colored that everyone looked at her rather than me. That, and they were all completely shit-faced.

But the real terror began when I realized she planned to take us right in the front door. I wrenched my hand from hers. "Nope. Not a chance."

"It's the only way," Stella said. "It'll be fine. We're going to go in and run right up the stairs."

I glanced at the door. "Right past the living room and library. Where there are people."

Stella grabbed my chin in her tiny hand. "This will work. I promise." She sounded so earnest; she looked so sincere. I couldn't help but believe her.

"All right," I said, knowing I'd likely regret it. "Let's go."

We raced through the door and up the stairs like Stella had promised. I thought I was going to make it without being spotted when a sweaty hand grabbed hold of my wrist. I turned around, expecting to find Ben or Coop, and found Blaise Lewis instead. He was trying to bring me into focus with his heavy, bloodshot eyes.

"I know you?" He stumbled into me, groping my fake breasts.

"Dude!"

"Huh?" Blaise's eyes flew wide with surprise and he tripped down a step.

Even laughing, Stella managed to extricate me from Blaise's manhandling and help me the rest of the way up the stairs, which wasn't easy in heels. By the time we got to Cassie's room, I was sweaty and pretty sure my heart was going to explode. Stella was still laughing.

"Can you shut up?" I said. There was nothing funny about Blaise feeling me up. I hoped he was too drunk to know what had happened or too embarrassed to tell anyone.

Stella covered her mouth with her hand, but the laughter leaked out around the edges.

It hit me that I was in Cassie's bedroom. A place I'd dreamed about for ages. It was just like I'd imagined, too. Pink and soft with all kinds of strange, exotic smells.

"She's a pig," Stella said. She ran her finger along the rim of a plate that was balanced on the edge of Cassie's dresser. There were water bottles on her nightstand and clothes piled on the floor. I wouldn't have called Cassie a pig, but the mess took some of the shine off.

"We're here," I said. "What now?"

Stella dug around in her purse, looking for God only knew what, and motioned toward the bathroom. "We hide."

"I don't get it," I said. "Ben and Coop will finish their job and Eli will be up here any minute. What are we going to do?"

"Hide. Are you deaf?" Stella stared at me like I was the one who'd lost his mind.

"Listen," I said, pretty much fed up. "I've done everything you asked, but I'm not moving another inch until you tell me everything."

Stella sighed and fished out the lipstick she'd stolen from Mrs. Castillo. "Fine. Ben and Coop are going to send Eli up here. We're going to hide in the bathroom." While Stella explained, she wrote, "Handcuff yourself to the bed and put on the blindfold," on the mirror in lipstick. She dotted the *i* with a heart. "We'll get Eli to handcuff himself to the bed and then we'll leave him here. With him out of commission, you'll be free to work your sexy voodoo on Cassie."

I couldn't deny that Stella's plan would definitely sideline Eli, but there was one thing I didn't understand. "If we're hiding in the bathroom, why am I dressed like Cassie's ugly cousin?"

Stella whistled and looked at the ceiling.

"Stella?"

"Okay," she said. "This wasn't part of the plan. I honestly thought it was going to be so much harder to convince you to dress like a girl, but you practically dove into the skirt. Not that I blame you. You make a damn fine woman."

"What?" My brain was having trouble processing Stella's confession. "Why?"

"Truthfully?"

"No," I said. "I prefer the lies."

She tsked. "No need to get snippy."

I made a gesture that was considerably more than snippy and she got the hint.

"It's a barter. One of Ewan's friends has this video game that's only available in Japan. He told me that he'd give it to me if I could get you to dress in drag."

"Are you fucking kidding me?" I yelled. I threw my fake hair against the wall.

"Don't wig out, Simone," she said, and grinned. "See what I did there?"

"Screw you," I said, really not in the mood for puns. "You dressed me like a hooker for a video game."

"It's not just any video game. It's Revenge of the Furry Bathtub Lickers, which is way more awesome than it sounds. It loses something in the translation."

I was about to tell Stella all the places she could stick the game when I heard footsteps in the hall and someone cursing to himself. It sounded like Eli.

"And, we're out of time. Get me a shirt from one of the drawers." While I fished a green shirt from Cassie's dresser and tossed it on the bed, Stella pulled out the handcuffs I'd seen in her car earlier. She laid them on top of the shirt and grabbed my arm.

"Hide." She pulled me into the dark bathroom and closed the door all but a crack as Eli entered Cassie's bedroom.

My anger drained away and was replaced by fear as I realized that I was trapped in Cassie's bathroom, dressed like a bad facsimile of a girl, with Eli just a couple of feet away.

Fuck.

Living the Dream

God hated me and was punishing me for some crime I'd committed in a previous incarnation. I was cursed to live out the remainder of my days under the ire of an all-powerful deity who had bent his limitless fury toward the single task of ruining my life. It was the only explanation for how I could have come to be trapped in Cassandra Castillo's bedroom with Eli Fucking Horowitz—her too-good-to-be-true ex-boyfriend, who actually happened to be that good. I was sure he usually spent his Friday nights rescuing kittens and saving old ladies from loud-music-blaring hooligans.

I stood in front of Cassie's bedroom door, holding the busted knob in my hand, feeling hopeless. Being beaten up by the school sociopath and trounced at beer pong by the girl I loved were turning out to be the high points of the night. I suspected that being locked in a small room with my mortal enemy might not even be rock bottom.

"You look like shit," Eli said. He'd moved into a sitting position and was now examining me, taking stock. I wasn't sure what he'd been doing prior to my arrival, but now all his attention was focused on me.

"At least I don't smell," I said. There were pieces of the door on the floor, pieces that I had no clue how to fit back together. With a shrug, I dumped the knob and shoved my hands in my pockets.

Eli didn't seem to take offense. He did, in fact, smell. It was an unwashed odor of rum and regret. Up close, he looked worse than he had at Gobbler's. Stubbly and unkempt. The way Coop and Ben and I looked when we came back from camping, only sadder and drunker.

"Well, this is awkward," I said.

"What happened to you?" Eli asked. I assumed he meant my face, but a quick glance in the mirror over Cassie's dresser revealed that I looked less like I'd been beaten up and more like someone had dumped a bucket of pig's blood on me.

"You should see the other guy," I said.

Eli nodded. "Sure." The way he looked at me and talked to me was infuriating. He was so authentically nice about everything. Eli was a parent's wet dream. Granted, at that moment, he wasn't living up to his potential, but Eli on his worst day was still better than most men on their best. He was certainly better than me.

As maddening as that was, he also put me at ease. I knew that I could tell him what happened and he would judge my actions honestly. So I told him about my fight with Dean without embellishing too much.

When I finished my story, Eli pointed at the bottom right

drawer of Cassie's dresser. "There's a shirt you can wear in there." He picked up a bottle of dark rum that had been hidden between his thigh and the bed and took a swallow.

The drawer was filled with clothes that were decidedly not Cassie's. A couple of pairs of jeans, some shirts. Boxers. I glanced back questioningly and he said, "They're mine."

"Thanks," I said. I chose a shirt at random and pulled it on. The thing was like two sizes too big. It was a green shirt with TEAM PLÁTANO written in red over a festive silk-screened menorah.

Eli chuckled. "Mr. Castillo had that made for me over the holidays. Every year he has a family contest. Last year was boys versus girls. Team Plátano versus Team Melón." I didn't get the joke, but it made Eli smile. I wished I could smile with him, but all I could think about was Eli celebrating Chrismukkah—or whatever inclusive hybrid religious holiday the Castillos had devised—with Cassie. Sitting around the table, part of the family, part of her life. It was all I could do not to rip off the shirt and burn it.

"You fucking her yet?"

I was so caught up in envying Eli and then hating him for making me envy him that I missed his question the first time. It wasn't until he said it again that my brain fired off the appropriate signals to my jaw, which, if I'd been a cartoon character, would have hit the floor with an audible thunk.

It wasn't the question itself that blindsided me. Firstly, it was how he'd asked it. Hearing Eli Horowitz ask something so crude was out of character. Secondly, and more importantly, it was the fact that he actually thought I had a chance of hooking up with

Cassie. Even if it was a jealous fantasy planted in his brain by a combination of alcohol and depression, it still meant that he believed me capable of such an act. Or better yet, that he believed Cassie would even have me.

"No?" I said.

"You don't sound sure."

"Definitely not," I said. "She won't even let me kiss her. Not that I tried. Well, I did, but it was an accident and she shot me down. I swear." Eli stared at me, not blinking, not twitching a single muscle on his face the whole time I babbled. He scared me more than Dean did, but my fear couldn't stop my diarrheal word geyser.

"Shut up, Simon." Eli held the bottle out to me. It was only half full and I hoped that Eli hadn't consumed the entire missing portion.

I held up my hands. "I've had enough liquor for two parties." The truth was that I barely felt buzzed. I'd danced off the tequila shot long ago, and what little beer I'd had was doing nothing but making me have to pee.

Eli shook the bottle at me. "Drink." It wasn't an offer, it was a command.

"Yeah. Sure." I sat down under the window and took the bottle. Eli watched me take a baby sip. "There. See?"

"For real this time."

Nothing got past Eli, drunk or not. I tilted the bottle back a second time and took a mouthful, holding it in my cheeks. The stuff tasted like rancid maple syrup and I didn't think I could choke it down. Eli slapped me on the back and I swallowed involuntarily, coughing and hacking as some of it went down the wrong pipe.

"Mazel tov." Eli grabbed the bottle back and took another shot like it was water instead of viscous liquid fire obviously distilled from gasoline by demons in the third circle of hell.

As the rattlesnake venom worked its way through my veins, I sat silently, trying to think of something to say that wasn't completely lame. For all that I'd envied Eli, I didn't actually know much about the guy. Ben had told me some stories, but Ben's stories are often more hyperbole than truth. From a distance, Eli appeared to have it all. A great family, a perfect future, more athletic prowess in his little toe than I had in my entire body, and a beautiful girlfriend. Ex-girlfriend, I mean. Upon close inspection, though, I could see the imperfections, the tiny cracks in his existence. Knowing that life sometimes sucked for Eli made him seem more human. Paradoxically, his flaws made him even more perfect.

"Don't ever fall in love," Eli said, his voice scratchy from drinking or crying—I didn't know which.

"Okay." What else was I supposed to say? I was already in love, had been for years, with the girl who had dumped him. God, how I wanted to feel like this was some sort of karmic retribution for all the years I'd spent pining for Cassie while Eli kissed her and hugged her and wormed his way into the tiny crevices of her life. But few people actually deserved the torment Eli was enduring, and I seriously doubted he was one such person.

Eli locked onto me with his big eyes. I'd never noticed how

they bulged out like a scared Chihuahua's. "Seriously, man. Love is bullshit." His words ran together, the rum deteriorating the spaces between them. But I got the message, loud and clear.

I nodded again, letting Eli know I'd heard, and then I realized that I had an opportunity that I might not have again. Cassie had chugged an entire beeramid rather than tell me why she'd broken up with Eli. Earlier, I'd suspected that the information might be important, but her stubborn refusal to answer the question had convinced me that knowing why she'd dumped her boyfriend of three years was essential to unraveling the puzzle that was Cassie—which I believed was the key to proving that I really loved her.

In a moment of clarity, free from the effects of the heroic mouthful of rum I'd been intimidated into swallowing, I decided that if I couldn't get the answers I needed from Cassie, maybe I could wheedle them from Eli. It certainly couldn't hurt to try. But first, I needed more rum. It took the edge off my war wounds and stiffened my courage, of which I was going to need every ounce.

We passed the bottle back and forth for a couple of minutes, each successive sip going down a little easier, until I felt my fear retreating.

"Sorry about Cass," I said, easing into it. Eli was fragile and I didn't want to push him too hard. Yet. He muttered something about love being bullshit again and I worried that I'd let him drink too much. He'd be useless to me if he passed out. "So, what happened with you guys?"

Eli glanced at me like he was gauging the shape and depth

of my question. I watched as his face cycled through all the emotions available to him in his intoxicated state—anger, desolation, hopelessness—before he finally settled into a quiet resignation.

"I don't know," he said, almost as if he was talking to himself and not to me. "We were good, then we weren't. No warning, no nothing. One phone call and we were over."

"She didn't say why?"

"Nope." Eli shrugged.

"Was she acting funny? Before she broke up with you, I mean?" It might have been because of the rum, but the longer I spent with Eli, the less I feared him. He was as pathetic as I was; in some ways he was worse.

But Eli didn't answer my question. I watched him fight the effects of the alcohol, trying to tread water in a depthless pool. "I know you're in love with my girl," he said. "Everyone knows." He looked triumphant as he let that nugget of information hang out between us.

"Yeah," I said. "It's pretty obvious, isn't it?" I thought back to that moment jumping on the bed with Cassie, when I'd told her that I loved her. Her lack of surprise. The way she'd brushed it off so casually. My similar reaction to Eli's statement clearly irritated him.

"Cassie laughed about it, you know? How pathetic you are." Eli was tossing bombs, and they hurt. His serious inability to speak in fully formed words robbed them of some of the sting, but not all.

I had a feeling that he wasn't trying to hurt me as much as he was trying to make himself feel better by lashing out at the only other person in the room who loved Cassie as deeply as he did. I could have fired back—in Eli's drunken state, it would have been so easy—but I didn't. Not even I could kick a man when he was so, so low.

"I came here tonight to tell Cassie I love her." I looked Eli right in the eyes as I said it. He deserved that much. "I tried to barter with her for a kiss."

Even drunk, Eli could have broken all 206 bones in my body. I watched him wrestle with his desire to do just that. But after a tense minute, he relaxed and sort of shrugged. A pitiable retreat. No matter what happened in the future, he'd never be Eli Fucking Horowitz to me again.

"Sometimes I think she liked you more than she liked me," Eli said.

"Don't bullshit me."

Eli took another swig from the rum bottle. It was definitely more than half empty now. "I'd been working up the nerve to ask Cassie out since I saw her in freshman assembly on the first day of school. Damn, she was fine." I didn't know where Eli was going with his story, but hearing that Eli had once been as afraid as I had to talk to Cassie validated years of procrastination and fear.

"Then I heard you'd asked her out," he said. He glanced over at me, some small bit of respect shining through. "She only said yes because she felt bad for you. No offense or anything, but you know how Cass is."

I wanted to puke. Cassie had felt bad for me? I was some

kind of pity case? No way. Cassie had obviously never told Eli about the eighteenth hole. I said, "I had a chance to kiss Cassie and I blew it."

Eli and I were past the point of being shocked or angry over our various Cassie revelations. We both loved her. We'd both do anything to be with her. In the arena, we might be enemies, but sitting in Cassie's room, trapped and not even trying to escape, we were just two lovesick high school boys drowning their miseries in a bottle of stormy rum.

"The first time I kissed Cassie was in a grocery store." Eli slurred more words than not, but it was like an accent I'd gotten used to.

"What?"

"We went for stuff to make cookies," he said, losing himself in the memory. "And I kissed her right in front of the chocolate chips."

Eli laughed. It was probably the first time he'd laughed since Cassie had broken his heart. But his smile faded and he took a huge gulp from the rum bottle to cover the tears that had formed in his eyes. I pretended not to see them.

"I don't know what happened. We had all these plans for our futures and shit. Then she fucking dumped me. It's like she doesn't care about anything anymore."

Nothing about the night made sense. Eli was right and I knew it. This Cassie—the girl who'd beaten up Blaise Lewis and trashed her house and jumped on her parents' bed—was not our Cassie. Somewhere along the way, she had changed and we'd missed it.

"How come you're up here?" I asked. "Shouldn't you be trying to help Cassie or get her back or something?"

"That was the plan. But then I saw the two of you dancing." The anger was back, but it seemed like he was directing it at himself more than at me.

I tried to put myself in Eli's shoes, watching me dance with the girl he loved. I would have run all the way home and hidden in my room until the end of days. But Eli had had the balls to stay.

Cassie was the same way. Fearless. But Eli was right: She seemed to move through the night like she was no longer responsible for anything. It was her apathy, her nihilism, that was different tonight.

The Cassandra Castillo I'd first met in freshman anatomy had been a brilliant, blinding star. But the Cassie who was throwing this party appeared to be going supernova. She was either going to explode or collapse under her own mass, destroying her whole life and everything she'd worked for.

Tonight was bigger than me, bigger than a kiss. I didn't just have to get to know Cassie so that I could kiss her; I had to find out what was going on so that I could help her save herself.

"I love her," Eli said.

"I know," I said. Eli was little more than an annoyance now that I thought I understood the seriousness of Cassie's problems. "Me too."

But Eli wasn't going to be dismissed. He grabbed my wrist in an iron grip. "You don't get it, Simon. I love Cassandra. Love. The way she walks and the way she gets all furious when she hears about animals being abused and how she's only ticklish when she's in the mood to be tickled and how she knows how to make me happy when no one else can and how she uses my hand to shield her eyes from the scary parts of movies. I love her. I suck at saying it. I can never make the words sound the way they do in my head, but I love her and I don't think I'll ever love anyone like I love her." Eli didn't sound drunk anymore. He spoke from a place inside him unaffected by the rum he'd consumed or the pain he'd endured since Cassie had broken his heart. Maybe his heart wasn't broken. Maybe it was only fractured and could be repaired.

"Tell her," I said. "Just like you told me."

"I can't."

My neck hurt from the awkward angle I'd slouched into and I pushed myself into a sitting position so that I could look at Eli dead-on. "You mean to tell me that after all the stuff I'm sure you guys have done, you still can't tell her that you love her?"

Eli shook his head. "I can tell her. Just not the way I want to."

"You're a pussy," I said. The force behind my words shocked even me, but like drinking the rum, the first time was the hardest and each subsequent swallow got easier and easier. "If Cassie loved me like she loves you, there's nothing I wouldn't do to show her."

I crossed my arms over my chest and waited for his reply. There was a chance said reply was going to come via a fist to the face, but I was prepared to accept the consequences. See, if I'd learned anything tonight, it was that Cassie was seriously fucked-up. I wanted to be the one to help her—doing so would be all the proof she needed that I truly loved her—but I wasn't delusional enough to believe that I could do it. If I was unable to pull Cassie back from the brink of self-destruction, I was putting my remaining chips on Eli Horowitz.

Instead of punching me or getting pissed, Eli simply stared at me for a tense moment before heaving himself to his hands and knees and crawling around the bed toward Cassie's closet. He disappeared into the deep recesses and I briefly entertained the notion that he'd gone in there and passed out. But he returned a minute later holding a cigar box in his hand. He found the indent his body had left in the carpet and settled back into it before handing me the box.

"Cassie will castrate us both if she finds out I showed you this."

I held the cigar box in my hands, trying to imagine what secrets Cassie had entrusted to its heavy, well-constructed protection. Clearly there was something inside that Eli wanted me to see, but I wasn't sure that I wanted to violate Cassie's trust. If I opened the lid and peered inside, whatever precious things she'd placed there wouldn't belong solely to Cassie any longer. They'd belong to me, too, and I hadn't earned that right.

But my curiosity won out. I justified it by telling myself that I was opening Cassie's box of secrets only in order to help her.

When I opened the lid, I was immediately disappointed. Instead of a treasure trove of artifacts, I saw only junk. "What is this crap?" I asked, picking through some movie ticket stubs and a dirty coin and a pack of jam.

Eli picked up the blueberry jam. "This is from our first date.

IHOP. Lame, I know, but Cassie wanted French toast more than life. We kept trying to talk, but the waiter wouldn't leave us alone. Cassie sent him on errands to keep him out of our hair, one of which was to find blueberry jam. It bought us five amazing minutes." Eli dropped the packet back in the box and motioned at me to keep digging.

I didn't see the point. "Great. Cassie kept some jam from your first date. Woo-hoo." Eli frowned at me as I picked through the trash. A tarnished silver cross, a pressed daisy, a USB drive, a water-stained picture of her grandmother. I was about to give up and return the cigar box to the closet when I spied a wrinkled slip of paper at the bottom. It was familiar and my hand gravitated to it, touching it without conscious thought.

"You know what that is," Eli said solemnly. He sounded like a man who, having completed his task, could finally rest.

I did know what the paper was. Or rather, what my brain thought it was. Because it couldn't really be that. Finding this paper in this box along with other things that Cassie had attached some sort of sentimental value to was like finding buried treasure.

I pulled the paper from the box and unfolded it. The scorecard was divided into two columns, just like I remembered. Cassie's name was written over one column and mine was scrawled over the other, in Cassie's messy script. The Pirate Chang's Booty and Mini-Golf logo was displayed in bold at the top and our scores were tallied at the bottom. Cassie had drawn a goofy smiley face next to my miracle shot at the eighteenth hole.

"Cassie kept this?"

"Obviously," Eli said.

All that time I'd spent pining for Cassie, thinking that she didn't remember that night, she'd kept the scorecard in her memory box. My mind raced with the possibilities. Clearly, Eli had been wrong. Cassie hadn't gone on a pity date with me. It had meant something to her. The proof was that she'd kept the scorecard. I couldn't help wondering how often she'd taken it out to look at and dream of what might have happened if I'd had the balls to kiss her when I should have. How our lives might have been different if Cassie and I had gotten together instead of Cassie and Eli.

And then I knew. I knew how I could show Cassie that I loved her, how I could turn a paper clip into a kiss.

"I have to get out of here," I said. I scrambled to my feet, accidentally dumping the contents of the cigar box to the carpet, but still clutching the scorecard. The effects of the rum hit me all at once. The room tilted, or I did, but everything was moving and I lost my balance, saved from falling back on my ass by the wall.

Eli watched me with curiosity. I didn't know whether he found my clumsiness funny or whether he was simply too inebriated to help me, but he maintained his position on the floor.

"What're you going to do?" Eli asked. His voice was clearer, no longer slurred.

I told Eli my plan. I hadn't worked everything out yet but I had the seed of an idea. Something had happened to Cassie, something bad. Whatever that was had turned her world upside down, causing her to act like a bizarro version of herself and spin out of control. All I had to do was give her something solid she could latch onto. I had to show her that I wasn't like other boys. That I would always be there for her. Once she knew that I really loved her, she could tell me what was wrong and we could sort it out and be together. The plan was brilliant in its simplicity. I'd been an idiot before. Of course telling Cassie I loved her wasn't enough. I had to show her. And thanks to Eli, I finally knew how.

When I'd finished, Eli stood up, steadying himself on the bed. "You think it'll work?"

I nodded. "I do."

He patted my shoulder and said, "Then go get her, champ."

There was something different about Eli now. Something had changed, but I couldn't put my finger on it. And truthfully, I was so busy trying to work out how to put my new plan into action that Eli could have been holding up a giant sign and I would have missed it.

"How do I get out of here?" I asked, looking at the broken doorknob. My brain was swimming in rum and it was difficult to line up my thoughts. They kept colliding and mixing and falling apart. I reached for the knob, but Eli grabbed the collar of my shirt and spun me around.

"Window," he said, pointing.

This suggestion seemed perfectly logical. Surely, if anyone had experience entering and exiting through Cassie's bedroom window, it was Eli Horowitz. He even undid the lock and opened it for me.

"Yeah?" I asked. Eli nodded.

The fresh air felt good on my face and I popped my head

out to take a look. There was a tree within easy reach with scuff marks on the closest branch from recent use.

There was no part of me that thought this was a bad idea, and I can only blame so much of that on alcohol. In reality, my judgment was clouded by the brilliance of my plan to win Cassie's love. Hell, if Eli had told me I was capable of stepping into the air and floating to the ground, I probably would have believed it. Okay, maybe I wasn't that stupid, but pretty close.

I was scared, but I kept repeating that if Eli could climb down the tree, then so could I. With one steadying breath, I mounted the windowsill and reached for the nearest branch. The bark was rough, but I had a good grip, so I held on tight and stepped out.

Instead of finding solid footing, I misjudged the distance and my shoe found only air. I panicked and let go.

One moment I was hanging on to the tree and the next I was on my back feeling like a thousand angry midgets had beaten me with tiny hammers.

Eli leaned out the window and said, "Sucker."

Reality Bites

I hid with Stella in Cassie's bathroom with the lights off and the door almost closed while Eli Fucking Horowitz moved around on the other side, only one thin piece of wood away from discovering me looking like a gang of color-blind drag queens had given me a drive-by makeover. I'd been stupid to trust Stella. If I could have magicked myself out of the bathroom, I would have abandoned her and never spoken to her again.

Instead I waited for Eli to see the note on the mirror telling him to put on the handcuffs and blindfold we'd left on the bed, praying that he wouldn't just barge into the bathroom and end the whole crazy charade.

"What the hell?" Eli stopped moving around in the bedroom and I could only assume that he'd seen the instructions on the mirror. I was too petrified to look through the crack in the door to find out for sure.

"I'm not in the mood for games, Cass," Eli said. "Some dog pissed on my jeans. You said we'd finish talking when you got back from the bathroom. So, come out of there and let's talk."

The plan was failing. Eli wasn't putting on the handcuffs or the blindfold. I looked at Stella to see what else she had up her sleeve, but even in the dark I could tell that her bag of tricks was empty. She'd expected Eli to comply and hadn't prepared for any contingencies.

"No," I said in my best Cassie voice. I sounded like a Muppet but hoped my one-word impression would fool Eli.

I pictured Eli standing there in his piss-soaked jeans, wondering how his life had come to arguing with his ex-girlfriend through a door about putting on handcuffs and a blindfold. If it had been me, I would have jumped into the metal bracelets, but Eli was made of stronger stuff. Or so I thought.

Eli Horowitz sighed so heavily that I heard it over the sound of Stella's breathing and the sound of the metal cuffs jingling. It was the sound of defeat. That sound should have made me happy, but something about this whole situation felt wrong.

"I love you," Eli said. He leaned against the wall next to the bathroom door. His voice carried through the crack like he was standing in the dark with us. "Remember your birthday last year? When I made us a picnic basket and we drove to Naples to watch the sun set over the ocean? You told me you loved me for the first time. Then we drove home and watched the sun rise over the ocean by my house. I told you I never wanted any other girl."

This wasn't Eli Fucking Horowitz. He wasn't some piece of debris cast from the side of Cassie's life, left to drift rudderless in a cold sea of apathy. This was the Eli who opened his heart to the girl he loved. This was the side of himself that he showed only to Cassie. Stella and I were thieves, picking through the bones of Eli and Cassie's private memories.

"I meant that, Cass," he said. "I still mean it. Whatever's going on with you, we can face it together. If you want me to play some stupid game with handcuffs and whatever, I'll do it."

There was so much honesty woven into Eli's simple declarations. He wasn't a guy just trying to get back together with a girl, willing to say anything to make it happen. He meant every single word he said. The depth of his feelings for Cassie made me question my own, which were based on a long-distance obsession and one night that had happened so far in the past that I wasn't sure she even remembered it. I'd never before doubted my feelings for Cassie and I didn't like it. The difference between Eli and me, though, was that while he and Cassie had a million perfect memories, Cassie and I had a future. A possible future—something Cassie had made clear she did not have or want with Eli.

"Do it," I said, my Cassie voice strong and hard. I still felt guilty doing this to Eli, but he'd had his chance.

Eli sighed again. It was the heavy, weary sigh of a man who didn't have much left to give. "Fine," he said. "But after that, we talk."

The cuffs rattled like chains as Eli put one end on his wrist and attached the other end to the wrought-iron bedframe. He could have easily faked it, but I had to trust that his devotion to Cassie would keep him honest. Though he and I were completely different people, we shared our love for Cassie. A love that would make a man dress like a woman or put on handcuffs and a blindfold.

Stella grabbed my hand and squeezed it, and I squeezed back, trying not to show her how sick this whole thing made me. I could justify it all I wanted—and I did—but deep down I knew what we were doing was wrong. Nothing was going to stop me from making a play for his girl, but Eli deserved to see me coming. Only I knew, as Stella must have too, that if I locked horns with Eli, I would lose.

"Done," he said. "Are you gonna tell me what's going on now?"

"What's next?" I whispered into Stella's ear.

Stella leaned in so that we were cheek to cheek. It sent a tingle down my arm and I shivered. "Now's your chance, big boy."

"For what?"

"You wanted to hook up with Eli, right?"

"What?" I said so loud that I feared Eli had heard. If Stella was joking, she hid it expertly.

"No? Then I guess we should leave and go get the girl." That was Stella's plan.

All I had to do was walk out of the room, find Cassie, and tell her that I loved her. I'd have to change first, obviously, but with Eli sidelined, there was nothing standing in my way. Stella had done as promised and given me my chance.

I still wasn't comfortable with the manner in which she'd gone about it or the part I'd played in her twisted game, but I couldn't deny the results.

Scared of what Stella might do if I hesitated any longer, I opened the bathroom door and walked out. The light was blinding after standing so long in the dark, but my eyes adjusted and I saw Eli sitting in his boxers in the middle of Cassie's bed with one arm appearing to hang in the air as if by an invisible thread. He was so pathetic that the wrongness of our perverse scheme socked me in the gut. Stella pushed past me and darted out into the hallway.

"If you're gonna leave me like this," Eli said, "the least you can do is give me one last kiss." I remembered the days and weeks following my failed date with Cassie as I spent count-less hours dissecting the details with Coop. I'd been beyond heartbroken. Back then, especially after I'd found out that Eli and Cassie were going out, I'd believed that my heart was beyond repair. That's how Eli sounded now. He could have torn off his blindfold and looked Cassie right in the eyes, but there wasn't enough fight left in him for even something that simple. He couldn't bear the thought of looking at his girl and not seeing his love returned.

Which is why I took two steps toward the bed, leaned for-ward, and kissed Eli lightly on the lips. Despite the fact that he was my mortal enemy, I couldn't abandon him handcuffed and blindfolded, believing that Cassie didn't care. There wasn't any rational thought behind my decision; I just did it.

What I didn't expect was for Eli to use his free hand to pull me in for more than a peck. He kissed me full on, sliding his tongue into my mouth like he must have done to Cassie a million times. The moment he realized something wasn't right—maybe it was my stubble or the fact that I'd forgotten to put the wig back on or even that my lips weren't as soft as Cassie's—Eli shoved me back. I slammed into the wall, stunned and breathless.

"What the fuck?" he yelled. He tore off the blindfold and blinked, the light blinding him. "Who the hell are you?" The resignation, regret, and despair that had gripped him to the core of his being disappeared, replaced by a fury that scared the shit out of me. The only thing that saved me from certain dismemberment was Stella's handcuffs.

I came to my senses and ran for the door. But before I left Eli shackled to the bed, I turned around so that he'd know that I was the engineer of his downfall. "I'm sorry about this, Eli," I said, surprised that I meant it. "But you had your chance." I slammed the door shut behind me, hoping that if Eli called for help, no one would be able to hear him over the sound of DJ Leo's music.

Stella ran through a pair of double doors near the top of the stairs and I followed her, not caring what room it was so long as it was empty. She shut the doors behind us and fell to the floor laughing so hard that she couldn't speak for an entire minute.

"Fuck you," I said, aiming all my ire at her.

I took a moment to catch my breath and get my bearings. The octagonal room was covered in pictures of the Castillo family. Cassie and her parents in Spain, in the Keys, at Disney. These were summer trips and Christmas trips and just-because trips. I followed the photos, watching Cassie grow from an awkward child into the self-assured girl I loved. Eli featured in some of the newest family photos, but I mentally photoshopped myself over his grinning image. When I hit the end of the Castillo photo parade, I nearly ran into an intimidating oak desk. I would have expected Mr. Castillo's office to be tidy and neat, but papers were scattered across the surface of the desk in a chaotic pattern.

"You making out with Cassie's ex was never part of my plan," Stella said like she was continuing an argument I hadn't been aware we were having. "You improvised that bit on your own." She picked herself up off the floor and hopped around the room, a fountain of manic energy.

"Your plan sucked balls." I stood at one of the floor-to-ceiling windows. There was too much light to see the stars, but they were out there and I wished on them that I'd never met Stella Nash, that I'd stayed out by the beach and drowned myself in the ocean. At least I wouldn't have been hiding out in Mr. Castillo's office, wearing Mrs. Castillo's clothes, trying to wipe the salty taste of Eli Horowitz off my tongue. I leaned against the wall and slid to the floor, not caring if the whole world saw my Superman underwear.

"This wasn't a joke to me, Stella. It was important." Even

though I knew that none of this was Stella's fault, I was still annoyed. What we did to Eli wasn't cool. Stella didn't know these people, though. To her, it was all fun and games. But I should have known better, and that's what annoyed me the most.

Stella sat down across from me. She pulled a bottle of water from her seemingly bottomless purse and took a swig before handing it to me. I accepted. Grudgingly.

"What's so special about Cassie anyway?" she asked. "She's a good kisser, but so are lots of girls, probably. What makes her worth all this trouble?"

"You wouldn't understand," I said.

"I am pretty dense. Try me anyway."

Stella stared at me with eyes so big they could eat my soul. In another world, one where I'd never known Cassandra Castillo, I could imagine liking Stella Nash. Except I didn't live in that world. So when I looked into Stella's ingenuous eyes, I saw only my own painted, pathetic face staring back at me.

"I have to get out of these clothes," I said. "I have to find Cassie before Eli Houdinis himself out of those cuffs."

Right. I didn't have any clothes to change into. There was no way that I was going to run through the house in a skirt and risk being sexually assaulted by Blaise again.

"Ben's bringing your clothes," Stella said as she sent a message from her phone. When she was done, she folded her hands in her lap. With nothing to do but wait, I found myself needing Stella to understand why Cassie was so important, why all this—even the skirt—was worth it.

"Cassie isn't the prettiest girl at Rendview High, but when she smiles at you, it's like the big bang. An entire universe explodes from her lips and forms around you." The memories of Cassie were like bullets whizzing by my head. Any one of them could have taken me out, but once I began telling Stella about her, I couldn't stop.

"We were lab partners freshman year. I don't know what made me think I could ask her out. For guys like me, it's not like in the movies. In real life, geeks never get the girls. They get friend-zoned into oblivion. They get cock blocked by better men. Footballers with muscle and money and shots at living extraordinary lives. But I was ignorant of the rules that were designed to keep me in my place. No one had ever shown me the way the world really worked. Back then, we were all so perfect, filled with limitless potential. Know what I mean?"

Stella didn't answer, but of course she knew what I meant. Even though she went to an all-girls school and had never kissed a guy, her informal education couldn't have been so different from my own.

"Anyway, I asked Cassie out and she said yes. It's stupid, I know, but I agonized about where to take her. A movie seemed like too much pressure—holding hands and making out and all that—but hanging out at the mall didn't feel like a proper date. It was Coop's suggestion to take her to Pirate Chang's Booty and Mini-Golf."

"They have tasty nachos," Stella said. Pirate Chang's is

famous for a lot of things, but the nachos aren't one of them. Stella had to possess an iron stomach if she actually ate and liked them.

"I'd never been more nervous in my life than in the days leading up to that night. Cassie and I didn't speak about it again except to confirm that I'd pick her up at seven, but every minute of every day, I obsessed over what I'd wear and what we'd talk about. I played every possible scenario out in my head. I even had contingency plans for rain and hurricanes and alien invasions.

"Everyone kept giving me advice. Ben told me to tell her dirty jokes, Coop told me to read all of Cassie's favorite books. But it was my mom who gave me the best advice. She told me to be myself. That was it. When she said it, I thought she was just being my stupid old mom, but as Cassie and I played through eighteen holes, I sort of understood what she meant. Once I'd told a couple of Ben's jokes and discussed who my favorite little woman was—Jo, by the way—all that was left was me. Simon Cross. I couldn't be Coop and I didn't want to be Ben. I had to work with what I had."

The door opened inward to admit Ben. Coop stayed in the hallway and he wouldn't meet my eyes. Ben held a bundle of clothes in his arms, which he tossed at my feet. "What happened?" Ben asked.

"He made out with Eli," Stella said. "There was tongue."

"Lucky bastard," Ben said, but his heart wasn't in it. I hadn't even thought that if I lost Coop's friendship, I'd lose

Ben's, too. In fact, the only reason Ben was probably here at all was to collect his prize for getting Eli up to Cassie's bedroom as promised. "There's some makeup remover in there too."

"Thanks," I said, knowing full well it was Coop who'd thought of it.

Stella dug around in her purse and tossed Ben the condom. He caught it and grinned. "I'll let you kids get back to doing whatever it is you're doing."

"Good luck," I said, trying to catch Coop's eyes. I wanted to go shake some sense into my best friend, but clearly that would have to wait.

"Uh, yeah," Ben said. "You too." He put the condom between his teeth and skipped out of the room, closing the doors behind him.

"Finish the story," Stella said.

I gathered my clothes and stood up. "I should change."

"So change."

"Do you mind?"

It took Stella a second to realize that I was asking her to turn around, and she made an O with her lips when she got the hint.

I continued talking while I peeled off my skirt and blouse and bra. "As far as dates go, it wasn't the worst. We played and talked and I thought it was going pretty well. All the way up to the eighteenth hole. You've been, so you know how difficult it is—"

Stella shook her head. "I only go for the nachos."

I laughed and told Stella she could turn back around. It felt good to be in my own clothes again—clothes with a crotch. I sat back down and held the makeup remover and cotton balls in my hands, unsure what to do. "How do you girls wear this shit all the time?"

"Let me." Stella took the bottle and scrubbed my face. She had a steady hand and I relaxed while she worked, wondering if she'd been serious about her job putting makeup on dead people.

"It's hard to describe the eighteenth hole if you've never played it. Pirate Chang built this crazy realistic fiberglass pirate ship. The hole is at the end of the walking plank in the center. To make that shot, you have to aim it between the crates holding the wenches, bounce it off the captain's peg leg, and get it to roll down the plank and into the hole. You get only one shot because under the plank is a watery vortex that's gobbled more balls than—" I coughed, embarrassed.

"Your mom?" Stella suggested, which made me laugh.

"Let's never put my mom and balls together in the same sentence again. 'Kay? Thanks." Stella winked at me and brushed my eyes closed so she could remove the caked-on mascara.

"Cassie and I were standing at the hole and I was feeling pretty okay with how our date had gone. It wasn't going to go down as the greatest date in the history of dates, but I'd done my best. Then, out of nowhere, Cassie told me that if I sank the shot, she'd let me kiss her."

I opened my eyes to see Stella's expression, but she wasn't wearing one. She was either really into removing my makeup or was deliberately hiding what she thought. I wasn't sure what I wanted her to feel. I knew that when we were done, she was going to go downstairs and make out with Ewan, but a tiny, dumb part of me wished she looked a little jealous. Since she didn't, though, I kept telling my tale.

"Obviously, I couldn't say no. If I made the shot, I'd go to school on Monday and everyone I passed in the hall would high-five me because they'd know that I was the guy who'd kissed Cassandra Castillo. We'd break out into a spontaneous song and dance number, like some kind of crazy flash mob."

Stella chuckled. "I thought that happened at only my school."

I smiled. "Making that shot was the scariest thing I'd ever faced. I put my blue ball on the mat and took aim. I didn't know whether Cassie actually wanted to kiss me or if she was bored and wanted to torment me. I hoped that she'd made the bet because she wanted to kiss me as much as I wanted to kiss her, but if I sank the ball, it wouldn't matter. She'd have to kiss me either way."

"Romantic," Stella said with a tiny hint of sarcasm that I ignored.

"I could do no wrong. Fate was guiding my hand. It felt like the whole universe was bending its will toward making sure I made the shot. Like I probably could have sunk it with my eyes closed. So I took aim, pulled back my club, said a prayer, and swung."

Stella let out a little *meep* sound and said, "And?"

The part of me that was still angry at Stella for tricking me into dressing up like a woman so that she could get a video game wanted to leave her hanging. But I couldn't do that to her. I couldn't stay mad.

"And Cassie grabbed my hand and pulled me onto the ship. Pirate Chang yelled at us from his little booth. He has a strict policy about boarding the ship and deals harshly with mutineers. But Cassie and I were impervious to his threats. We ran down the deck, following my ball as it bumped off the corner of the wench cage and banked off the captain's peg leg at the perfect angle. I thought I was going to puke as my ball rolled onto the plank, heading for the hole. It circled once, twice, three times, and then fell in. I let out a holler so loud that people on the other side of the golf course stopped what they were doing to stare at us.

"Hell, I nearly forgot Cassie was even there until she hooked her finger through my belt loop and pulled me up against her. I hadn't hit my growth spurt yet, so Cassie and I were at the same eye level. God, I'd never been so terrified. All my preparation for this date and I had absolutely no fucking idea how to kiss a girl. Was I supposed to open my mouth? Did I use my tongue? How was I going to breathe? But it didn't matter, because I was going to kiss Cassie. She actually wanted me to kiss her."

Stella held the dirty cotton balls in her tiny, tight fists. "So you kissed her?"

"No."

"What happened?"

I let out a sigh. "That's the question, isn't it?" The way Cassie looked, the way she smelled, the sound of her breath in my ear. Those things were as vivid as the night they happened. "I told Ben and Coop that Pirate Chang pulled me off of her before I had a chance, but that was a lie."

Stella put down the cotton balls and pushed Mrs. Castillo's castoff clothes to the side. There was nothing between us now but the air we breathed. "What's the truth?"

"I was afraid," I said. "Not of kissing Cassie, but of what would come after that."

"What's changed?"

I hadn't thought about that. In so many ways, I was still that stupid kid at Pirate Chang's, too scared to kiss the girl of his dreams. I still wasn't sure what would happen if I went for it.

"The future," I said. "It's going to happen whether I'm ready for it or not. And Cassie may shoot me down and I might barely escape this party with a shred of my pride intact, but if I don't face the future now, I'll spend the rest of my life living in the past."

Stella and I sat quietly for a few moments. My face felt dried and puckery. There were no mirrors in the room, so I had to trust that Stella had done her job well.

"Thanks," I said. Stella probably thought I meant for the

makeup, but she'd helped me realize that it didn't matter what would happen when I told Cassie everything tonight; it only mattered that I do it. "I should get on with this."

"Yeah. It's probably only a matter of time before Eli figures out that those are trick cuffs."

"What?" I scrambled to my feet, gawking at Stella. "Why didn't you tell me earlier?"

She began collecting her things, moving like she had all the time in the world. "The catch is difficult to find and Eli doesn't look all that bright."

I took a deep breath to quiet the voices that were screaming in my head, the ones that wanted me to murder Stella. When I'd calmed down I said, "Wish me luck."

"Me too," she said. "Ewan's waiting downstairs."

I stopped at the doors and looked back. Stella stuffed Mrs. Castillo's clothes into her purse along with her other things. "How do you fit all that crap in there?"

"It's bigger on the inside," she said with a halfhearted grin.

I itched to find Cassie before Eli escaped, but there was something about the way Stella looked that made me feel guilty for leaving her. I mean, she was the reason I was getting my shot with Cassie at all. "Maybe we can hang out sometime," I said.

"Sure." Stella crossed the room and kissed me on the cheek. It came out of nowhere and I barely had time to react. Then she said, "You're still perfect, you know. You always were." And she was gone.

Living the Dream

Coop's was the first face I saw when I opened my eyes. He was talking, but I couldn't hear the words. Someone had muted the world, drained all the color from it. Everything was gray. I sat up, which was a mistake. The earth tilted and spun, and I puked until I was certain that I was going to turn inside out, forced to wear my guts like a macabre tuxedo.

"Drink?" was the first word I heard. Ben handed me a lukewarm bottle of water. I swished and spat first and then swallowed a mouthful but didn't think I'd ever rid my mouth of that tangy vomit aftertaste.

"I think someone hit me with a car." My whole body hurt. I wiggled my fingers and toes to make sure everything still worked and was in its proper anatomical location. The fall from Cassie's window wasn't far, but it was still a miracle I hadn't broken any bones.

Coop was dangerously close to a full-blown panic attack. "What the fuck were you doing?" he asked. His voice was an octave higher than normal, and when I looked closely, I could see the veins in his temples pulsating. I had to calm him before he did something stupid like call an ambulance, if he hadn't already.

"Practicing for the Olympics," I said. "My landing needs some serious work."

Ben chuckled and helped me up. "He's fine. In fact, I think the concussion improved his sense of humor, not that the bar was high to begin with."

I steadied myself on the tree, trying to keep the ground from shifting under my feet. The back of my head hurt, but when I touched it, there was no blood or anything. Overhead, light still shined out of Cassie's window, but Eli was gone. His last word echoed in my head and I replayed everything, wondering how much of what he had told me was made up. I still clutched the scorecard in my fist, though. It didn't matter what else Eli might have lied about because the scorecard was undeniable proof that that night had meant something to Cassie. That I meant something.

"Nice shirt," Coop said. His nuclear core was beginning to cool, but there was still an aura of frantic energy around him, and he could melt down if I didn't keep assuring him that I was okay.

The problem was that I wasn't okay. I'd been duped by Eli Horowitz. Somewhere along the way, Eli had realized that I had an actual shot at proving to Cassie that I loved her. He'd tricked me into telling him my plan, and then had all but shoved me out the window to sideline me so that he could get Cassie for himself. I briefly wondered if I'd have been capable of something so underhanded if I'd been smart enough to think of it but brushed the thought aside. Time was against me and I still had a lot to do.

"Can we move away from the puddle of puke?" Ben asked. "Those fries are starting to make me hungry."

Coop groaned and led us around the house. He kept a hand on my arm, for which I was grateful. I couldn't admit to him how badly I hurt. The bruises from my fall were layered on top of the bruises I'd earned during my fight with Dean. My throbbing brain insistently demanded a handful of aspirin and a twenty-four-hour nap, but I knew that by the end of the night either Eli or I was going to be with Cassie. It was one of those rare prescient moments. The knowledge took root with such certainty that I'd have wagered my entire future on it. My injuries would have to wait.

We sat down on the couch Cassie had stashed on the patio for safekeeping. It was quiet here, cool under the fan, and I was able to make an honest attempt to organize my thoughts. I was running on adrenaline and fear, but neither of those would carry me across the finish line.

"What the hell is Sia up to?" Ben asked. He was looking behind him at the pool. It was lit up with primary colors and filled with inflatable animals. But this was no haphazard arrangement. The alligator was tail down, tied to the steps, and someone had decorated the waterfall with a series of interlocked inner tubes. Other kids I recognized from the drama club scurried around like ants converging on something tasty. I spotted Aja Bourne standing off to the side, watching Sia with a bemused expression. No . . . bemused wasn't the right word. Aja was watching Sia the same way Coop watched

Ben. With pride, admiration, and a sliver of mortification. In short, she looked happy. I didn't know what that was all about, but it was kind of cool.

"I need to go home," I said. Coop and Ben had been arguing about what the drama kids were up to, but my statement grabbed their attention. My time with Eli had strengthened my resolve. It had brought the entire night into perfect focus. I had one chance to show Cassie that I loved her. Everything else had been a red herring. Roadblocks Cassie had thrown in my way to keep me from finding her. But I knew the truth now and I knew what I had to do.

Coop nodded and grabbed his keys. "Agreed. We should probably think about stopping by the hospital first to get you checked out. I don't know if you've noticed, but you look like hell."

"No," I said. "I need to get something from my house and bring it back."

"You do realize you just fell out of Cassie's window, are reeking of rum and puke, and that you probably have a concussion?" Ben said.

I nodded, which was a terrible idea.

"Is this a Cassie thing?" Coop asked.

"Isn't it always?" Ben said.

Coop wasn't joking, though. He was still King Serious, ruler of Grimland. "You fell out of a window. I heard a rumor that you got into a fight with Dean over a Ping-Pong ball. And I'm guessing it all somehow relates to Cassie."

"Please," I begged. Coop already knew the truth; I was at

his mercy. Coop could refuse to drive me home and there was nothing I could do about it, but I hoped that he would hear my desperation and help me one last time.

"Fine." It was all he said to me. A few minutes later we were idling outside of my house.

Ben threw a pack of gum at me and said, "In case you run into your folks."

I popped two sticks of gum into my mouth and got out of the car. As I walked around to the side door of the house, I used the time to compose myself. Puking had rid my body of some of the rum I'd consumed with Eli, but I'd absorbed enough of it that, combined with my likely concussion, I would have a difficult time convincing anyone of my sobriety, least of all my parents, whose alcohol-sensing skills were razor sharp.

I stopped to take a leak in the bushes and didn't notice that the lights in the kitchen were on until I saw my dad staring at me through the window over the sink. He was wearing his angry face.

"Shit," I said over and over as I finished watering the Christmas cactus and zipped up. In another time or place I might have been able to come up with a perfectly good explanation as to why I was pissing in the bushes, but right then, my mind was blank.

The only thing to do was man up and walk inside like everything was normal, like I peed in the garden every single day.

"What's up, Dad?" I said, and tried to walk by him casually, not making eye contact.

"I'm not even going to ask what I just witnessed," Dad said. "But you're not moving a muscle until you tell me what happened to your face, why you smell like a frat house, and why you're wearing a Hanukkah shirt in April."

Dad stood at the kitchen island wearing one of Mom's silky bathrobes. The fridge was ajar and there was a can of whipped cream and strawberries chilling on the counter. Based on my dad's tone, I knew I needed to do some fast talking to avoid being imprisoned in my bedroom until graduation.

"I got into a fight chasing the girl of my dreams and my shirt got covered in blood so I had to borrow this shirt from the girl's ex-boyfriend, who tricked me into drinking a ton of rum and climbing out a window, which isn't as easy as it looks on TV."

Dad tapped his finger on the tile counter and stared at me. I couldn't read his expression, which was always a bad sign. "Are we talking about that Cassie girl?"

"Yeah," I said. "I came home only so that I could get something that would prove to her that I really love her."

I thought Dad was going to lock me in the attic, but instead he got a bag of peas from the freezer and tossed it at me. He sat down on a bar stool and motioned for me to do the same. I wanted to tell Dad that I didn't have time to sit, but I knew that would make the situation much, much worse. So I sat and held the peas to the lump on the back of my head. The cold hurt so good.

"You and I never really talked about girls—" Dad couldn't look me in the eyes and it was all I could do not to run screaming from the conversation. Solitary confinement might have been preferable.

"I'm sorry for the drinking," I said. "For the fighting and all of it, but this is important. I've waited a long time to tell Cassie how I feel and now I finally have my chance." To Dad's credit, he turned off Dad mode and treated me like a man.

"So you really believe this is the right time for you to tell her that you're in love with her?" I nodded, hoping that Dad would see the urgency of my situation and let me go. Instead he sighed and said, "Simon, I'm afraid I've failed you as a father."

That wasn't the response I'd expected, and I didn't know how to react.

"Do you know how I met your mother?"

"In college," I said, annoyed. Time was running out. Every second I was here, Eli was there. With Cassie. "You had a class together or something."

Dad nibbled on a strawberry. "Sort of," he said. "The only reason I took Renaissance literature was because of this girl I fancied."

"'Fancied,' Dad? Really?" I tossed the melting bag of peas on the counter and pushed back my stool. "The girl was Mom and you fell madly in love. The end. Can I go?"

"Sit." Dad pointed at the stool and I dropped back onto it. "The girl was Nancy Stadler. The first time I saw her was in registration. I bribed her roommate to give me Nancy's schedule."

It was difficult to picture my dad bribing anyone. He was the kind of guy who wouldn't even jaywalk. "How very *Mission: Impossible* of you."

Dad gave me a wry smile. "It took me all semester to talk to her. I memorized this poem. 'Come live with me and be my Love—'"

"This walk down Old Geezer Lane has been fun and all, but the clock's ticking."

Dad gave me a look that told me I was lucky to get a story and not a beating, so I shut my mouth. "Anyway, I waited until class ended and then I stood on my desk and began to recite the poem. What I failed to notice was that Nancy had left and I was wooing an empty room. When I realized I was alone, I hopped down off the desk, slipped, and hit my head on the wall. Your mother saw the whole thing from the hallway and helped me up. We've barely been apart since."

I stood up again, and this time I wasn't going to sit back down. "So what you're saying is that I inherited my sense of timing and balance from you?"

"What I'm saying," Dad said pointedly, "is that sometimes love hurts, but it shouldn't be so hard."

"Thanks for the words of wisdom and the hilarious mental image of you crashing into a wall. Can I go now?" Somewhere, in the undamaged part of my brain, I knew that my dad was trying to tell me something important, to have a big father-son moment that would change the course of my life, but that part was buried too deeply for my father's dubious wisdom to penetrate.

Dad sighed. "Fine. But tomorrow you and I are going to have a discussion about drinking." He paused. "We can keep your mom out of it."

"Thanks, Dad." I looked around the kitchen. "Speaking of Mom, is she asleep?"

Dad's eyes flicked to the whipped cream and strawberries and he turned the color of the fruit on the counter. I wished I'd never asked.

"Dad! Gross!"

"What? It's perfectly natural for your mother and me to have relations."

I covered my ears with my hands. "Jesus, Dad, can you never say the word 'relations' again?"

"Sex is a beautiful thing between two adults who love each other."

"La la la la!"

We were saved by Coop, who popped his head in the door without knocking. "Hey, Mr. Cross."

"Cooper," Dad said. "I trust you haven't been drinking this evening."

"Sober as a stone," Coop said. My parents trusted Coop more than they trusted me, and my dad just nodded. "Simon, if we're going to go back to the party . . ." Coop sounded like he would have preferred not going back, but that option wasn't on the table. Not for me.

"Yeah. One second." I ran up the stairs and tore my bedroom apart until I found what I'd been looking for. When I showed it to Cassie, she'd know that I loved her. She'd be able to tell me what was going on, and we could be together. It was perfect. Nothing could stop me now. I was panting when I got back to the kitchen, but I ignored every ache, every pain.

"You and Mom have fun," I said to Dad before I left.

"Remember what I told you," Dad said, but I was already out the door.

No one spoke as we left my neighborhood. It wasn't until we got up to the beach road that Coop asked me what my plan was.

"I'm sort of improvising," I said.

Ben laughed. "You don't improvise well. Remember that time—"

"Fuck!" Coop slammed on the brakes as something white ran into the middle of the road. It looked like an albino raccoon. A girl in a yellow tank with bright red dreads chased after the animal. The seat belt bit into my shoulder and I cussed up a storm.

"What was that?" Ben asked, but Coop was too busy yelling out his window to answer.

The girl in yellow scooped up the furry white animal that had nearly become roadkill and ran back to the sidewalk.

"Did that just happen?" I asked.

Coop drove off in silence. We were almost back to Cassie's house when Coop said, "Are you sure you want to go back to the party, Sy? We can go to Howley's. Get some loaded fries, crash at my place." It was the kind of question Coop had asked me a million times because it was the sort of thing we'd done a million times. But his voice had an urgency to it now that I didn't comprehend.

"That's low," I said. "Tempting me with loaded fries." I was joking, but when I caught Coop looking at me in the rearview, I knew that he wasn't. Something was going on that had nothing to do with fries. I pulled out of my pocket what I'd gone back to my house for and held it up for Coop and Ben to see.

It was the blue ball from Pirate Chang's Booty and Mini-Golf. The one I'd sunk on the eighteenth hole. I didn't have to tell them what it was. They knew.

"We're going to this party," I said. "And I'm giving this ball to Cassie. The rest is up to Fate."

Ben actually looked impressed. Coop, not so much. "It's okay, baby," Ben said. "We can go to Howley's after Simon humiliates himself."

Coop shook his head. "No, we can't."

I didn't know what he meant by that and I didn't have time to unravel the enigma that was Cooper Yates, because we were back at the party and the only person on my mind was Cassie.

I'd found my paper clip. It was time to go turn it into a house.

Reality Bites

I felt like I was living in a pop music video as I descended the stairs into the belly of the party. While Stella and I had been hiding in Cassie's bathroom, tricking Eli into handcuffing himself to the bed so that I could make my move on Cassie, the party had continued without us. Whatever semblance of civility people had arrived with, they'd shed it and devolved into a PG-13 hedonism that would have sent their parents into apoplectic fits. Shane Durban streaked from the front of the house to the back, his hairy ass disappearing into the chaotic tumor of dancers in the family room, screaming about the end of the fucking world. Shane was a straight-A Mormon vegan who I'd never seen wear anything other than khaki pants and button-down shirts. Tonight, he'd gone native.

And he wasn't the only one. The lights in the library were out and the distinct sounds of sucking face told me that the game of Contact Scrabble was over. Kids were dancing on the tables. Various articles of clothing hung from sconces and door handles, their owners nowhere to be seen. The party had peaked and the air was thick with laughter that was too loud and screams that were too shrill. Soon, it would collapse under its own weight. A fight would break out or the cops would show up. People would try to grab their dignity and scram, but I was sure that photographic evidence was already on Facebook, telling the whole sordid story of the night.

As much as I felt like I was in the middle of a memory I'd carry with me for the rest of my life, I also felt out of place. These people, compatriots with whom I'd gone to war in hell, were lost, whereas I was finally found. They were drifting aimlessly through the party, pulled in whatever directions their amped-up hormones deemed gave them the highest probability of getting laid. But I, I had purpose. And I moved through the party with one thought in my head: *Find Cassie.*

Okay, okay, that's not entirely true. I was also thinking about the last thing Stella had said to me before she'd gone to find Ewan. The part about me being perfect. What the hell did she mean anyway? She didn't know me. She didn't know a damn thing about me except that I was gullible, which wasn't exactly a state secret. If Stella knew me, she'd know that I wasn't perfect. There were so many things wrong with me that I'd given up keeping track of them a long time ago. If Stella thought I was perfect, then there was something seriously wrong with her. No wonder she'd never kissed a guy before.

Stella wasn't around, though. She was probably trading those humiliating pictures of me in drag for that stupid video game. Whatever. The only thing she'd done all night was distract me from my true purpose. It didn't matter if she thought I was perfect or the pope. Stella Nash was not Cassandra Castillo.

With that settled, I continued my hunt for Cassie, but I didn't get another step before someone pulled a pillowcase over my head, and calloused hands grabbed me and yanked me off my feet. I heard muffled laughter but I couldn't make out what the voices were saying. I struggled, kicking and clawing—I even bit someone who was stupid enough to put their hand near my mouth—but my captors were strong and I couldn't break free.

In less than a minute, it was over as I was thrown onto grass. I scrambled to my feet and pulled off the pillowcase. I recognized it from Mr. and Mrs. Castillo's bedroom.

"He don't look like a girl," Derrick Fuller said. He wasn't the brightest kid on the best of days, but drunk, he was a total moron.

Blaise stood at the apex of his idiot brigade, his brutish grin aped by his minions. Derrick Fuller and Seth Portnoy on his left, and Jesús Gomez and Fat Duke on the right. Everyone called him Fat Duke because he was fat. Really fat. And the way he held his thumb told me that he was the unlucky bastard I'd gotten a mouthful of. Urinal Cake stood off in the shadows, watching me with a satisfied grin. Part of me wished I'd helped him earlier.

"I'm telling you, he was wearing a skirt and he tried to grab my dick." Blaise's words wove and stumbled, but I knew I was screwed no matter how drunk he was. Alone, I might have been able to outrun Blaise, but five against one was a recipe for a serious beat down. The funny thing was that I wasn't worried about broken bones or bruises. My only thought was that my opportunity to tell Cassie I loved her, bought and paid for with my humiliation, was slipping away.

I couldn't let that happen.

"Do I look like I'm wearing a dress?" I asked, pleading my case to a jury of half-wits. "Blaise is so lit he probably felt himself up."

Fat Duke laughed, but a vicious snarl from Blaise silenced him.

"I know it was you, Cross." Blaise pointed at me. "And I'm going to fuck you up." Blaise motioned at one of his guys, and Derrick grabbed me by the neck and pulled my left arm up behind my back. Bombs of excruciating pain detonated in my shoulder and I bit my tongue to keep from crying out.

I glanced up at Blaise, blinking away the tears that formed in my eyes. He looked triumphant, like he could already taste my apology. But I wasn't ready to surrender. "It's nothing to be ashamed of," I said. "My best friends are gay. I just don't like you that way."

Blaise punched me in the stomach with a lead fist. It knocked the breath from me and I would have crumpled to the ground if Derrick hadn't been holding me up. He wrenched my arm back even farther and the pain in my shoulder offset the agony in my gut. Or it did, until Blaise followed his right hook with his left.

"Tell 'em you were dressed like a girl!" Blaise yelled. "Tell 'em you grabbed me on the stairs." Blaise hocked a loogie and spit it in my face. The mucus hit my eye and slid down the bridge of my nose.

Blaise Lewis wasn't playing around; I'd seriously misjudged the situation. I didn't have time to dig out the childhood trauma that had turned a silly encounter on the stairs into the catalyst that caused Blaise to lose his damn mind, but I knew that if I didn't defuse him, he was going to fuck me up.

"I'm sorry," I said quickly.

"Yeah, you are." Blaise's lips pulled back into a cruel rictus that had a serious serial-killer vibe.

I was alone. Ben and Coop weren't going to come to the rescue. Stella was probably inside snogging the face off Ewan McCoy, and . . . that was it. There was no one else.

Blaise pulled back to punch me again and I punted. "Wait!"

"What?"

"It was me on the stairs," I said.

Seth and Jesús laughed. They were so drunk that they were little more than prop pieces in Blaise's drama. Derrick and Fat Duke were the ones I had to watch out for.

"It was me, but it isn't what you thought."

Blaise relaxed slightly and said, "Yeah?"

I nodded. "Yeah." And then I made my move. Because I could have stood there and admitted to Blaise and his goon squad that I'd dressed like a woman as part of a bigger plan to ensnare the heart of the girl I loved, but it wouldn't have mattered to them. So I stomped hard on Derrick's foot, causing him to loosen his grip on my arm. It wasn't much, but it was enough to twist free. I launched forward at Blaise and lowered my shoulder, crashing into him and toppling him into Fat Duke. Both boys went down in a tangle of arms and legs. The only person in my way was Urinal Cake, but he stood aside wordlessly.

Without a second's hesitation, I fucking ran. I heard Blaise screaming for someone to get me, but I had a huge lead and I wasn't about to let them catch me. I ducked around the side of the house and headed for the patio. I looked behind me and was running so fast that I didn't see Aja until I nearly ran her down.

"The fuck, Simon!"

I put a hand over her mouth and dragged her into the bushes. Aja didn't struggle but she gave me a withering glare. A moment later, Blaise and his posse tore by. They didn't stop. After they passed, I counted to ten and then let Aja go.

"Fans of yours?" she asked.

I nodded.

"What'd you do?"

"It's a long story," I said.

Aja brushed the grass off her jeans. "I'm betting it has something to do with Cassie, and no, I don't want to know what it is."

"This really shouldn't be this hard," I said to myself.

"What?"

"Nothing."

Aja and I stood there for a moment, she staring at me curiously and me catching my breath. I still wasn't used to the idea that Aja and I could share the same air without fighting or making out.

"Sia's got the drama geeks putting on an aquatic version of *Romeo and Juliet*," Aja said. "It's amazing. Or mental. I'm not sure which yet." But I could tell that Aja was impressed, which was something many had tried and few had accomplished.

"Why aren't you watching?" I asked.

She held up her phone. "Had to call Gran to let her know I'm alive so she didn't send in the Marines."

"Gotcha."

"I should get back."

"Listen," I said. "I feel like a dick for asking, but have you seen Cassie?"

Aja nodded but didn't say where. I tried deciphering the expression on her face but she sort of looked like she'd drunk a big cup of rotten milk. Then she said, "If you tell Cassie how you feel about her, she'll hook up with you."

"How do you know?" I asked.

"I just do."

"Thanks," I said, and turned to go.

"But not for the right reasons," Aja called. That pulled me up short, dampened some of my fire.

"Go on."

Aja got the rotten-milk look again. "You're not stupid, Simon. You know something's up with Cassie. She's a Goody Two-shoes, not a party girl. Until a week ago, she and Eli were married in all but name. Think about it."

I knew all this. I'd already thought about it. Ben and Coop had warned me. But so what? Yeah, something was wrong with Cassie. It didn't change the way I felt about her.

"If you know something," I said, impatient to be on my way, "tell me."

Aja patted my cheek. "Maybe I was wrong," she said. "Maybe you are stupid."

Yells echoed down the narrow passage between the house and the hedges and I flinched before realizing that they were coming from the back patio, probably from Sia's play, and not from Blaise. "I'm not doing this with you."

"Cassie's broke," Aja said abruptly.

I didn't know what to say to that. It was ludicrous. Obviously Cassie wasn't broke. We were standing right outside her expensive house. "Bullshit."

"I thought I'd enjoy this," Aja said.

"Enjoy what?" Aja wasn't making any sense and I suspected she might be playing a game. Maybe it had all been a game.

"Cassie's downfall." When it was clear I had no clue what she meant, Aja sighed and said, "Sia's dad is a Realtor. The Castillos lost this house. Her dad got canned. I even heard they can't afford to send her to college."

It wasn't true. It couldn't be. "You're a liar, Aja. Always were."

Aja threw up her hands. "Believe what you want, Simon. Maybe you and Cassie do deserve each other." There was no more to say and she walked toward the patio without another word.

I waited until Aja was gone, trying to process what she'd told me. It might have been a lie, but it had the feel of truth. And Cassie losing everything would explain why she'd been acting so strangely. So unlike herself.

What it didn't explain was why it would make Cassie hook up with me if I told her how I felt. Aja had seemed as certain about that as she had about the rest. But it didn't make sense.

It also didn't matter. I could sort it out when I found Cassie.

I followed the sounds of the play to the back patio. Half the party was out there watching what was likely the most elaborate poolside production of *Romeo and Juliet* that had ever been staged. They were waist deep in the masquerade scene, and the audience was so enthralled that I was able to move through them with ease.

Ben and Coop were watching from the couch by the grill. Sia and Aja were by the deep end of the pool. I ran into people I hadn't even known were at the party as I wandered around. The only person I couldn't find was Cassie.

But I knew she was out there.

I would have spent all night looking for Cassie, but my

time was up. Eli ran out of the house in his shirt and boxers, with murder in his eyes. He locked onto me with laser precision and tore through the crowd. Most people were too busy watching the play to notice that Eli was coming at me, probably to tear my head from my neck. I still didn't see Cassie and I didn't know what else to do.

So I did the first thing that popped into my mind. I climbed up the rocks to the summit of the waterfall and shouted, "Cassandra, Cassandra! Wherefore art thou, Cassandra?" And then waited for the shit to hit the fan.

Living the Dream

Cassie's barter party was winding down toward its inevitable collapse. I knew it the moment I opened the front door. The party had the weary, frantic look of a marathon runner at the end of a torturous race. People were still drinking and dancing and bartering their last bits of pocket lint for whatever they could get, but these were the actions of the desperate. Last drinks, last dances, last attempts to find someone, anyone, to make out with. Coop and Ben and I usually vacated parties before they got to this point. Me because when I didn't, I ended up with Aja Bourne, and the boys because they had each other.

Tonight, though, I was staying. I had to. Cassie was somewhere in this house and I had to find her and show her my blue ball. I had one last chance to prove my love.

As I pushed my way through each room, I kept an eye out for Eli. There was no doubt in my mind that he was still plotting against me. He wouldn't have thrown me out of a window unless I was a threat. I only wished I hadn't been so gullible. Every time my head ached or some drunk asshole ran into me, sending shockwaves of pain through my body, I cursed Eli Horowitz.

"She's not in here," Dean said. He was in the same chair he'd been in the last time I'd seen him, with one leg up, relaxing like he was the king.

"About earlier," I said.

"No need to apologize."

"I wasn't," I said. "Just wanted to thank you for not killing me."

Dean chuckled. He looked around but there wasn't anyone watching us. The Ping-Pong table lay abandoned and forgotten. A beer puddle that looked suspiciously like Lake Okeechobee stained the green surface. A couple I didn't know was sucking face in the far corner, but we could have pulled out rapiers and dueled and they wouldn't have noticed.

"The rumors of my homicidal tendencies are slightly over-stated," said Dean. "You should take a break. You look like shit." He pointed at a chair.

My body ached and my legs were shaking. Sitting down would have been the end of me. But I wanted to so badly. I wanted to relax and shake out all my worries into a dusty pile on the floor, let the wind blow them away. "I can't," I said. "I have to find Cassie."

Dean leaned to the left and looked down the hallway. "Pool," he said. "Prima donna Sia's putting on a show."

"A what?"

"A play. You know, the kind with actors and shit? Shake-speare, I think."

I wondered if that was what Sia had been doing when I'd

been on the patio earlier. My head injury made my memories somewhat fuzzy around the edges, but it made sense in a random sort of way. "Thanks," I said.

Dean nodded and pulled a wrinkled joint from behind his ear. He offered it to me but I shook my head. That was the last thing I needed. Dean sucked in a lungful of the sweet smoke and said, "Watch out for Eli."

So Eli had fixed the doorknob and escaped. That didn't surprise me. The only thing I didn't get was why Dean had warned me. Based on everything I knew about him, not only would he have enjoyed watching Eli and me tussle, but he would have made a fortune taking bets on the outcome.

"You're not really a bad guy, are you?" I said impulsively.

Dean shrugged. If I was expecting some kind of outpouring of emotion or an admission of the tragic past that had shaped Dean Kowalcyk into the man he was now, I was going to leave disappointed.

And leave is exactly what I did.

I tore a path down the hall and through the kitchen, picking up more bruises along the way as people who shouldn't have been able to stand got in my way. DJ Leo looked haggard but proud. He'd spin until the last person was standing.

When I emerged onto the patio, half the party was crowded around the pool watching Sia's masterstroke. I never imagined a pool could be transformed into Verona, with inner tubes and alligators and a cartoon inflatable shark forming the various set pieces, but Sia Marcus had done it. It was something like magic.

The play had only just begun and I stood in awe for a whole scene before remembering why I'd risked permanent brain injury to return to the party. I elbowed my way through the audience, standing on my toes to look over people's heads. I finally saw Cassie on the other side of the pool, standing alone. She looked radiant dressed in shadows, her eyes reflecting the multicolored lights of the pool. For a moment, I thought she saw me but I was mistaken. The blue golf ball burned a hole in my hand and I knew it was time.

"She's so pretty, isn't she?"

Urinal Cake stood beside me, looking at Cassie with so much admiration it was embarrassing. He wasn't even trying to hide the fact that he was staring at her, watching her, thinking about her.

"Yeah," I said. "She's beautiful."

"I think I'm in love with her," Freddy said.

"That's cute," I said, not meaning to be condescending. "You don't even know her."

Freddy shrugged and kept staring at Cassie like there weren't a hundred people gathered around the pool watching an improvised production of *Romeo and Juliet*. He was hyperfocused on her in a way that I kind of admired. "I love her. I'll never love anyone else."

When Freddy said those words, I didn't hear him. I heard myself. I heard myself the night Coop and I snuck into Pirate Chang's to steal my ball back. The same ball I held in my sweaty fist. I'd said those exact same words with the exact same amount of slavish devotion. In an instant, I saw Urinal Cake's entire future stretch out in front of me.

"You don't love her," I said. "You only think you do." When Freddy tried to interrupt me, I put my hand over his mouth. "Shut up and listen."

A girl shushed me and I pulled Freddy to the back of the crowd so that we wouldn't disturb anyone. "Listen to me, kid. Cassie only saved you from Blaise because she felt bad for you. She doesn't love you; she doesn't have any feelings for you. She probably doesn't even remember your name. There are tons of girls who are better for you than Cassandra Castillo. Girls who will love you. If you don't forget about her right now, you're going to miss out on so much."

I didn't know whether I was talking to Urinal Cake or to myself, but all the words made sense. Eli had told me that Cassie had gone out with me only because she felt bad for me. She'd kept the scorecard, but maybe she'd just had a good time that night, maybe it had nothing to do with me at all. I was so fucking confused and my head hurt and I wanted to scream.

It might have been too late to save myself, but Urinal Cake still had a chance if I could get through to him.

"Have a nice fall?" Eli detached from the shadows and strutted toward us. He wore a jack-o'-lantern grin and didn't appear the slightest bit drunk. I couldn't help wondering how much of that rum-soaked slurring had been an act for my benefit.

"Eli."

"Whatcha doing?"

"Talking to my friend." But when I looked over, Freddy Standish was gone, disappeared into the crowd. "Or not."

While I scanned the audience for Freddy, Eli grabbed the blue golf ball out of my hand and held it in front of his eyes. "Is this the ball that made the famous shot?"

"Give it back," I said, trying to avoid drawing any attention. But it was too late. Cassie had seen Eli and me together. She eased through the gaps between people on an intercept course. Explaining to Cassie how I felt about her with Eli standing here wasn't my first choice for how this was going to go down, but I'd do what was necessary.

"So, you actually went home and got it," Eli said. I wished I'd never told him my plan. He wasn't the guy I'd shared rum and stories with in Cassie's room. We weren't compatriots anymore. This was the gladiatorial field and we were locked in a battle to the death.

I made a grab for the ball, but Eli's athletic reflexes bordered on superhuman. "Give me my ball back," I growled.

Cassie reached us and did not look amused. In fact, she looked a bit green and swayed when she tried to stand still. The beer she'd chugged during our game did not appear to have agreed with her. "What the hell's going on?"

People were beginning to watch us rather than the play. Sia directed a sour frown at us that said we'd better shut up before the drama queen went full-on Carrie.

"Maybe we should go inside," I said. Eli waved me off. He kept my ball hidden behind his back. He either didn't want Cassie to see it or he planned to reveal it at the worst possible moment. I'd broken into a mini-golf course, kept it safe, and braved the wrath of my father to get the ball to this moment. I refused to let Eli Horowitz ruin it.

Cassie shook her head. She looked exhausted. Not just from the night but from everything. Weariness clung to her bones, to her soul, and she looked like she'd never shake it. Gone was the girl who'd met me at the door, the girl who'd dragged me to dance, the girl who'd jumped on her parents' bed for the first time. The Cassie in front of me bore her wounds like rocks in her pockets that would inevitably drag her down. And I don't mean her bruised knuckles or the foot I'd gracelessly trampled on. Cassie's hurts were deep. Even stripped down as she was by booze, her injuries were so profound that I doubted they could be found and fixed in one night.

"I don't know what's going on, but can you not do it now? I can't take anything else tonight."

I wondered if Eli had reached the same conclusion about Cassie as I had, because some of the fight drained from him and he reached out to his once-and-former girlfriend. "We were just—"

Cassie held up her hand. "I know what you were doing, Eli. I'm not stupid."

Behind us, Sia Marcus had decided that if she couldn't shut us up, she could drown us out. The actors shouted their lines, which were a clever bastardization of Shakespeare and hip-hop. I might not have liked Sia as a person, but she had genuine talent on- and offstage.

"I'm not doing anything," Eli said. His voice had dropped the edge he'd used with me and he was pleading his case. He still had my ball behind his back and I felt powerless to do anything but stand by and watch him steal Cassie away from me again. "You know how I feel about you, Shana."

"Don't call me that," Cassie said. I tried to gauge Eli's chances of success in Cassie's bloodshot eyes, but nothing he said seemed to reach her. Cassie had fortified her walls, she'd filled the cracks I'd seen earlier.

Eli's nostrils flared as he breathed heavily. Whatever plan Eli had devised was falling apart, and I could practically feel the frustration building inside of him. I understood the feeling intimately. I'd been so sure when I'd gone home to retrieve the blue ball that I'd show it to Cassie and everything would fall into place. But nothing was working out like I'd hoped. "I'm trying here," he said.

"You're pathetic." Cassie directed her insult at both of us even though I hadn't said much.

I waited for Eli to tell Cassie the things he'd told me in her bedroom, to show Cassie the depth of his feelings for her in some way that could break through the barriers she'd erected. Eli had the words; I'd heard him say them. I wasn't sure if they were strong enough to breach Cassie's defenses, but I thought they might be. The only problem was that Eli hesitated. He stood like an actor who'd forgotten his lines, the hot stage lights burning away his confidence, the eyes of the audience stripping him naked, each second that ticked away increasing the pressure on him to do something. Anything.

But he didn't. He froze.

We were about to lose our Cassie. She was about to turn

around and disappear from our lives forever. I saw it in the way her honey eyes lost their shine and in the way her shoulders relaxed ever so slightly. Most kids think they're wise—they think that sixteen or seventeen years of living makes them world-weary experts on everything. Not me. I knew I was an idiot. It helped that Coop constantly reminded me of my terminal dim-wittedness. However, I did know, even then, that life seldom offers more than one opportunity to do a thing. If you wait, if you hesitate, if you let fear pull your puppet strings, you may spend your entire life living in that moment, wondering where it all went wrong.

I was an idiot, but I knew that I had to act.

"I love you, Cassie," I said. This time I didn't blurt it out accidentally. The words didn't stumble from my tongue. I owned those words. They were mine and I offered them to Cassie.

Cassie rolled her eyes. *"Eres tan estúpido como un perro."*

"Yeah," I said. "I don't know what that means, but I'm guessing it's not a compliment."

"You're worse than he is," Cassie said, pointing at Eli. "Take a hint." Cassie turned to leave.

Fear was my bitch. I was SIMON FUCKING CROSS. Nothing could stop me from wresting my ball from Eli's iron fist and showing Cassandra Castillo that I really did love her. Except that I had one question I needed answering first.

"Did you only go out with me because you felt sorry for me?"

"What?" Cassie asked. "Are you serious? That was years ago, Simon. Move on."

Our show was competing with Sia's and winning, a fact

about which I genuinely felt bad. People were shooting pictures with their phones and I was certain at least one person was recording video of the whole thing. Hell, I could probably get the instant replay on Facebook right now if I wanted. But those concerns were for later. Cassie was the only person on the patio who mattered.

"Answer the question," I said, and I knew that this time Cassie would. There was no beer to drink, nowhere for her to run. "Why did go out with me?"

Cassie seemed to finally realize that we had an audience and she began to shut down. I closed the distance between us and took her hand. She was so beautiful, so amazing. All I wanted to do was show her the golf ball and kiss her all night long. But I had to know.

"It's okay," I said, keeping the words between us. I was aware of Eli still standing there, but I blocked him out.

"I'm going away," Cassie said.

"What?"

"I'm leaving. I may not even be around for graduation." The words were so difficult for Cassie to say, but the moment they were out, I could actually feel her relief. These were the wounds that had been festering in Cassie all night and for who knew how long. By peeling back the bandages, finally letting them breathe, they'd begun to heal.

"Why?"

Cassie blinked away tears. "Does it matter?" she asked. "My parents lost everything. It's all gone. College, home. Everything."

The details seemed unimportant because everything finally made sense. Cassie's behavior, the party, Eli. Something had happened that had upended Cassie's life and she was foundering without an anchor. Cassie, the girl who had her whole life planned, was suddenly working without a net, and it scared the shit out of her.

"I'm sorry," I said, though it felt inadequate.

"It's not your fault."

"I know . . . still."

"Thanks." Cassie saw me for the first time that night. She'd looked at me before, but this time she actually saw me. The last time I'd felt like that was when I'd made the shot at Pirate Chang's. She smiled and said, "Yes."

You'd think it would be difficult to forget that there was an entire party going on around you, but it's actually pretty easy when you're standing with the girl you've loved for so long you can't remember what it was like before you didn't love her, and she's looking at you and you're looking at her and you're thinking about all those moments you wished you could kiss her, knowing that now, right now, you might finally get your chance.

"What?" I shook my head to clear it.

Cassie squeezed my hand. "Yes, I went out with you because I felt bad for you," she said. "But when I made that bet with you at the golf course, I really did want you to kiss me." Cassie inched forward.

Eli still had my blue ball. Now was the perfect time for me to show it to Cassie, to show her that I really loved her and that I'd always be there for her. I could be her anchor. I could be her true north. It was ballsy, but I put my free hand behind my back and held it palm up, hoping that Eli would accept defeat with grace.

And he did. Eli Horowitz dropped the ball into my hand; the weight of it felt right. I drew in breath, prepared to show it to Cassie and tell her how I felt about her when a shout ripped through the night and we all turned.

Urinal Cake stood at the summit of the waterfall, a warrior, a conqueror, a man with a mission. "Cassie!" he shouted again. "I love you! I love you so much!"

Seriously? Was this kid fucking kidding me? But I already knew the answer to that question.

Freddy Standish displayed his feelings for everyone to see. And everyone laughed. Not with him, at him. It started off small, but pretty soon the laughter was a symphony of cackles and giggles that rose toward a crescendo. None of which caused Urinal Cake to falter.

"Get down from there!" Cassie yelled over the crowd. She pulled her hands from mine and pushed her way toward the edge of the pool.

"But I love you."

"You don't love me," Cassie said. "You're a kid with a crush. Now get down from there before you hurt yourself."

Urinal Cake was deflated but not deterred.

It might have been somewhat funny if I hadn't seen Blaise and Derrick sneaking up behind Cassie, laughing to each other. Whatever they were up to, it wasn't good. I glanced at

Eli, but he was sitting on a lounge chair, retreating back into his depression.

Blaise and Derrick crept into position behind Cassie as she argued with Urinal Cake, oblivious to their existence. In an instant, I knew what they planned. Blaise was going to take watery revenge on Cassie for busting his nose and his pride.

"Cassie!" I yelled to get her attention, but she didn't hear me over the laughter. I pushed my way through the crowd of people, shoving them when necessary, not caring who got in my way. But I wasn't going to get to her in time. Blaise and Derrick stood on either side of Cassie and prepared to grab her. I was so close; only a clutch of debate geeks and Crystal Whatshername stood in my way. I dove toward Cassie, calling her name.

Cassie finally turned as I made a desperate grab for Blaise. He twisted and stiff-armed me, using my momentum to propel me forward.

For a moment, I felt like I was flying, like I really was Superman.

And then I hit the water and went under, too heavy to swim. I sucked in a mouthful of air. Except it wasn't air at all.

Reality Bites

Sophomore year of high school, I'd briefly joined the debate team. Yes, the same debate team that spent most of Cassie's party playing Contact Scrabble with the lacrosse team. My mom had convinced me that it was important to be well rounded if I wanted to get into college—and her definition didn't include spending every night chowing Cheetos and spanking my monkey.

I turned out to have less talent for debate than I did for singing, which anyone who's heard me sing will gladly tell you is worse than being trapped on a plane with a screeching baby. During my first and only competition, I had decided I'd take my beating, show my mom that I wasn't cut out for competitive bickering, and quit the team.

As it turned out, a debater existed who was worse than me. A short, timid girl with dishwater hair down to her butt and braces colored in with green rubber bands. I never found out whether her tendency to drool was a naturally occurring phenomenon or a byproduct of her anxiety, but before she finished reading her six-minute affirmative construction, the front of her green dress was damp with shame. I wasn't particularly harsh during cross-ex, but I didn't even get to ask her two questions before she broke down right in front of the judges and ran out of the room.

For the rest of the day, I was the guy who'd made a girl cry. Everywhere I went, people stared at me like I'd been branded with a scarlet D for "douchebag." I skipped the rest of my rounds and hid in the bathroom playing Bejeweled on my phone.

So having people gape at me like I'd dropped my drawers and flashed them my kickstand wasn't a new thing for me. But that didn't make it any less awkward.

"You're ruining my play, you mentally deficient poop noodle!" Sia Marcus muscled her way around the pool, screaming impressive new combinations of obscenities at me. Some of the others, especially Sia's actors, booed and threw cups of beer at me—not all of them empty.

"I'm sorry," I said from my perch atop the waterfall, and meant it. "This looks cool and all, but in the immortal words of Shakespeare himself: Cassie, I'm crazy for you."

"That's Madonna!" Ben shouted. I hadn't seen him but I recognized his voice. I searched him out and saw him sitting alone by the windows, recording my humiliation with his cell phone.

I'd lost track of Eli in the shadows, but it wouldn't be too difficult to locate a rabid dude wearing boxers covered in tiny turkeys. Anyway, I wasn't afraid of him anymore. I'd seen Eli at his lowest, his most vulnerable, and nothing would ever be the same.

Blaise and his moron patrol were nowhere to be seen, but it was only a matter of time before they noticed the commotion and busted in to ruin the rest of my night. My stomach still hurt, but it was nothing compared to the pain I'd be in if they caught up to me.

Half the damn party stood on the patio, staring at me as I wrecked Sia's show, but they were minor players. I was the star now.

The thing about being the star, about standing under the spotlight, is that you have to know your lines. Unless you're good at improv, which I wasn't. I'd seen shows where people froze up onstage and it never ended pretty. In truth, I probably would have imploded right then and there if it hadn't been for Stella.

Stella stood at the fringe of the audience with Ewan Fucking McCoy. Ewan was ruddy and smiling, and I couldn't help wondering if he'd already kissed her. I knew that if I'd kissed that crazy chick, I'd have been smiling way bigger. Stella was grinning. Not at Ewan, at me. At what I was doing. She held her tiny fist in the air and offered me an enthusiastic thumbs-up. Even after what she'd said to me in Mr. Castillo's office, she was still cheering me on.

I'd been mad at Stella when she'd told me that she'd tricked me into wearing Mrs. Castillo's clothes, but as I stood on the summit of the waterfall, everyone at the party gawking at me, Eli plotting my death, Blaise sneaking around to flank me, Ben recording every excruciating moment, I knew that I wouldn't be here without that girl. We'd taken the round-about way, but she'd kept her end of the bargain. I owed it to her to see it through.

"We want *Romeo and Juliet!*" someone yelled from the crowd. I thought for a moment that it might have been Natalie Grayson. People took up a chant of "Romeo, Romeo!" and I knew I had to act or risk losing them.

"Fuck all this *Romeo and Juliet* crap," I said. My voice filled the night as my confidence grew. "Who kills themselves because their parents won't let them hook up? They should have caught a train out of Verona and gone on the lam— Bonnie and Clyde–style. Robbing apothecaries and blowing shit up." I raised my arms in the air and yelled, "I'm your Romeo now, bitches!"

The roar of the crowd was intoxicating. The applause, heroin. Neurons fired in my brain, sending the signals to flood my body with adrenaline and dopamine and all those feel-good chemicals that turned me from bumbling Simon Cross into a goddamn superhero.

"Get down!" Sia grabbed the cuff of my jeans and tried to pull me off the rock. When that didn't work, she pushed. I didn't blame her. It was like Aja had said: I was only the hero in my life. In Sia's, I was the terrorist who'd hijacked her show. Yippee-ki-yay, motherfucker.

"Five minutes," I begged shamelessly.

Sia was fury, she was rage. I didn't want to be the one to tell her that, as awesome as her play had the potential to be, we were at a party. Shit happened and she needed to loosen up and roll with it. Because I knew if I said those things, she'd punch through my rib cage, tear out my liver, and eat it raw. Luckily for me, Aja did not share my fear.

Aja slid in beside Sia and put a hand on her back. It was weird to see a girl I'd made out with so many times touching another girl, especially a girl who clearly wanted to maim me. It was also cool, and not in a porny way. "He's an idiot," Aja said, just loud enough for me to hear. "And he doesn't deserve five minutes from anyone, but could you maybe do it for me anyway?"

Sia glared up at me with more hatred than I knew a human face was capable of holding. Then she relented with a nod so sharp it nearly sliced me in two. "Asshole," she said, and then left.

"Don't fuck this up, Smoochie," Aja said. Then she ran after Sia to repair the damage standing up for me had done.

When I took center stage again, the night air was still. The water lapped against the edge of the pool, and someone was blasting music from their car by the road, which was bound to attract the police, but other than that, it was dead silent and all eyes were on me. There was no one left to get in my way. Well, okay, Eli and Blaise were out there, but I was the only person who knew that. To the audience that had gathered, I'd destroyed my enemies and had only to claim my prize.

Cassandra Castillo.

I saw her standing at the shallow end of the pool with her arms crossed over her chest, her hip jutted out, looking at me with a frightening mixture of anger and curiosity. This was not the girl who'd bet me a kiss on a pirate ship three years ago. The same girl who'd met me at the door a couple of hours ago and kissed a stranger who'd picked me up on the side of the road. The Cassie who'd broken up with her boyfriend and thrown a party about which epic poems in tenth-grade creative writing classes would be composed. The Cassie who didn't seem to care that her parents were going to imprison her for life when they returned and saw the damage that had been done to their house.

No, the Cassie watching me, waiting for my next move, was a girl who looked as though she'd woken from a bad trip. A girl who was sobering up after a binge, seeing the swath of destruction she'd cut through her life. A girl who had opened her eyes and found herself face-to-face with the decisions she'd made, and didn't like what she saw.

Still Cassie, still the girl I'd been in love with since freshman anatomy, but damaged, though not beyond repair.

"Come on then, Romeo," Cassie said. "We're all waiting." She shifted to her other foot but her eyes remained locked on mine. I couldn't tell whether Cassie was being sarcastic. There was a definite bite to her voice, but it could have been because I hadn't simply shined the spotlight on myself, I'd dragged her into it with me.

Now that I had Cassie's undivided attention, I wasn't sure what to say. Coop had advised me to be direct. Aja had told me that Cassie would hook up with me if I told her how I felt. And my mom had told me long ago to be myself. But none of those things seemed to apply here. I'd spent years dreaming of this moment, but it wasn't anything like I'd imagined. My best friend had dumped me, my sort-of-ex-girlfriend had turned gay, a girl I'd known only a couple of hours thought I was perfect, the girl I loved was hiding a life changing secret from everyone, and, for the first time since I'd met Cassie, I had doubts.

Not about whether I loved her, but about whether I should.

"I know about your parents," I said. "About college and all the other stuff."

Revealing the possible reason for Cassie's sudden personality change in front of everyone wasn't the smartest tactic, but when I opened my mouth to tell Cassie that I loved her, that I'd been in love with her for ages, those were the words that came out instead. The funny thing was, as soon as I said them, I knew I'd done the right thing.

Cassie, clearly, didn't share my convictions. "Shut your mouth, Simon." Cassie was looking from side to side like a trapped animal. "You don't know what the fuck you're talking about."

Which was true. I was making it up as I went along. Still, I felt like Fate was guiding me, showing me the correct path. "I know you're scared," I said. "But you can't let fear dictate your whole life."

People were starting to whisper. I'd been vague enough that no one really knew why her life was falling apart, but speculation ran rampant anyway. And Cassie's face grew frantic.

"Forget them," I said. "It's just you and me talking."

"Fuck you."

"If you're lucky," I said. Cassie frowned. "Wrong time for jokes. Got it." I wiped my sweaty hands on my jeans. "Remember that night at Pirate Chang's?" Cassie nodded. My memories of that night were high fidelity; Cassie's might have degraded, so I reminded her. "You bet me I couldn't sink the shot at the eighteenth hole, but I did. You bet me a kiss."

"I remember, Simon." Cassie looked exhausted, and not just from the party. "So what?"

"I didn't kiss you at mini-golf because I was scared. Scared of you, scared of the future, scared that I'd accidentally suck your face off." People laughed but I ignored them. "You have no idea how much I regret screwing that up."

Cassie's bottom lip quivered like she was going to fire off another retort, but she didn't. "That was a good night," she said.

"The best." Cassie's anger began to disintegrate so I pushed onward. My five minutes were up, but Sia didn't rush to stop me. "I know that you did all this—the party and everything—because you're scared. But you can't be afraid,

Cassie. Otherwise, you'll spend the next three years wishing you could go back in time and do it all over again. You can't change who you are. Putting on a sexy dress and trashing your parents' house isn't going to make facing the future any easier. No matter what, Cassie, you're perfect."

"Is that how you really feel?" she asked. God, it was like I'd been waiting for her to ask me that my whole life. I'd been so lost, waiting for Cassie to find me, and now she finally had.

I nodded, unable to form words.

"Stay there." Cassie kicked off her shoes and descended the steps into the pool.

My moment of glory was sweeter than I'd ever imagined. Kids I'd known for years, some of whom I'd known my whole life, hooted and hollered at my triumph. I watched Cassie swim toward me, smiling up at me. And then hands grabbed my ankles and yanked my feet out from under me. I didn't have time to fight back as my knees ground into the porous faux rock, tearing through my jeans and into my skin.

"You're dead now, asshole." Blaise and Fat Duke pinned me to the back of the rock.

An hour earlier I would have pissed myself, but finally telling Cassie how I felt had given me confidence I'd never known. Instead of flinching in anticipation of the punch I knew was coming, I said, "Do your worst, Blaise. But remember this day. It's the day you became what everyone always figured you'd become: a mouth-breathing Neanderthal with nothing to look forward to but drinking lukewarm cases of

Keystone Light at the beach and beating up people smaller than you."

I'm not sure if what I said to Blaise made any impact, because I hadn't finished speaking when Coop yanked Blaise off balance and shoved him into the hedges. Coop brushed himself off and stood prepared to fight.

"You can take me, Duke," Coop said. "But I know about locker 237." He touched his finger to the side of his nose and smiled.

Fat Duke turned pasty white and ran.

Blaise tried to get back to his feet, but he was so drunk that he tripped over low branches and fell back into the bushes, cursing and yelling. No one bothered to help him. In a way, I felt bad for Blaise. Unless he became a better man, high school really was going to be the best years of his life.

"I thought you were done with me," I said to Coop.

Coop shrugged. "You looked better in the skirt." He slapped my arm and said, "Juliet's waiting."

Shit! I'd forgotten about Cassie. I scrambled back up the waterfall, my knees burning like crazy, bloody and torn. When I got to the top, Cassie was treading water below me. I descended the side and pulled her up. Cassie's black dress stuck to all her curves, making it difficult to concentrate on anything but how amazingly perfect she was.

"Isn't Romeo supposed to be the one who climbs the tower?" Cassie asked.

I shrugged. "We're updating the story."

"What happened to you?" Cassie pointed at my skinned and bloody knees. They burned but I was too busy for pain.

"I was jumped by some Capulets behind the waterfall." I hiked my thumb over my shoulder to where Blaise was still trying to extricate himself from the dense hedges.

Cassie laughed. "I never liked him. I heard he made some kid drink a cup filled with all these different liquors."

"Yeah," I said.

Then it was just Cassie and me. Sure, there were all those other people—watching, waiting for me to make a fool of myself—but fuck 'em. I didn't know what to say, what Cassie expected me to say.

"I wished you'd kissed me that night," she said.

I was blown away. For years, I'd figured that the kiss had been little more than a bet to Cassie, that she'd probably been relieved when I'd chickened out. But I'd figured wrong.

"You can kiss me now," she said.

"Yeah?" I'd been reduced to one-word answers. When I'd asked Natalie to come to the party with me, I'd decided that it was time to let go of the past and move on with my life. Obviously, that hadn't worked out, and here I was, about to kiss Cassie. Again.

Then I did.

I kissed Cassandra Castillo. No more waiting, no more talking, no more fear. I closed my eyes, put my lips to her lips, and kissed her.

The earth didn't move, the sky didn't light up with spontaneous fireworks, I didn't see my future with Cassie spread out before me like a slow, winding road. None of the things I'd expected to happen happened. I'd fantasized about kissing Cassie for longer than I could remember, and yet now, I felt nothing. It was a good kiss, a nice kiss. Cassie had soft lips that tasted a little like peanuts and she knew just what to do with her hands.

I should have been ecstatic. Over the moon. I was standing atop a rock, in front of a couple hundred of my peers, kissing the girl of my dreams.

Only, this was real life, and I'd finally woken up.

"Simon?"

I looked toward the house, scanning the crowd for the one person I'd been thinking about while I kissed Cassie. But Stella was gone.

"Simon, what's wrong?"

Cassie was looking at me like I'd slapped her in the face. I felt like a dick. I'd been such a moron, but it had taken kissing the girl I'd loved forever to realize that forever isn't so long after all. That love isn't always what you think it ought to be.

"You're perfect, Cassie," I said. "Just not perfect for me."

I turned to climb down off the waterfall when Eli sucker punched me in the nose and I fell backward into the pool, his grinning mug the tombstone that leaned over my watery grave.

Living the Dream

Movies will make you think that when you're about to die, your entire life flashes before your eyes so that, if you live, you'll know all the mistakes you made and be able to spend the rest of your days fixing them and being the man you were meant to be before you made some bad choices and turned into a magnificent asshole.

That's all bullshit, of course. After I hit the water and began to drown in Cassie's pool—a victim of my misguided need to save Cassie from the drunken machinations of Blaise, who'd only wanted to soak Cassie as revenge for punching him in the face and ended up nearly killing me instead—my life did not, in fact, flash before my eyes. I panicked, I swallowed a gallon of chlorinated water that one of Sia's actors had very likely peed in, I even looked up Cassie's skirt, though the water blurred out all the good bits, but I didn't watch any of Simon Cross's funniest home videos as my oxygen-deprived brain slowly shut down.

What I did do was black out. And the next thing I remembered with absolute clarity was making out with Cassie. She was sitting on top of my chest, bouncing up and down while she kissed me. Before I opened my eyes, I thought about how I'd dreamed of kissing Cassie for years and that the reality was pretty much a letdown. Cassie kissed like she was having a go at hoovering off my lips with her mouth.

Cassie kept yelling my name and I wondered how she could be kissing me and talking to me at the same time. Maybe when she kissed me, we developed spontaneous ESP. I could hear her in my mind and she could hear me.

Then she wasn't kissing me anymore. My chest burned. Cassie was stabbing me with a sword made of wasps. My lungs screamed. I had to breathe, but Cassie was on me. She wasn't kissing me, she was stealing the air from my body, slowly starving my cells.

I tried to fight back but my limbs wouldn't move. Someone was restraining me.

"Simon!" Cassie called again. But I knew it wasn't in my mind this time.

When I tried to ask Cassie how she could kiss me and speak at the same time, no words came out, but I turned to the side and coughed. Suddenly nothing in the world was more important than breathing. Than getting whatever Cassie had put into my lungs out. Someone slapped my back and I hacked so hard I felt my lungs tear. When I was able, I dragged in the deepest breath possible, unsure whether Cassie was going to try to steal it from me again.

And then I opened my eyes.

Cassie stood over me, her face ashen, tears running down

her cheeks. Coop and Ben knelt at my feet. I'd never seen either look more scared. But they weren't the ones I really saw. It was Eli Horowitz to my left. He wiped his mouth with the back of his hand and asked me if I was all right.

"What the fuck?" I said weakly. My chest felt like someone had hit me with a car. And was that rum I tasted?

"Don't talk," Cassie said. "Eli saved you. You were drowning and he gave you mouth-to-mouth." She sounded awed. Scared. My life hadn't flashed before my eyes, but I was willing to bet Cassie's had.

"Blaise?" I asked.

Coop tried to talk but he couldn't. Ben said, "That freshman chased him off. Kid's got balls. But if I see Blaise—"

"Yeah," I said. I tried to stand up, but I didn't have any strength in my legs so I propped myself up on my elbows.

Cassie wiped her tears with the back of her hand. "Simon. About what you said—"

Coop threw up his hands. "Are you fucking kidding me?"

"Coop, chill." Ben put his arm around Coop but Coop ducked it.

"Don't tell me to chill," Coop said. "Simon nearly died; he needs to go to the hospital."

I managed to sit up all the way. "Coop, just give us a minute. Just a minute, I swear."

The guy was my best friend for a reason. No matter what he said or what I did, Cooper Yates and I would always be friends. "Whatever." Coop and Ben went back into the house.

But Cassie and I still weren't alone. Everyone who'd come out to see Sia's version of *Romeo and Juliet* had decided Cassie, Eli, and I put on a far more entertaining show. "Let's go over there," I said, pointing to the couch. "It's more private."

"Private" was clearly a relative term to describe the patio, but it was our best option short of going inside, which I didn't feel strong enough for. After all the abuse my body had taken, I figured I was going to need a year to recuperate.

Eli stayed by the pool as Cassie helped me totter over to the couch, but he made it clear that we weren't through. I felt like a douche. He'd saved my life and thought I was going to repay him by stealing his girl.

When Cassie and I sat down across from each other, she touched my hand and looked into my eyes and liquefied my carefully planned speech. I forgot everything in that moment. Cassie was sweaty and flushed and the night had been unkind, but she was still beautiful. Still the girl I loved.

"Simon," Cassie said. "What's this?" She turned over her palm and revealed the blue golf ball. I'd lost track of it when I'd taken a header into the deep end.

"You know what it is," I said.

"And?"

I sighed. "And it belongs to you."

Cassie turned the ball over in her hand. It was the proof that I loved Cassie, and I saw the recognition of that in her eyes.

"Do you love me?" Cassie asked in a voice so near a whisper that a stiff breeze could have snatched it from me. I didn't need to answer her question to hold up my end of our barter; Cassie held my reply in her bruised fist.

"Yes," I said anyway. Because I had to say the words, and Cassie had to hear them. "But there's someone who loves you more." I looked over my shoulder at Eli. *Romeo and Juliet* had resumed, and he was pretending to watch.

Cassie frowned. "Eli?" This was not the direction Cassie had expected our conversation to take. I was triumphant. I'd proven my love to her, but it wasn't enough anymore.

"He loves you, Cassie." I took Cassie's hand and held it between my pruney fingers. "I can't begin to know what you're going through right now. All that stuff with your parents and your house. But Eli—he knows who you are even if you've forgotten, and he'll be there for you no matter what." I couldn't believe I was talking about Eli Horowitz, my nemesis. He'd stolen Cassie from me in ninth grade and I was sending her right back into his arms.

Cassie didn't appear to believe it either. She'd seen only half of what I went through to get to her, but that half was pretty impressive, and it was inconceivable that, in my moment of triumph, I'd concede.

"I thought you loved me."

"I do. I probably always will."

Without another word, I stood up. Adrenaline alone kept me from collapsing into a bag of bones and allowed me to walk away with my dignity mostly intact.

For me, the party was over. Sure, it would probably go on until the cops showed up or Cassie realized that she'd only thrown it to get back at her parents for ruining her life, but I had had enough.

As I marched inside, people opened a path for me. They

weren't going to do song and dance numbers in my honor, but my peers seemed to look at me with a newfound sense of respect. I didn't need to be Superman or SIMON CROSS. Plain old Simon was good enough.

At the sliding glass doors, Eli stopped me. "Hey."

"Hey," I said. "Thanks for saving my life."

Eli nodded. "We're even, then." When I looked at him quizzically, he said, "I use a ladder when I climb in and out of Cassie's window."

The part of me that wasn't bruised wanted to laugh. I wouldn't have believed he had it in him, but when it came to Cassandra Castillo, there didn't seem to be anything the boys who loved her wouldn't do.

Eli and I were no longer enemies—no longer two men on a collision course toward the same beautiful prize—but that didn't make us friends, either. I knew that the only reason he was even talking to me right now was because he wanted to know what Cassie had said to me. No, he needed to know. I'd seen only a small portion of Eli's story that night, but I suspected he'd overcome his own share of obstacles to get to this moment. That didn't entitle him to the details of my private conversation with Cassie, but it was the reason I said what I said next.

"Cassie doesn't need a boyfriend," I told Eli. "She needs a friend. That's how you show her that you love her."

When I walked back into the house, I should have felt like a failure. The only lip action I'd gotten had been from Cassie's ex-boyfriend. Instead I felt like a champion. Sure, maybe my night would have turned out differently if I'd taken Coop and Ben's advice and talked to Natalie Grayson—who was passed out on the couch next to Ewan McCoy. He'd snaked her phone and was posting fake status updates to her Facebook. According to her feed, she'd pooped her pants twice. But I was coming to terms with everything that had happened. I felt like my life had been on pause since that night at Pirate Chang's and I was finally ready to play again.

Coop and Ben found me in the kitchen. Ben threw his arm around my shoulders, babbling about how awesome the party was. Coop was less enthusiastic but he gave me a solid grin, which was exactly what I needed. Once the hub of the party, the kitchen was now a wasteland. The keg was empty and there were red cups perched on every surface. Someone had raided Cassie's cupboards and spilled a bag of yellow rice on the tile floor. The grains crunched under my feet.

"Buck up," Ben said. "We'll find you another girl. Maybe even one who doesn't mind if you don't shower for three days and that your idea of cooking a gourmet meal is microwaving Hot Pockets."

"Whatever," I said. "It's cool."

Coop was looking at me the way he looked at pictures of naked girls, with curiosity and confusion. "Why?" he asked.

I knew the why he was speaking of. It was the why that had defined my life for years. If anyone deserved an answer, it was my long-suffering best friend. "When I saw that Urinal Cake kid up on the waterfall, I realized he was me. That I was a fool. I took a shot of tequila, jumped on a bed, fought a psycho, got trounced at beer pong, drank a shit-ton of rum with Eli, fell out a window, and nearly drowned. My dad was right: Sometimes love hurts, but it shouldn't be so damn hard."

Neither Coop nor Ben said anything right away. Coop probably wanted to do the dance of joy, but he held his glee in check for my benefit. Instead he took Ben's hand and kissed the top of it. They were in love. They had to work at it, sure, but it wasn't a titanic struggle. The way they knew what the other felt and fell into each other's sentences. That was real. That was love.

I knew I'd really been in love with Cassie and that maybe she could have loved me too, but it wasn't enough. Love wasn't always enough. That thought should have brought me down, sunk me into a deep depression, but it actually made me smile. Because if Cassie wasn't the girl for me, then maybe that girl was still out there somewhere, being awesome.

"I know what'll cheer you up," Ben said.

"This better not be like the time you tried to order me a Russian bride on the Internet."

"Kasia loved you," Ben said. "And you rejected her. Do you know how that made her feel? Do you?"

Coop chuckled, and the pall that had settled over us burned away like morning fog. "Rewind, baby. What's the plan?"

Ben rubbed his hands together, making sure he had our attention. "Strawberry-stuffed French toast," Ben said. "Smothered in syrup. And cheesy fries. And maybe a burger. I've been craving a burger for like an hour. And water. I'm parched."

As we left, I saw Eli sitting on the couch with Cassie, letting her cry into his shoulder.

The rest of the party people were outside watching the best version of *Romeo and Juliet* ever staged in our shithole town. A couple of hours earlier, I might have thought it was beautiful that Romeo was willing to kill himself for the girl he loved, but now I realized how stupid that sentiment is. That isn't romance, it's mental illness. No girl is worth dying for, not even Cassie.

I looked at Coop and Ben—my best friends. Everyone I wanted to hang out with was right here in this room.

"Sounds awesome," I said. "I'm done here."

Reality Bites

As I sat on the pool steps, letting the watery blood stream out of my nose while Eli and Cassie argued behind me and Sia tried to corral her actors back into position so that she could finish *Romeo and Juliet,* I admitted to myself the one thing that I wouldn't have admitted to anyone else: I'd deserved what I'd gotten.

I'm not just talking about the bloody nose. Though I did have that coming. Not only had I lured Eli into his ex-girlfriend's bedroom and tricked him into handcuffing himself to her bed, but I'd kissed Cassie right out in the open where I knew he'd be able to see.

It was more than that, though. Because I'd dicked over Natalie, pissed off my best friend, and lost the one girl who might have actually liked me. My phone had taken on more water than the *Titanic* when Eli had punched me and I'd fallen into the pool, so I couldn't even text Stella and apologize for being an asshole. Maybe she was still around the house some-where, but I wasn't sure if she'd want to talk to me, especially not if she and Ewan were making out, a thought that turned my stomach.

I was dateless, friendless, and phoneless, and my nose felt like it was filled with bees. There didn't seem to be much lower to go. Clearly I was wrong.

Cassie sat down next to me and sighed. "Did you really dress up like a girl and kiss Eli?"

"What happens at spring break parties, stays at—"

"I'll take that as a yes," Cassie said. I thought she was going to throw me out of her house, but she laughed and patted my arm. "How's your nose?"

I shrugged. It felt surreal to be sitting here talking to Cassie like nothing else had happened all night. Like we were friends now or something. But it was cool. Realizing Cassie wasn't the girl of my dreams didn't diminish the feelings I'd carried for her all those years. I still loved her. I simply wasn't in love with her. When I imagined my future, Cassie was still in it, just off to the side, a supporting character who got less screen time as I grew older.

"I'll survive."

"Where's Coop?"

"Lost track of him," I said. "Maybe he left." The truth was that I didn't know. After he'd saved me from Blaise, I hoped that Coop would come to his senses and decide not to end our friendship, but as I sat there in the water, I wasn't sure I deserved to have a friend like Cooper Yates.

I was staring at the water and the way the ripples

reflected the moon, but when I looked up, Cassie was smiling at me and doing that thing with her tongue and the gap in her teeth. It was still sexy as hell. "You're different," Cassie said. "I like it."

I'd waited years to hear Cassie say something like that, but the thing was that I didn't feel any different. Older, wetter, bloodier, but still like a total fuckup who seemed destined to do the wrong thing in every situation.

"You gonna be okay?" I asked.

Cassie looked over her shoulder at Eli. He was sitting on the couch in his boxers, watching my every move. I suspected I'd made an enemy tonight; not that I thought Eli and I could have ever been friends—not really. We'd loved the same girl, and in a competition like that, there are rarely any winners.

"He wants to get back together." Cassie looked at me again. "But I don't know. I think . . . I think maybe I need some time alone. You know, to figure things out." She looked embarrassed. "When my parents told me about the house and college—I sort of lost it."

"Are you going to finish the year?"

"I'm going to try," Cassie said. "You know Aja Bourne, right?" I nodded. "We've never been good friends or anything, but we had a couple of classes together. Earlier, she told me that if my parents had to move, I could stay with her until graduation. Isn't that weird?"

Aja was just full of surprises tonight, and all of them amazing. "You should do it," I said. "Aja's a cool chick. And her grandma used to be a chef in France and cooks shit you can't even believe."

Cassie gave me a curious smile. "I'll keep that in mind." Cassie glanced back at Eli again. "I should go. . . ."

"Yeah," I said. "I should look for a ride home."

"What about that girl you came with? She was cute."

"She's with . . . someone else." I shrugged and looked back toward the house, hoping I'd see Stella. I didn't. "It's cool." Losing Stella to Ewan was another thing I deserved. My myopic focus on Cassie had kept me from seeing the amazing girl that had been right in front of me.

Cassie graced me with a pitying frown. "You'll find someone." There was a moment of silence, and then Cassie kissed me on the cheek and walked back to Eli.

I sat on the steps until Sia grabbed me by my wet collar and wordlessly dragged me out of the pool. Despite the fact that she'd lost most of her audience, she was determined that the show would go on. I admired her dedication. Aja waved at me from the sidelines and I waved back before going inside.

The house was stained with the evidence of the night's festivities. There was no way that Cassie was going to be able to scrub it clean before her parents returned home. Which might have been a good thing. Maybe seeing what Cassie had done would make them realize how much their decisions affected her. That's what I told myself anyway. Sure, I could have stayed to help clean up, but this was more than a two- or even a twenty-man job, and I just wanted to crawl into bed and let tonight become the past.

I wandered through the house, looking for Ben and Coop, hoping that maybe I'd find Stella, but the rooms were occupied by people who had passed out or fallen asleep or who were otherwise engaged in the sort of activities that don't usually require an audience. All in all, I thought Cassie's party had been a success. It was certainly not the night I'd envisioned when I'd left Gobbler's with Natalie, but I doubted that anyone who'd attended would soon forget Cassandra Castillo's barter party.

When I reached the front of the house and hadn't found anyone to give me a ride, I resigned myself to the fact that I was going to have to call my parents after all. If I'd called them when Natalie had dumped my ass on the side of the road, I probably could have avoided the events of the entire night, but I realized that, even in my current predicament, I wouldn't have wanted to.

"Simon!"

I turned to the spiral staircase and saw Ewan McCoy running down it, carrying something white and furry under one arm. "Ewan?" When I realized he had Falcor, I about jumped out of my skin with excitement.

"What's up?" Ewan asked when he got to the bottom step.

"Nothing." I was about to explode with curiosity. Why did Ewan have Falcor, and where was Stella? I listened for her singular voice in case she was lagging behind but heard nothing resembling Stella Nash.

Ewan pointed at my nose. "That's gotta hurt. You should hear what people are saying. Apparently you took out Eli and half the football team to get with Cassie."

I laughed at the way the events by the pool were already morphing into the stuff of legend. By Monday morning people would be telling each other I'd swooped out of the sky on a helicopter made of beer cans and rescued Cassie from Eli's clutches. Or not.

"Awesome," I said. Ewan fist-bumped me and we shared a chuckle over the whole thing. "How are you and Stella getting along?" I asked, no longer able to contain myself.

Ewan looked down at Falcor, who was acting squirmy. Neither seemed comfortable with the other. "That's what I wanted to talk to you about."

"Did you guys . . ."

"She's a cool girl, but she wasn't into me." A choir of angels sang in the background and it took me a moment to realize it was part of an actual song and not a gang of divine beings celebrating on my behalf.

I did my best to look nonchalant despite the fact that I was dancing on the inside. "That sucks. Where is she?"

Ewan glanced toward the front door. "She took off." He held up Falcor like he was plague infected. "Left me with this."

Falcor now hung limply in Ewan's hands. "No," I said. "She's got to be here somewhere. She'd never leave Falcor."

"I'm telling you, man. She split while you were doing your thing with Cassie."

I wasn't sure if Stella had stuck around to see me kiss Cassie, but whether she'd seen it or not, though, she very likely assumed I'd achieved my goal. It was too bad she hadn't waited around for the finale. Maybe not the part where Eli decked me, but definitely the part where I realized that Cassie wasn't the girl for me.

"What're you going to do?" I asked.

Ewan shoved Falcor into my arms. "I'm not really an animal person. Can you take him home?" Falcor bathed my face, his tongue snaking up my right nostril, licking away some of the dried blood. "Yeah," Ewan said. "That's just gross."

I wanted nothing more than to be Stella's white knight, the guy who saved her dog and returned him to her unscathed. There was only one problem. "I don't know where Stella lives."

Ewan arched his eyebrow. "I thought you were friends. She talked about you all night." Ewan shrugged. "It's tough making a play for a girl when she won't shut up about another guy. Know what I mean?"

"Yeah," I said. The fact that Stella had spent the entire night talking about me made me feel both amazing and totally douchey. Amazing because it meant that maybe she liked me. Douchey because I might have ruined my chance to find out.

"So," Ewan said. "Can you?"

"Yeah."

Ewan broke out in a grin, looking relieved. "Sweet. I totally owe you one." He rubbed his hands together. "Now, if you'll excuse me, I've got a lady friend waiting for me." Ewan dashed back up the stairs and left me standing in the foyer.

Falcor licked my chin and I realized that I wasn't just stranded at Cassie's party, I was stranded at Cassie's with Stella's dog. I decided to go outside and see if I could find someone with a cell phone I could borrow.

The night air soothed my nose. I still felt like Eli had hammered railroad spikes into my skull—the guy had one hell of a right hook—but the throbbing was beginning to settle into a dull ache. I looked for the huddle of smokers you could usually find outside at parties—outcasts even among outcasts—but they'd either gone home or migrated to another location.

I thought I was going to have to go back inside to beg a phone off of Cassie when I heard a familiar voice say, "Looking for a ride, hot stuff?" Ben cackled, his voice carrying across the lawn.

"You couldn't afford me," I said.

Ben and Coop were sitting on the hood of Coop's Kia, holding hands. It was fitting that my night was ending the way it had begun: with my best friends.

Coop looked me up and down when I approached, and chuckled. "Cold?" I nodded. I was still damp from the pool and my clothes stuck to my skin. Coop got up and went around to the trunk, returning with a bright yellow T-shirt that had MY OTHER RIDE IS YOUR DAD written across the front.

"Thanks," I said as I traded it for my own. "I thought you'd left."

"Probably should have," Coop said. "But Ben's hungry and I'm broke and you sort of owe me for saving your sorry ass."

I'd always taken it for granted that Coop would be around. He'd been there for so long that I didn't know how I was going to survive life without him when he and Ben went to college. Friendships are like that though. You rarely recognize how much you need someone until they're gone. I didn't know how to tell Coop all that though, so I just said, "Sorry." And that was that.

Ben pointed at Falcor. "What's with the mutt?"

Falcor was sleeping in my arms. I'd almost forgotten about him. "Stella left him. Ewan asked me to take him home, but I don't know Stella's address."

"Ugh," Ben said. "I'm pretty sure you ate lead paint as a child." He slid off the hood and grabbed the small metal tag hanging off Falcor's blue collar.

On the front, it said: MY NAME IS FALCOR. On the other side were Stella's number and address.

I said, "Mind taking a detour?"

Coop let out a disgruntled sigh, but he was smiling. Ben tapped his chin and said, "My brain says sure, but my stomach says I'll cut a bitch if I don't get some stuffed French toast."

"Didn't you already get stuffed once tonight?" I asked.

Ben said, "It's on now, boy," and put up his fists, dancing around me like a champion boxer.

"Get in the car before I change my mind and leave both of you here." Coop grabbed Ben around the neck and kissed the top of his head.

I hopped in the backseat with Falcor, unable to hide my shameless optimism.

Coop looked in the rearview mirror. "You got everything?"

Falcor licked my hand and I nodded. I watched as we drove away from Cassie's house, leaving the party behind. Everything I needed was right here.

Well, almost everything.

Living the Dream

Coop, Ben, and I sat in a booth at Howley's, staring at the gluttonous amount of food on the table. Our waitress, Trish, wore her frown like a badge of honor. Despite the fact that we always tipped generously and were mostly well behaved, Trish saw it as her sacred duty to disapprove of the way we stumbled in: bruised and reeking of liquor and looking like hooligans.

Other than Trish and us, there were only four other customers. A red-haired girl who appeared to be having a conversation with herself; an elderly couple arguing the merits of the *Alien* movies; and a homeless guy at the counter who'd been nursing the same cup of coffee since we'd arrived.

Howley's was our favorite late-night hangout. The seats were hard, the music was stuck in the eighties, the cook was surly, but it was like a second home. Trish even yelled at us to eat our veggies.

It had taken a lot of convincing to keep Coop from driving me directly to the emergency room, but I'd promised to buy breakfast, which had instantly brought Ben over to my side. I was definitely in a lot of pain, but nothing that would leave permanent scars. Plus, God hadn't invented an injury that a waffle sandwich couldn't cure.

"I'm not sure what was funnier," Ben said. "You getting your ass handed to you at beer pong or you making out with Eli."

I savored every bite of Howley's famous waffle sandwich. It consisted of two crispy Belgian waffles surrounding two eggs, three slices of bacon, one slice of ham, and enough cheese to stop my heart. The whole mess was covered in syrup and whipped cream.

"First of all, I didn't make out with Eli, he gave me mouth-to-mouth, and it wasn't all that funny from my perspective." I pointed with my waffle-loaded fork, swinging syrup all over the table. "And you weren't even there for the beer pong." I shoved the whole bite in my mouth, relishing it a little too much.

Ben chuckled. "Is it true that Cassie got you to admit that you masturbated to Mrs. Tanaka's yearbook pictures?"

"The librarian?" Sticky drool leaked down the front of my shirt. Coop handed me a napkin. "She's a hundred and uses a walker."

Ben held up his hands. "I don't make up the rumors, I just spread them."

Coop playfully backhanded Ben's arm. "Ben!"

"Fine, fine," Ben said. "I might have been the one to start that particular rumor. Either way, if Tanaka gives you the eye on Monday, I say go for it."

I laughed in spite of the fact that my night had been little more than a string of poorly planned disasters. It was strange imagining life without Cassie. But it was freeing, too. A whole world of possibilities was open to me now.

While Coop and Ben bickered, I stole one of Ben's bacon-wrapped bacon bites. It was comforting to know that even if I was doomed to be forever alone, Coop and Ben would be together for a long time. I was getting used to the idea of a future without Cassie, but I couldn't imagine one where Coop and Ben weren't disgusting and happy and so fucking in love.

"Hey, so what happened to you guys tonight?" I asked.

Coop glanced at Ben and then blushed so furiously that I thought he might stroke out. "It's complicated," Coop said.

I leaned back against the booth, put my arms behind my head, and smiled in spite of the pain. "Either you did the deed or you didn't," I said, watching them squirm. "Did you even find a condom?"

"Yes," Ben said. "And you have no idea what I had to go through to get it."

"We," Coop said.

"What *we* had to go through."

"Do tell," I said.

Ben looked at Coop, who sighed and nodded. "It started with Claudia Wisneski . . ."

Over the next ten minutes, I ate my waffle sandwich while Ben related the convoluted story of how he and Coop managed to secure a condom. I laughed, I cried, I blew root beer out of my nose, which hurt, by the way.

"After I finished Photoshopping Carl's face onto all the

pictures in Harmony's Facebook, Cole finally gave me the lighter that got me the notebook that I traded for the keys to the teachers' break room so that I could get the stupid condom." Ben popped a fry into his mouth and tried to play like that was the end of the story, but I refused to let the boys off that easily.

"So you got the condom," I said. "Did you . . . you know?" I made an obscene hand gesture right as Trish walked up to clear some of our dishes.

"Do I even wanna know?" Trish asked. She had a light New England accent that tickled my ears.

"No," Coop said, but I jumped in with "I'm trying to find out if Coop and Ben got busy at Cassie's party."

Coop covered his face with his hands while Ben took a sudden interest in the wall. For all their bravado, both boys were kind of prudish. Trish left without saying a word.

"The answer's no," Coop said when he was sure Trish was out of earshot. He said it low like anyone in the diner cared. Ben shot him a dirty look, but Coop said, "He's going to hound us until he gets the truth."

Ben sighed and said, "Fine, but I don't see how it's any of his business." Which was funny since Ben thought everything was his business. "We got the condom. And I'd paid a freshman to set up a guest room with candles and shit."

"What happened?"

It was what I'd been thinking, but I wasn't the one who said it. Neither had Coop. We all turned around and saw the red-haired girl in the booth behind us, kneeling backward in her seat, resting her chin on her arms. She was cute in an awkward way. Her red dreads dangled like vines and her yellow tank had been clean once upon a time. But it was her eyes that wrecked me. They were big and the color of bacon and . . . wow.

"Who's the Nosy McSnooperson?" Ben asked.

The girl rolled her eyes. "Is that the best you've got? You have so much to learn." Then she rotated 180 degrees and disappeared in her booth.

Coop and Ben and I exchanged puzzled looks. "Do we know her?" Coop asked.

"Maybe she goes to our school," I said.

"I don't think so," Coop said. "But she looks familiar."

Ben snapped his fingers. "We almost ran her down near the beach."

"Yes!" I said. She'd been the girl in the road we'd nearly hit on our way back from my house. That drive was sort of a blur, but it was definitely her. I glanced back at her booth. She was facing forward but definitely still eavesdropping.

"Finish the story before I grow too old to care," I said, but the truth was that I'd already lost interest in the Amazing Adventures of Coop and Ben.

"It's stupid," Coop said.

"To be fair," Ben interjected, "I told you not to open it that way."

"I was trying to be sexy."

Coop and Ben looked at each other and then at me. "Coop bit through the condom trying to open it with his teeth."

"It was hot!"

"It was dumb."

"Fine," Coop said. He crossed his arms over his chest. "If I'm so dumb, then I'll take my raging case of herpes and find someone who really loves me."

Ben frowned and then wrapped his arms around Coop. "Now why would you want to do that when you know that *I* really love you?"

Coop melted and kissed Ben.

"Seriously, guys. I just ate." But they didn't hear me. Knowing they could be at it for a while, I stood up and walked over to the red-haired girl's booth. It hurt when I smiled, but I gave her my best.

"I'm Simon," I said. "Did we almost run you over tonight?"

The girl shook my hand. "Stella," she said. "You'll have to be more specific. It's a fairly common occurrence."

This whole talking-to-girls thing was weird. Before, it had always been easy because in the back of my mind, they'd been not-Cassie. Placeholders. But now that I'd come to terms with my feelings, everything felt new, scary. There were real consequences. I was walking a tightrope without a net and it felt fucking amazing.

"What were you doing in the road anyway?"

Stella put her finger to her lips and looked around. Coop and Ben were still sucking face, and Trish was chatting up the homeless guy. Stella pointed at her purse as a white dog popped up, its tongue lolling from its mouth. It barked and Stella gave it a stern look, causing the dog to retreat.

Trish glared at us and I said, "That was me. Something in my throat." I barked loudly, trying to imitate the dog. If Trish could have given me the finger, I'm sure she would have.

"Thanks," Stella said. She tore off a piece of toast and fed it to her purse. "Falcor thanks you too."

"His name is Falcor?"

Stella nodded. "He's also blind. And a little dumb."

"He's cute," I said. "So are you."

"I know," Stella said with an easy smile, like strangers complimented her every day. Who knows, maybe they did. "Are you going to ask me to come sit with you guys? My psychic said I'd meet a nice boy tonight and I'm kind of hoping one of your friends might be the one."

Coop and Ben were doing their best not to be obvious snoops, but their keen interest in an empty milk shake glass gave them away. "I'm not sure you're properly equipped."

Stella sighed. "Pity. I do so love a challenge."

The girl was crazy. Brilliant and mad and so unlike Cassie in every way. "So listen," I said. "How about a trade?"

"I'm all ears."

"Come sit with me—pretend you maybe like me a little—and I'll share my cheesy fries with you."

"Don't listen to him!" Ben shouted. "He never shares his cheesy fries with anyone!" Ben laughed while Coop mouthed, "Sorry," and shrugged.

Everyone was staring at us, which was nothing new. Ben was a one-man spectacle. For once, I didn't care.

Stella tapped the table with her finger as she seemed to consider my offer. "No deal," she said.

My shoulders fell and I tried to think of something witty to say that would let me slink back to my table with my pride intact. But Stella wasn't finished with me.

"I'll sit with you only if you tell me how you got beat up." Stella pointed at my nose. The swelling had gone down some, but I still couldn't breathe properly.

Maybe I should have been embarrassed to recount the entire night's events to this strange, beautiful girl, but when I looked into her eyes, when she smiled, I couldn't say no. "Deal."

Stella collected her dog, and I carried her plate and drink to our table. She slid into the booth first as I said, "Guys, this is Stella. Stella, this is the Unambiguously Gay Duo."

They traded introductions. Ben made an ass of himself as usual. Trish brought us a fresh plate of steaming cheesy fries. When she dropped them off, she flashed me her dimples, which I'd seen only once before.

"So," Stella said. "Who beat the ugly into you?"

I looked at Coop and Ben, and then at Stella. The whole night washed over me like the incoming tide. So much had happened. So much had changed. It would take me until dawn to tell Stella the whole story, but there was nowhere else I wanted to be. I began at the beginning.

"I guess it started when I tried to turn a paper clip into a kiss."

Reality Bites

Stella's house was one side of a duplex on a quiet street near the railroad tracks. Somehow Falcor seemed to know where we were, because the closer we got, the more he barked and panted and danced in my lap. I knew how he felt. The whole way over, I wondered if Stella had left Falcor at the party on purpose. Would she be happy to find me on her doorstep in the middle of the night or would she be disappointed I wasn't Ewan? I wasn't sure if I should even knock on the door at all, but it wasn't like I could go creeping around outside her house, peering through windows to find the one that belonged to her.

"Are you going to do it, or what?" Coop asked. We'd been sitting outside her house for five minutes and I hadn't moved. I couldn't stop replaying in my mind the last thing she'd said to me. Did she honestly believe I was perfect? That maybe I'd be perfect for her or that we'd be perfect together? I'd never know if I didn't get out of the car, and that's exactly what scared the shit out of me.

"I'm working on it," I said. We waited another minute and I could sense the boys growing restless. I tried to distract them. "Hey, you never told me what happened with you guys tonight."

Ben was rummaging through the glove box for a candy bar he was sure he'd stashed in there. "With what?"

"The sex," I said. "Did you do it?"

Ben turned around in his seat and grabbed the front of my shirt. "Simon, I'm hungry. Under any other circumstances, I'd tell you to go screw yourself, but since I know you're just stalling, I'm going to tell you." Ben glanced over at Coop, who held up his hands. "We did it. It was awesome. Happy?"

Coop shook his head that they hadn't actually done it, but he was smiling. I knew I'd get the whole story eventually, but it honestly didn't matter. My best friends were happy and in love. The rest was gravy.

"Fine," I said. "You're a stud."

Ben let go of my shirt. "Damn right, and I love this idiot over here. Now go give that girl her dog so we can go eat."

There was nothing else to do, so I got out of the car. The moment Falcor's tiny paws hit the ground, he ran toward the house. I thought he must have some kind of supernose to smell that he was home. It all smelled the same to me, but somewhere in this stew of scents, Falcor smelled Stella.

I chased the dog to a green door, in front of which he stopped and sat down. Before fear could get the best of me,

I knocked three times, wincing at the hollow drum beat that echoed through the night.

Lights turned on inside and I subconsciously began taking shallower breaths. Falcor wagged his little tail and panted, acting on the outside how I felt on the inside. I tried to think of something clever to say to Stella, but my words dried up when the door opened.

A large, hairy man in a pair of dingy white briefs stood in the doorway, holding a Louisville Slugger. The light framed him, blunting his features with nightmarish shadows. He had a sleeve of tattoos and a large misshapen scar on his abdomen. Honestly, I nearly peed my pants in fear, and I'm not ashamed to admit it. That dude had "psycho killer" written all over him.

"Uh . . . uh . . . shit." The words dribbled out as my brain melted from sheer terror.

The yeti brandished the bat menacingly. "Boy, you better have a good reason for waking me up." His voice was gravelly and deep and promised unimaginable pain if I didn't provide a satisfactory answer.

The truth was, I had a great reason for knocking on this brute's door in the middle of the night, but I was in fight-or-flight mode, and my words had obviously chosen to flee.

"You got till the count of three before I beat your ass."

There wasn't a doubt in my mind that he'd do it. That crazy dude looked like he'd dismember Girl Scouts for Caramel deLites. But I froze.

"Oscar, leave him alone. He's slow."

My breath whooshed out of me as I turned and saw Stella standing outside the door of the adjoining house. She was wearing pajamas covered with unicorns pooping rainbows.

Oscar frowned—a truly frightening sight. "Fool woke me up."

Stella waved him off like he was an annoying toddler and not a seven-foot-tall bloodthirsty giant. "He's stupid, not a burglar. I'll take it from here."

With a grunt, Oscar slammed the door in my face.

"I fully expect to find out one day that Oscar has a freezer full of human corpses," Stella said. She leaned against her door with her arms over her chest. If she was self-conscious about me seeing her in her pj's, she didn't show it.

"Is that your dad?" I asked.

Stella laughed so hard that she snorted. Even that was moderately cute. "That's not my house," Stella said. She pointed at the numbers on the doors. I was standing at 606. Stella's house was 608.

"I really am slow," I said.

"No argument here."

"You left your dog."

Falcor was already at Stella's feet, standing on his back legs, trying to get her to pick him up. The moment felt awkward because Stella wasn't acting like she was even remotely happy to see me. I'd hoped that she'd left Falcor so that I could find her, but that was dumb, right? Maybe I'd misunderstood. Maybe she'd really just forgotten about him.

"And you brought him home." Stella turned to leave.

"That's all?"

"Thanks, I guess."

I panicked. I didn't know what to say to Stella, so I said, "I kissed Cassie."

"Me too!" she said. Then she rolled her eyes.

I was blowing it big-time and I had to do something or I would never see Stella Nash again.

"But then I realized I didn't want to kiss her," I said. "I mean, I wanted to kiss her, but then I didn't. I wanted to kiss you. I think. Fuck, I'm screwing everything up." I took a deep breath and said, "I thought kissing Cassie would change everything. But it didn't."

"Sorry," Stella said. She actually sounded like she meant it.

"I'm not."

Stella sighed. "Listen, I'm happy for you, but it's late and I'm tired and dead people don't put makeup on themselves. Unless they're zombies, but I'm pretty sure we don't have any of those right now."

Falcor scampered around our feet, yapping at the air. I had to admire him. He never knew where he was going but he didn't let that stop him.

"Listen," I said. "I'm not perfect. And neither are you. I'm an idiot and you're odd. Really odd, actually."

"You suck at compliments," Stella said.

I didn't know what I was trying to say, but, like Falcor, I

refused to let that get in my way. "Yeah," I said. "You're odd and I have dick tendencies, and I like you. I think you like me too."

Stella shrugged, giving nothing away. "My psychic said I'd meet a tall stranger. I assumed she was talking about the guy at the gas station who tried to sell me stereo speakers out of the back of his van, but I suppose you might do." A smile peeked out from behind her dreads and it was the most beautiful sight in the world.

"Kiss her, you idiot!" Ben yelled from the car. I looked back in time to see Coop wrestle Ben away from the window.

When I turned back around, Stella was holding Falcor. "Well, thanks for my dog. Good night."

"Wait."

"What now?"

I reached out to pet Falcor, and touched Stella's hand instead. "I'm not sure I should let you have Falcor."

Stella got this pouty, indignant expression on her face that made me want to kiss the shit out of her. "He's my dog."

"You abandoned him. When I found him, he was doing shots with Dean Kowalcyk and trading paw jobs for bacon strips. I'm not sure you're responsible enough to have a dog."

Stella chewed her lip. "I see what you mean. How do you propose we resolve this situation?"

"How about a trade?"

"A trade?"

Emboldened by the events of my night, I laid it all on the

line. Stella wasn't perfect, but maybe she was perfect for me. The only thing I knew was that I'd never know until I tried.

"Now, this isn't personal, but I have to know I'm returning Falcor to someone who really wants him."

"Name your terms, Simon Cross."

"For this dog—"

"Which rightfully belongs to me—"

"Which you abandoned," I amended. "I will trade you one first kiss."

Stella whistled. "That's a steep price to pay for a dog." She looked at the fluffy mutt in her arms. "And a defective one at that. I've got some Vegas dice you can have. I hear they're lucky."

I reached out to take Falcor from her. "If you're not interested, I have a buddy who works at a Chinese restaurant . . ."

"On second thought," Stella said.

"Yes?"

"I am kind of attached to him."

"The dog, you mean?"

Stella nodded. "Of course." She paused. "And if kissing you is the only way to get him back, then I might be willing to make that sacrifice."

My palms were sweaty and my mouth was cotton dry. "Do we have a deal?"

While Stella looked from me to the dog, seemingly weighing her options, I couldn't help wondering what would have happened if I hadn't gone and talked to Natalie Grayson at Gobbler's. This was certainly not how I'd expected my night to turn out, but I supposed that life was like that. You could get dumped on the side of the road by a crazy pretend ketchup fanatic and end the night kissing the girl of your dreams, who might not be the girl you thought was the girl of your dreams.

"Deal," Stella said. "But first you have to kiss Falcor."

"That wasn't part of the bargain," I said.

"Ewan did it."

"Ouch," I said. "That's low."

Stella held Falcor out to me. "A girl only gets one first kiss."

Falcor probably had terrible dog breath, but luckily, I couldn't breathe through my nose. I dove in to trade slobber with Stella's blind dog. When I came back up for air, Stella was laughing so hard she had to hold her side.

"Wow," she said. "I didn't think you'd do it."

"Seriously?" I wiped the dog drool away with the back of my hand.

Stella grimaced. "Seriously. I'm not kissing you after that." Before I could argue, Stella walked into her house and slammed the door behind her. A moment later, the porch light flicked off.

"Stella?"

The house went dark next. It was just me and the night, standing in front of Stella's duplex with no dog and no kiss, looking like a complete tool. I waited for a full minute before admitting I'd been duped again and turning to leave.

Before I'd made it even half a step, Stella opened the door, grabbed my shirt, and spun me around.

"What—"

"Shut up and kiss me, idiot."

So I did.

Stella wrapped her arms around my neck and I pulled her tightly to me, kissing her like the first time, like the last time, like all the times in between. I didn't think about Cassie or Eli or the fact that Stella smooshed my nose so hard that my face felt like an exploding grenade. People aren't meant to be perfect. We're all imperfect people looking for perfect moments to share with other imperfect people.

I'd found one such moment, and I never wanted to leave.

I could have kissed Stella until the sun rose, except Ben honked the horn and I was afraid Oscar would reappear with a chainsaw instead of a baseball bat.

"You're definitely a better kisser than Cassie," Stella said.

"Thanks," I said. "I think." I looked back at Ben and Coop. "We're going for breakfast. Wanna go?"

Stella sighed and shook her head. "I wasn't joking about the dead people."

"Oh," I said. I didn't want to leave her. I wanted to stay on her front porch, kissing her all night long.

"But there's always tomorrow," she said, which made me smile. "I hear Pirate Chang's has a killer eighteenth hole."

I shook my head. "My mini-golf days are behind me."

Stella linked her fingers in mine and kissed the palm of

my hand. "You should go before Ben wakes up the whole neighborhood."

"Yeah," I said. Except that I kissed Stella again. Because, you know what? Fuck it. I was seventeen, imperfect, and kissing a brilliant girl. Ben and Coop could wait.

Acknowledgments

FML wouldn't be the book it is without the help and guidance of a lot of amazing people.

First, I want to thank my family for being so patient and amazingly awesome. Rachel Melcher for being honest when I needed it most. Margie Gelbwasser for spending countless hours reading and rehashing plot points with me. Pamela Deron for telling me when I needed to suck it up and get back to work. All the Tenners for their constant support.

All the wonderful folks at Simon Pulse deserve a huge thanks. I may not get to name you all, but you are all awesome and deserve raises . . . and by raises, I mean cupcakes. But this book wouldn't have existed without Emilia Rhodes, who came to me with a cool idea and then let me run with it; Anica Mrose Rissi, who gave me the support I needed and the space to make it work; and my copy editor, Stephanie Evans Biggins, whose heroic efforts saved me from looking like a dummy.

I also want to thank Chris Richman and the whole team at Upstart Crow. You guys are the best.

Lastly, I'd like to thank Matt Ramsay for always being there at the end of the day when I've run out of words.

About the Author

Shaun David Hutchinson lives in South Florida with his partner and two dogs and spends way too much time watching *Doctor Who*.

You can find him online at shaundavidhutchinson.com.

JIMMY
October 17, 9:07 P.M.

The eyes were beautiful.

They were mad huge, anime-hero huge, staring out of the darkness.

Something brushed his cheek too, rhythmically. Like kisses.

Jimmy smiled.

Kisses happened all the time to guys like Cam, who expected them. Never to Jimmy.

So he would always remember that moment, how weirdly tender and exciting it was on that deserted road on that rainy October evening, before he blinked and realized his world had gone to shit.

9:08 p.m.

It wasn't the taste of blood that brought him to reality. Or the rain pelting his face through the jagged shark-jaw where the windshield had been. Or the car engine, screaming like a vacuum cleaner on steroids. Or the glass in his teeth.

It was the sight of Cam's feet.

They were thick, forceful feet, Sasquatch feet whose size you knew because Cam bragged about it all the time (14EE), feet that seemed to be their own form of animal life. But right now, in a pool of dim light just below the passenger seat, they looked weightless and demure, curved like a ballerina's. One flip-flop had fallen off, but both legs were moving listlessly with the rhythm of the black mass that lay across the top half of Cam's body—the mass that was attached to the eyes that were staring up at Jimmy.

"Shit!"

Jimmy lurched away. The animal was twitching, smacking its nose against his right arm now, flinging something foamy and warm all over the car. It was half in and half out, its hindquarters resting on the frame of the busted windshield, its haunches reaching out over the hood. The broken remains of a mounted handheld GPS device hung from the dash like an incompletely yanked tooth.

For a moment he imagined he was home, head down on his desk, his mom nudging him awake with a cup of hot cocoa. It was Friday night. He was always home on Friday night. But this was real, and he remembered now—the deer springing out of the darkness, running across the road, legs pumping, neck strained. . . .

"CAAAAAM! BYRON!"

His voice sounded dull, muffled by the rain's ratatatting on the roof. No one answered. Not Byron in the backseat.

Not Cam.

Cam.

Was he alive? He wasn't crying out. Wasn't saying a thing.

Jimmy fumbled for the door handle. His fingers were cold and numb. With each movement the engine screamed, and he realized his right foot was stuck against the accelerator, trapped between it and a collapsed dashboard. He tried to pull it out and squeeze the door handle, but both were stuck. He gave up on his foot and looked for the lock.

There.

The door fell open with a metallic *grrrrrock*. Jimmy hung on to the armrest, swinging out with the door, as a red pickup sped by. It swerved to avoid him, and Jimmy tried to shout for help. His foot still stuck, he spilled out headfirst, twisting so his shoulders hit the pavement. As his teeth snapped shut, blood oozed over his bottom lip. He spat tiny glass particles.

The pickup was racing away, past a distant streetlight, which cast everything in a dim, smoky glow. From the car's windshield, the deer's hind legs kicked desperately in silhouette, like the arms of a skinny cheerleader pumping a victory gesture.

As Jimmy yanked his own leg, not caring if the fucking thing came off at the ankle, he felt the rain washing away the blood. Through the downpour he could see the long, furry face on the seat—nodding, nodding, as if in sympathy. *That's it, pal. Go. Go. Go.*

His ankle pulled loose, and he tumbled backward onto the road, legs arcing over his head. As he lay still, catching his breath, he heard someone laugh, a desperate, high-pitched sound piercing the rain's din.

It took a moment before he realized it was his own voice.

9:09 p.m.

"Jesus, it's still alive!"

Byron's voice. From the backseat.

Byron was okay.

Jimmy jumped up from the road. He struggled to keep upright, his leg numb. He spat his mouth clean as he made his way around the car. Through the side window he could see Byron's silhouette, peering over the front seat. Jimmy looked through the driver's side window. The deer's back was enormous, matted with blood and flecks of windshield. Under it he could make out only the right side of Cam's body from the shoulder down, but not his face.

Cam was completely smothered.

"Oh God, Jimmy, what did you do?" Byron said.

"I—I don't know. . . . It just, like, *appeared!*" Jimmy had to grip the side of the car to keep from falling, or flying away, or completely disintegrating. He blinked, trying desperately to find the right angle, hoping to see a sign that Cam was alive. "Push it, Byron—push it off!"

"It's a monster—how the fuck am I supposed to push it? *Shit, Jimmy, how could you have not seen it?*"

"*I did!*" Jimmy screamed. "I braked. I tried to get out of the way—"

"Dickwad! You tried to outmaneuver a *deer*? You don't *brake!* That makes the grill drop lower—lifts the animal right up into the car, like a fucking spoon! You just *drive*. That way you smack it right back into the woods."

"*If you know so much, why weren't you driving?*"

"With what license?"

"*I don't have one either!*"

"You told me you did!"

"I never told you that! I just said I knew how to drive. I never took the test—"

"Oh, great—the only person in Manhattan our age who knows how to drive, *and you don't bother to get a license.*" Byron leaned closer, suddenly looking concerned. "Jesus Christ, what happened to your mouth?"

"It's what I get for applying lipstick without a mirror—"

"Awwww, *shit!*" Byron was looking at something in his hand. "My BlackBerry's totaled."

"*How can you think about your BlackBerry while Cam is under the deer?*"

Byron looked up with a start, then immediately leaped out of the car. "Oh fuck, Cam. Is he dead?"

"*'Oh fuck, Cam'*? You just noticed him? You're yelling at me, and you just thought of Cam?" Jimmy's hands trembled as he pulled his cell phone out of his pocket. "I'm calling 911."

"No, don't!" Byron said, snatching the phone from Jimmy's hand.

"Are you crazy?" Jimmy said. "What's wrong with you?"

"We're in East Dogshit and the GPS is busted—do you even know what road we're on? What are you going to tell the cops? *Um, there's this tree? And, like, a ditch? And a road?* And then what, we wait? We don't have time, Jimmy!"

"But—"

"Think it through, Einstein. What's your story? One, you wrecked a car that's not yours. Two, you don't have a license. Three, you killed a deer. And four, look at Cam. You planning to go to Princeton and room with Rhodes scholars? How about a guy with three teeth who can't wait for you to bend over? Because if we don't stop talking, dude, you're facing murder charges."

"He's not dead, Byron—"

"Just put the fucking phone away and let's get Bambi off Cam." Byron threw Jimmy the phone and raced to the back of the car. "Throw me the keys. I'll get a rope out of the trunk. When I give you back the keys, get in the car."

Jimmy reached into the car, tossing the phone onto the dashboard. Quickly removing the keys from the steering column, he threw them to Byron. He eyed the driver's seat. The deer was still moving, still trying to get away. *No way* was he going back in there.

But he couldn't abandon Cam.

If only he could think straight. His brain was useless. In that moment, he was picturing a cloud of small, hungry ticks hovering over the front seat. He tried to shake it off, but it was like some weird psychological hijacking brought on by his mother's lifelong vigil over the mortal threat posed by proximity to deer, which turned every suburban outing into a preparation for war.

"What are you fucking worried about, Lyme's disease?" Byron shouted. "Get in there!"

Jimmy cringed. "It's *Lyme*," he muttered, grabbing the door handle. "Not *Lyme's*."

"What?" Byron shouted.

"Nothing. What am I supposed to do—in the car?"

"What the fuck do you think you're supposed to do?"

As if in response, the deer gave a sudden shudder. Jimmy jumped back, stifling a scream. "I—I'm not sure . . ."

"When I give the word, put it in reverse, Jimmy. And gun it."

Byron yanked open the trunk and threw the keys to Jimmy, who kept a wary eye on the deer as he opened the door. It was motionless now, its snout resting just below the gear shift.

As Jimmy climbed inside, the car rocked with Byron's efforts to shove stuff under the rear tires for traction.

Breathe in. Breathe out.

Jimmy tried to stop himself from hyperventilating. He eyed Cam's feet, blinking back tears. He had never liked Cam, or any of the smart-ass jocks who treated the Speech Team kids like they were some kind of lower life-form. Since freshman year he had devoted a lot of time conjuring horrible fates for most of them, fates not unlike this.

In ... Out ...

Jimmy hadn't wanted to go on this drive. It was Byron who'd pushed the idea. *Cam* wants us to go, *Cam* says suburban parties are the best ever, *Cam* says Westchester chicks are hot for NYC guys. *Cam* wants to be friends. It would be stupid to miss a chance at détente between the worlds of sports and geekdom.

In ...

Until this time, Jimmy couldn't imagine that Byron would be friends with a guy like Cam. Byron the potty-mouthed genius, Cam the football guy. Was this some kind of crush? Was *that* the reason for—

"Wake up, douche bag!" Byron shouted. "Now! *Go!*"

With his foot on the brake, Jimmy threw the car in reverse. The accelerator was touching the bottom of the caved-in dashboard. Carefully, he wedged his foot in and floored it.

The engine roared to life, the tires gripping the debris. As the car lurched backward, the deer's head rose slowly off the seat with the force of the rope. Something warm spattered against the side of Jimmy's face.

"AAAGHH!" he screamed, yanking his foot away from the accelerator.

"*WHAT?*" Byron cried, running around the side of the car. "Why'd you stop? We almost had it!"

"*It puked on me!*"

Byron shone a flashlight into the front seat. "It's not puke. It's blood."

"Oh, great . . ." Jimmy's stomach flipped. *This couldn't be happening!*

"Here. This'll protect you." Byron was throwing something over the animal's head—a rag, a blanket, it was impossible to see. "Don't think about it, Jimmy. Just step on it! And put on your seat belt."

Jimmy felt a lightness in his head. His eyes were crossing. *Focus.*

He buckled his belt and put the car in reverse again, slipping his foot under the wreckage of the dashboard. As he floored it, the car began to move, the engine roaring. The animal's hulk rose up beside him, away from him—scraping across the bottom of the windshield, slowly receding out of the car and onto the hood.

The blanket fell off the deer's head, as the carcass finally slipped off, the car jerked backward.

SMMMMACK!

Jimmy's head whipped against the headrest. He bounced back, his chest catching the seat belt and knocking the wind out of him.

"Are you okay?" Byron cried.

"Fah—fah—" Everything was white. Jimmy struggled to breathe, his eyes slowly focusing on the image in the rearview mirror, the twisted metal of a guardrail reflecting against the taillights.

Byron was leaning in the open passenger window, training a flashlight on the dim silhouette of Cam's lifeless body, now freed from the deer. "This does not look good. . . ." he said.

"Is his chest moving?"

"I don't know! I don't think so, but I can't—" In the distance a muffled siren burst through the rain's din. Byron drew back, shutting the flashlight. "Shit! Did you call them?"

"No!" Jimmy said.

"Then how do they know?"

Jimmy thought about the red pickup. "Someone drove past us, just after the accident. Maybe they called."

"Someone saw us?"

"This is a New York suburb. Occasionally people drive on the roads."

"Oh, God. Oh, God. Oh, God. Oh, shit. Oh, God." Byron was backing away from the car, disappearing into the darkness.

"I'm the one who's supposed to be freaking out, not you!" Jimmy

leaned toward Cam's inert body, his hands shaking. The cold rain, evaporating against his body, rose up in smoky wisps. *Don't be dead don't be dead please please please please don't be dead.*

"C-C-Cam?" Jimmy slapped Cam's cheek and shook his massive shoulders, but Cam was limp and unresponsive. His body began to slip on the rain-slicked seat, falling toward the driver's side. Jimmy tried to shove back, but he was helpless against the weight. Cam's head plopped heavily in Jimmy's lap.

"Aaaaghhh!" He pushed open the door, jumped out, and looked around for Byron. "I think he's . . . he's . . ."

The siren's wail was growing closer. How would he explain this? *You see, officer, in New York City no one gets a license until they're in college. But my dad taught me to drive on weekends, on Long Island. No, I don't have the regi-stration either. The car belongs to— belonged to . . . him . . . the deceased.*

He'd have to get out of here before they came. He looked past the car. There was a gully, a hill. It was pitch-black. He could get lost in the night.

Asshole! No, the cops would figure it out. Fingerprints. Friends knew he was driving—Reina Sanchez, she had to know. She was all over Cam. She'd tell them. So it wouldn't only be manslaughter. It would also be leaving the scene of the crime. What was that? Life in prison?

Stay or go, he was screwed either way. Because of a deer. A fucking stupid deer. Without the deer, everything would have been all right.

"BYRON!" he shouted.

In the distance he heard Byron retching, with characteristic heroism.

Cam was now slumped into the driver's seat, his right shoulder touching the bottom of the steering wheel.

He used me. He convinced Byron to get me to drive so he could go to a party. And now he will never ever be accountable. Because he's...

Dead. He was dead. He would never move again, never talk.

And that opened up several possibilities, some of which were *Unthinkable.*

An idea was taking shape cancerously fast among his battered brain cells. If you were thinking something, it wasn't unthinkable—that was Goethe, or maybe Wittgenstein, or Charlie Brown. The idea danced between the synapses, on the line between survival and absolute awfulness, presenting itself in a sick, Quentin Tarantino way that made perfect sense.

It was Cam's dad's car. It would be logical that Cam would be driving it.

No one will know.

He grabbed Cam's legs. They were heavy, dead weight. He pulled them across the car toward the driver's side, letting Cam's butt slide with them—across the bench seat, across the pool of animal blood and pebbled glass.

Jimmy lifted Cam into an upright position, but his body fell forward, his torso resting hard against the steering wheel.

HONNNNNNNNNNNK!

The sound was ridiculously loud. Around the bend, distant headlights were making the curtain of rain glow. No time to fix this now.

Jimmy bolted for the woods.

"What are you doing?" Byron called out of the dark. He was standing now, peering into the car. "Jesus Christ! You're trying to *make it look like Cam drove?* What if he's alive? He'll tell them you were driving!"

Jimmy stopped, frantically looking around for something blunt. He stooped to pick up a rusted piece of tailpipe, maybe a foot long. It would do the trick. He knelt by the driver's door and drew it back.

"JIMMY, ARE YOU OUT OF YOUR FUCKING MIND?"

Byron's eyes were like softballs. He grabbed Jimmy's arm.

Jimmy let the tailpipe fall to the ground. He felt his brain whirling, his knees buckling. He felt Byron pulling him away.

As the cop cars squealed to a halt near the blaring car, he was moving fast but feeling nothing.